The Checkout Girl

The Checkout Girl

Susan Zettell

EDITIONS

Cover design by Doowah Design.
Photo of Susan Zettell by Carol Kennedy.
"All Along the Watchtower" by Bob Dylan. Copyright©1968; renewed 1996 Dwarf Music. All rights reserved. International copyright secured. Reprinted by permission.

This book was printed on Ancient Forest Friendly paper.
Printed and bound in Canada by Marquis Book Printing Inc.

We acknowledge the support of the Canada Council for the Arts and the Manitoba Arts Council for our publishing program.

Library and Archives Canada Cataloguing in Publication

Zettell, Susan, 1951–
      The checkout girl / Susan Zettell.

ISBN 978-1-897109-26-7

      I. Title.

PS8599.E77C44 2008   C813'.54   C2008-905747-3

Signature Editions
P.O. Box 206, RPO Corydon, Winnipeg, Manitoba, R3M 3S7
www.signature-editions.com

for Daniel and John

"It's all about ice," Charlie told Kathy. "No ice, no skating; bad ice, crappy skating. Start right and you'll have perfect ice all winter long."

Her father talked as they whapped their way up and down the yard, tamping the snow with coal shovels. Their mingled breath shushed into the cold air.

"You have to be patient," he said. "You have to wait until at least four inches of snow has fallen to make a solid base. Six inches is better, but four works. Most of all, you have to wait for the cold."

They started after supper. Kathy's mother, Connie, opted to stay inside to clean up. "Get out of here so I can read the newspaper in peace," she told them, pretending to be cross, pretending she didn't want them around. "Dress warm," she scolded.

Charlie wore earmuffs, no scarf, the buttons of his car coat open at the neck. A clear bead of snot dangled from his nose. He wiped it on his sleeve when it got precarious. The frayed stitching on his old Sunday gloves exposed a thin beige lining. He said the felt slippers he'd tucked inside his galoshes kept his feet toasty warm.

Though the pompoms on her toque bobbled, Kathy's scarf was wound so tight she couldn't move her head. With flannel-lined jeans and an extra sweater under her leggings and parka, she looked like a sausage. Minutes after stepping outside, her toes were frozen inside her rubber boots, but she didn't complain.

Charlie wasn't going to use boards; he said when you didn't have much, boards were a waste of money. Instead he'd mound snow around the perimeter of the rink, pack down the bank, and square off the top and the inside. His plan was to flood the snow wall from the outside with a gentle spray of water from the hose, being careful not to over-saturate it. He didn't want water to flow through the wall onto the base, didn't want anything to mar the smooth snowpack he and Kathy were preparing. He explained every detail to Kathy as they worked.

"I'm going to make a windbreak near the back door," he said, dabbing his nose on his sleeve, "with hay bales from Schultz's farm. Five or six for the wall and a couple for a bench. Keep our bums all snuggly warm."

"Charlie," Connie had called at that exact moment, and she had leaned her warm bum against the storm door to hold it open. She handed Charlie a steaming mug of coffee. "There's a shot of rye in it," she said.

Connie was often benevolent, but not always. She let the door slam shut and returned with a mug of hot cocoa for Kathy, marshmallows glowing like the moons of Jupiter.

"Don't forget Kathy has school," she said. And because she knew they weren't listening—and because she couldn't help herself—she added, "Don't stay out too long."

They stayed out until she came to the door again, pounding on the frosted windowpane, motioning with her thumb for them to come inside. They came in then, not because Connie wanted them to, but because they knew it was time—and only fair—to share their happiness with her. After putting Kathy to bed, Charlie went out alone and flooded the snowpack, methodically laying the first layer of ice.

The night the rink was ready, the ice a wide glassy runway through the yard, they wolfed their grilled cheese sandwiches. They smacked their lips and laughed too loud and left the dishes on the table. Their skates, sharpened, waited at the back door, lined up side by side: Connie's—the same skates she'd worn since she was twelve—brightened with white shoe polish. Charlie's brown and worn, a pair he'd found at the church bazaar. Kathy's brand new, because Charlie insisted she start right. Hockey skates.

Connie glided around the rink, one, two, three times, and then into the centre, fast. She was terribly beautiful. She brought her skates together, crossed her arms and twirled. They waited, hushed. She tipped her toe pick into the ice and stopped.

"You did it!" she called to them. They breathed, for they had been holding their breath, and they joined her on the ice.

They skated, each of them alone—Connie and Charlie orbiting Kathy, who click-clacked up and down the middle of the rink—until Connie grabbed Charlie's hand and skated with him to Kathy. They each took one of her hands and they skated together in the dark.

"Yippie-yi-yo-ky-yay," Charlie shouted.

What did Kathy say? Not a word, for on this cold, clear night she wore a new pair of hockey skates. The gleaming ice on which she skated, she had made with her father. Her beautiful mother held one of her hands and her father the other. There was nothing to say. So she listened, and all the sounds—her parents' voices, the slish-slish of their skates on the ice, the whooshing of their breath and the sigh of the wind in their wake—were sounds of love.

It was 1955, the year Kathy turned five, the first time she and Charlie flooded the backyard to make Rausch's Rink. They'd moved that year to a brand new bungalow in Pleasant View Subdivision in the east end of Varnum. They made a rink every winter until 1959, the year Shelly, a distant and fretful baby, was born. As if contagious, Shelly's unhappiness spread through the family, first to Connie, then to Charlie and finally to Kathy. The next year Charlie was killed in a car accident.

1955 was the same year a hockey coach named Anthony Gilchrist wrote Punch Imlach and told him he might want to send out a scout to watch a young player from Parry Sound, a twelve-year-old. Gilchrist told Imlach he might want to get the boy on the Toronto Maple Leafs' signing list before some other scout got to him. Bobby Orr was the kid's name.

Of course, Charlie didn't know anything about Bobby Orr, and Kathy didn't either, not then. But in 1966, when Bobby started playing for the Boston Bruins, anybody who knew anything about hockey knew he was the Canadian hope that was going to save the Bruins, and maybe some day take them to the Stanley Cup. What Kathy came to know about Bobby, the thing she knew Charlie would have seen too, that even Connie could see, was that Bobby Orr could skate. He laced his bare feet into a pair of hockey skates and once he hit the ice he was part of it; he never looked down, always knew where his feet were, where the puck was, where the opening was going to be. Always knew when to shoot. Bobby Orr skated as if the ice spoke to him.

Yes, Charlie would have liked Bobby Orr. And everything Kathy hadn't learned about skating from her father before he died, she learned later from watching Bobby.

Winter, 1970

Let me say it flat out right here: skating is the single most important part of the game of hockey.
— Bobby Orr

Snow-filled cracks traverse the ice. Kathy zigzags her way down the rink avoiding them. Barry, on the other hand, hits every one.

"Mother of God," he whines. His cheeks are red, his ears are redder, the tip of his nose the reddest of all. His too-big borrowed skates tap-tap-tap as he baby-steps his way to equilibrium. He hits another crack, bends forward and twists.

"Shee-it."

His arms windmill; his windbreaker rises at the back, exposing tender flesh. Kathy catches him on the turn. She grabs the bottom of his jacket and yanks it over his goose-bumped skin. With her arm tucked around his waist, she skates beside him, holding him up, propelling him faster and faster.

"I told you to wear a warmer coat," she sings into his right ear. "It's winter, Barry. You know, true north strong and free?" She skates behind him, switching arms and sides. "Hey, man," she says into his left ear, "you're Canadian, right? You remember snow? Cold? Ice, maybe?"

She lets go his waist. Barry stumbles, leans back and thumps down on his bum. He groans.

Kathy turns. She smiles at him, big and hard. "I bet you remember ice now," she says as she skates away.

"Come back," Barry calls after her. He pulls the waistband of his chinos down, showing off his left buttock. "Look here. Bruises."

Skating backwards, Kathy glides away. Cross-stepping the turn, leaning into it, she picks up speed. When she hits the stretch she imagines a puck on the far side of the rink, changes direction, crosses over to it. Imagines balancing the puck on her stick, an offenceman coming toward her. She sidesteps him, cups the puck with her stick, changes direction and skates forward. Holds the puck. Holds it. Patient. Moves to the net. She shoots.

"And she scores," she screams, throwing her arms in the air. "Bobby Orrette scores!"

"What?" Barry asks as she does a little jig. Barry's sprawled on his side, elbow on the ice, head in his hand. He's been watching her.

"How did you get so good?" he asks. Turning onto his belly, he pulls his knees up under him and struggles to stand.

"My dad. Then Bobby Orr. Everybody watches Bobby play hockey," Kathy says, "I watch him skate."

"Who scored?" he asks again when he's upright.

"Me," Kathy says. She's skating circles around him. "Kathy Orrette. Best damned girl offensive defenceman Canada ever exported to the U. S. of A. Saviour of the Boston Bruins. Don't you know anything?"

"I know who Bobby Orr is," he says.

Kathy ignores the hurt in his voice. That's what this night-time skating trip is all about. Ignoring Barry. And more than just the hurt in his voice, and the bruise on his buttocks. She's ignoring the fact that he wants to sleep with her.

Kathy skates away. She's not going to let Barry ruin this first skate of the season. Because this is when she's happy, this is part of the reason she left Vancouver and came back to Varnum, to be outside in real cold, on real ice, with the hockey skates on her feet as natural as eyelashes, as fingernails, as teeth. Ever since she and her father made their first backyard rink, this is all she ever wanted.

"I haven't skated since grade eight." Barry follows her with his voice. "Compulsory PE. Fucking freeze your feet off, not to mention the family jewels. Some smart-ass saying, 'let's play crack-the-whip,' so they can let you go at a zillion miles an hour. And you're scared shitless, so you look like an idiot even before you get the snot smashed out of you when you hit the boards.

"Bigger guys with hockey sticks trying to whack your ankles. They couldn't find mine because I was skating on them. And to top it off, tear-factory Maureen Zimmer peeing her pants, every single skating class, and then crying and telling everyone she peed them. That girl had no dignity. Made me sick, all of it. Hated skating. And I hate it now."

Kathy slows to skate beside him. "Feel better now that's off your chest?" she says.

"How'd you ever talk me into this?" he asks.

"Sex," Kathy says, the word flying out of her mouth.

"I'm absolutely sure Barry won't mind," Penny said when she offered to rent a room in her basement to Kathy, and Kathy had accepted.

Kathy had known Penny McDonald forever, though she wasn't Penny McDonald any more. She was Penny Lehman. In grade school, Penny was a four-foot-ten potato of a girl with dull stringy hair always drawn back in an elastic, one of those almost invisible kids who hit high school looking exactly the way they always did. Then part-way through grade ten, the Tuesday after the Easter holidays to be exact, Penny arrived in homeroom looking at least two inches taller. Her hair—glossy black shot through with copper—almost touched her bum. She blinked four-inch, teased and hair-sprayed bangs up and down on eyelashes so stiff with mascara they looked like shelves. Her lips were frosted white, her breasts 36B, her waistline cinched tight in a wide white vinyl belt.

But the real holy-shit-how-did-this-happen moment came after school when Penny told Kathy she wasn't going for french fries and gravy with her girlfriends. She was going with Pete Lehman. Sloe-eyed, dark-haired and languid with a bad-boy rep, Pete had been in grade twelve when they entered grade nine. After graduation he'd started working part-time at the university maintaining the labs. Rumour was, he made LSD in one of the labs at work, and grew marijuana downtown among the peonies and asters in the perennial beds in Regent Park.

No one—none of her friends at least—was surprised when Penny quit school in grade eleven and moved in with Pete, then went to work at the cookie factory. Nor were they surprised when she had an empire-waist wedding the next summer and produced a big fat baby boy five and a half months later. She named her baby Rhettbutler. She'd read *Gone with the Wind* while she was pregnant, a copy that had a picture of Clark Gable and Vivien Leigh on the cover. The baby had curly black hair and thick black eyelashes and Penny said she hoped he'd turn into a handsome, good-hearted rogue just like the Clark Gable Rhett. And like his father, Pete, of course.

After Rhettbutler, Kathy didn't see much of Penny. At the occasional party where Kathy and Penny would chat while Pete sold a few nickels and dimes of marijuana or hashish. Once or twice when Penny was out walking the baby in Regent Park. So when Kathy literally bumped into Penny at the schnitz and shoofly pie counter at the farmers' market a week after she moved back to Varnum, they hadn't talked in over a year.

"Kathy Rausch," Penny said. "I thought you were out west. When'd you get back?"

"October," Kathy said.

"Where's Doug?" Penny wanted to know.

"Vancouver," Kathy told her. "I think."

"You think?" Penny asked.

"I'm pretty sure."

"Did you break up?"

"Sort of," Kathy said.

Doug had been down in Gastown panhandling when Kathy left. That's what he did then, panhandled and picked up his welfare cheque, smoked dope, did a little acid, shot a bit of speed. She was supposed to be at work at the store, but she'd given her notice the week before. She hadn't told Doug because they weren't talking much. Besides, he knew everything anyway, or so he let on. She'd packed her bag, got in her car, and abracadabra—well, maybe not that fast, but she didn't do any sightseeing along the way—she was back in Varnum.

"How'd he take it?"

"Don't know," Kathy said. "I haven't talked to him. He calls my mother, but she won't tell him anything. Connie never liked Doug."

"Kathy, Kathy," Penny said, shaking her head. Then she laughed and asked Kathy where she was staying, and when Kathy said the Y, she offered her the room.

"There's a snake in it," she warned.

"Who, Pete?" Kathy asked.

Penny laughed again and told Kathy it was a pet snake named Freddy and he lived in a cage Pete built, a very large, very secure cage. That was the deal. She said she and Rhettbutler hated snakes. Kathy asked if they had any other pets and Penny said a tame one they let out occasionally. They called him "Little" Barry Bender and he'd be thrilled to have a cute hippie chick living down the hall. Even if he was engaged.

"How little," Kathy asked, "is Barry Bender?"

"Very little."

"Shorter than you?" Kathy asked.

"Looks it," Penny said. "He's small all over: little nose, little hands, little feet."

"Sure he won't mind?" Kathy asked.

And Penny said, "Abso-fucking-lutely not."

A blush rises up Barry's neck and turns his cold cheeks redder when Kathy says the word sex. She wishes she hadn't said it, because it's the last thing she wants: to have sex with Barry. It's why she dragged him out skating tonight. Because when Freddy hit the glass she didn't want a Barry rescue.

Freddy the snake is a boa constrictor, seven feet long and as thick as Kathy's arm. He lives in Kathy's room in a Plexiglas cage that takes up most of one wall. He's pretty quiet most of the time, lies at the back of his cage in a mottled, muscled coil. But every once in a while, for no particular reason Kathy can figure, he shoots straight out from where he's resting and slams his nose, BAM, into the Plexiglas. The first time, Kathy screamed. Now she tries not to scream because when she does, Barry comes running into her room.

"Ta-da," he sang when he came in tonight. "Barry Bender to the rescue."

During the week, Barry works as an electrician up on the Bruce, at the Douglas Point Nuclear Plant. Shutdowns began almost as soon as the plant opened, and Barry's one in a large pool of workers hired to fix the problems and keep the plant running. He makes big bucks, which is good because he just bought a shiny new Corvette Stingray, and because he's saving to marry The Virgin Goddess, the beautiful, platinum blonde, Westmount-born-and-bred Rachel Anderson.

When he's home on weekends, Barry takes Rachel to expensive restaurants, where they talk about The Wedding. Rachel lets Barry make out with her on Barry's basement bachelor bed, but she won't let him Go All The Way. (That's the way Rachel talks, raising her eyebrows and opening her eyes wide for words with especial meaning.) For that, Barry waits for Freddy to make Kathy scream. Then he can run into her room and rescue her.

Kathy sleeps in the buff. Barry used to pretend he did, but Kathy now knows he wears old-man pyjamas, and not just because Rachel told her one Friday night when they were sitting together at the Lehmans' kitchen table drinking instant coffee while Rachel waited for Barry to arrive home from the Bruce. Rachel said she doesn't want to see Barry naked until after their marriage, so she buys him those cute flannelette pyjamas with button flies, white or beige with little blue anchors, or brown and red pheasants all over them. She gets them at Ahrens Department Store.

Once she bought him a pair with Disney characters, novelty pyjamas, Rachel said, that she got when she went with her family to Disneyland. She was disappointed, she said, because Barry wouldn't wear them. Barry's allowed to take his clothes off when they make out, but he has to wear pyjamas, Rachel told Kathy. You know how men are, Rachel said. They dribble here and there when their "thing gets big." She didn't want to get any of that stuff on her. Rachel kept her bra and panties on at all times, and she wore a long-line panty girdle for extra protection.

So Kathy believed Barry when he told her his sex life woes. His blue balls, as he called them, and how Rachel wouldn't touch him and didn't want to see him naked before they get married. Kathy thought that if Rachel ever saw Barry's penis, she'd find another man to marry, invest in a potentially larger growth fund.

Barry's little penis works, as Kathy found out the first time Freddy hit the Plexiglas. Kathy screamed and Barry stood in front of her so quickly it was as if he'd spent every night waiting for this moment, had been practising this particular rescue all his life. Kathy stopped screaming. As she sat naked at the side of her bed, she watched Barry's penis stiffen inside his flannel Disney pyjamas.

(She'd have to remember to tell Rachel he did wear them. Then again, maybe it would be better not to tell Rachel anything.)

Daffy Duck grew bigger and bigger, and moved closer and closer, until he was almost touching Kathy's nose. When Barry dropped his drawers, the edge of his pyjama top lifted and fell with the gentle bobbing of his little swelling. Kathy sat on the edge of the bed and gripped the mattress. She tried not to laugh. And her eyeballs crossed, she was trying so hard not to look. Barry looked down at her naked breasts.

"Oh, Kathy," he said.

His penis reminded her of an aging Pinocchio, a slowly growing nose-like woody making its way from between two wee wrinkled whiskered puppet ball cheeks. Barry sat down beside her on the bed and his little penis poked up between his legs. Kathy had to look away.

"Kathy," he said again.

Kathy felt so sorry for him she let him into her bed. *I'm freezing*, she told herself as she slid back under the covers. Barry came in after her. Kathy was being nice to Barry. Trying to make him feel better about his tiny penis, that's what she told herself.

Kathy's breasts are small and firm. She tells herself that's why she felt sorry for Barry that first time. She had a sense of what he must go through worrying all the time about the size of his appendage.

"More than a handful's a waste," Doug used to say about her breasts every time they made love. Or in front of friends, or at a restaurant, always loud enough for strangers to hear. It never made her feel better. Partly because she had never thought much about her breasts until Doug started commenting on them, never worried about their size until he reassured her they were adequate. She felt this was Doug's way of making fun of her, of saying they were very, very small and he didn't like them. Doug excelled at the backhanded compliment. That's partly why she left him in Vancouver.

Once with Barry was enough, Kathy had told herself. After she found out his little penis actually did what it was supposed to do, Kathy felt they didn't need to test it again. Barry did, though. He wanted to marry Rachel, The Virgin Goddess, and he wanted Kathy too. Just not to marry.

"Don't you believe in free love? You're a women's libber, aren't you?" Barry asked her one night when she was putting him off.

"Love's never free," Kathy told him solemnly. She'd heard that in some movie. Lovers discussing their future. It had sounded so profound. Now it sounded like the sorry excuse it was.

Barry lets Kathy take the Corvette for spins, its powerful motor thrumming under the hood (Rachel isn't allowed to drive it so Kathy is supposed to stay away from her neighbourhood in Westmount), and he buys a little hashish from Pete for her. He brings home dope munchies and cigarettes and beer, all in the hopes that she'll once again have pity on him and take him into her bed.

Kathy can walk to work from the Lehmans', walk to the library, walk to Regent Park, walk to market to get winter apples or maple syrup or schnitz pie, then have a beer at the Eby Hotel or a club sandwich in the Grill Room at Ahrens Department Store or just hang around downtown, see if some friends show up. When she lies in her bed at night she can hear the trains stop at the station going to, or coming from, Toronto. Soothing hopeful sounds, hisses and clanks, slow groaning starts.

Kathy would like to hold out on Barry. She likes to think she's superior to him. So it makes her sick. Not the sex, because Barry's so gentle and timid, so anxious to please that she can't feel bad about the actual sex. It's how sorry-ass and weak she is. That's what she can't understand right now: The way she didn't stand up to Doug, and left Vancouver without telling him. The way she doesn't say no to Barry. The way she likes Barry's warm body in bed next to her at night even though he's engaged to Rachel. She has nothing against Rachel, who's a really nice girl. In fact Kathy's glad he's engaged to Rachel because it means he doesn't want anything from her but the sex, but that's one more thing she doesn't get about herself right now.

Kathy likes Barry's wannabe rich-boy smell: Ban roll-on deodorant and Breck shampoo, and on alternating days Canoe or English Leather cologne. Likes the softness of his breath on the back of her neck as he falls asleep, each exhalation so full of gratitude.

Sometimes Kathy wonders how she got into this mess.

And when she's being honest, she even has to admit that Barry is fun to be with in an aspiring-to-Westmount electrician kind of way. Barry wears loafers and white socks, straight leg chinos, never, ever bellbottoms. He wears psychedelic print shirts with pointy collars and his hair, though shaggy, is neatly trimmed. He shaves every day and uses aftershave, and his sideburns are an ordinary length. He has a big watch. He's generous and likes to indulge Kathy, likes what he calls her wild side, will do almost anything she asks as long as it won't get him in trouble with Rachel. Sometimes they smoke dope and laugh and talk without making love. It feels so good to laugh.

But tonight Kathy decided to take Barry skating instead of smoking dope or having sex with him. She hadn't been skating since she got back from Vancouver, and on her way home from work at suppertime she noticed that the local rink was flooded and ready to go. She wanted to test the ice, test herself, because she hadn't been on skates for way too long.

But there's another reason to put Barry off. She's having supper at her mother's tomorrow and she doesn't want to betray herself, doesn't want to go home with even an inkling of Barry because she thinks her mother might be able to tell. Her mother's unhappy with her these days, and is only too willing to tell her so. Connie uses all the ammunition she can find against Kathy to press her to change her life, so Kathy has to stay alert. She doesn't want anything to distract her from whatever defence she'll have to mount against her mother, because, except for skating, she really doesn't know what she wants and it takes enormous effort to disguise the fact. To maintain that what she's doing right now is all she really wants to do.

When Freddy hit the glass and Barry ran into her room, Kathy told him to get dressed, they were going skating. When he said he didn't own skates, she dug out a pair from a pile of old sports equipment in Pete and Penny's furnace room. She told him to put on warm clothes. She told him it was skating or nothing.

Barry listened to her. He got dressed, got into her car, put on his borrowed skates. There he is now at the end of the rink, moaning and muttering about the cold, trying to keep his balance. Kathy skates hard, getting a sense of the ice, beginning to sweat. She stops hearing Barry's complaints; she pushes her mother's voice away. Worry slides from her shoulders, down her back and legs and into her feet, which slice the ice, over and over, slice it. Her body takes charge, as she hoped it would, and all she thought she'd lost returns. She is a skater.

"Listen to this," Connie calls out. She knows Kathy and Shelly are around the house somewhere, but it doesn't matter. She talks to herself. And she reads the newspaper out loud, has done since Charlie died in the car accident ten years ago. Not that she'd been shy of the sound of her own voice before his death. But after he died there was far too much emptiness and she felt compelled to fill it in whatever way she could. The newspaper teemed with words, all of them soothingly impersonal and so removed from the rawness of her own pain that they became necessary, and she was soon in the habit of reading them aloud.

Supper is cooking, a pot roast especially for Kathy. Ever since she broke up with her no-good boyfriend, Doug, and moved back to Varnum from that hippie commune where they were living in Vancouver, Kathy comes every Monday after work at the grocery store to share a meal with Connie and Shelly.

Connie had read out how Egyptian President Nasser is promising an army of a million men to liberate Palestine, and before that how there's going to be a boost in their very own twin city population—Varnum and Sand Hills—as people move from Quebec. Some want to get away from the political unrest and financial insecurity caused by the separatist movement. Some are fleeing because the FLQ continues to set off bombs in mailboxes and they're afraid for their lives.

Now she's reading about Cassius Clay. Connie likes Cassius Clay, likes his solid Negro good looks, his quick smart-ass bravado with the press, and the lyrical provocations he tosses out at his opponents, both other heavyweight fighters and now his political foes as he fights to stay out of jail after refusing the US draft to Vietnam. He gave up his slave name and changed it to Muhammad Ali when he became a member of the Nation of Islam, but Connie can't get used to the change, so she still calls him Cassius Clay. He says his religion doesn't condone war, except those in the name of Allah, which is part of why he says he'd rather go to jail than fight.

Connie remembers when he first got in trouble, when he told the draft board—and the press, of course, for he never could keep his mouth shut—"I ain't got no quarrel with them Viet Cong. They never called me nigger." Connie has some views on the military herself, especially how Canada never formed a coherent strategy for its Forces after World War II, but she thinks the war in Vietnam is over for the Americans, and they'd do well to bring their boys home alive rather than in body bags.

Connie wonders why Negroes are changing religion. Her theory—Connie prides herself on her theories—is that it's linked to being underdogs. American Negroes are underdogs and they need a clear way to distinguish themselves from whites that's not based entirely on skin colour. A distinct culture—the Negro Nation of Islam culture, for instance.

She supposes the same thing could be said about French Canadians, the ones who say they're fighting to protect their culture and language, that is. On a good day she'll admit they have a point, but their fight scares her, especially the terrorism, because it's so close to home. She can understand why people are leaving Quebec. If she lived there, as an English person, she'd at least have to think about it. For Shelly's sake, her argument goes, if nothing else, because if anything happened to Connie…

And that's as far as Connie gets with her French Canadian liberation musings, because even though Connie has seen a lawyer and made arrangements for Shelly to live at the Sunshine Home if anything ever happens to her, she doesn't like to think about what Shelly's life would be like there. And she will never ask Kathy to take Shelly on. It wouldn't be fair. One life completely devoted to a retarded child's care is enough. Connie's taken out an insurance policy that will help cover everything. (Though if she ever became a cripple that would be another story.) She learned from Charlie's death what a godsend an insurance policy could be.

Connie's reading from the *Varnum Recorder*, the twin cities' main newspaper. She's leaning sideways in her chair to catch the best light from the lamp beside her. Her dressing gown, a full-length pastel pink terrycloth, new at Christmas—a gift from Kathy—opens across her breasts, revealing a deep, shaded cleavage inside a serviceable but well-fitting white bra. Connie might be a widow, but she hasn't let herself go, prides herself on not letting herself go in fact.

Her figure is full: wide shoulders, big breasts, small waist, round hips and bum. Strong and compact, but not fat. She doesn't work at keeping trim, but she doesn't overindulge, either. She wears a long-legged panty girdle to work every night, but under it her belly and thighs are still tight.

Occasionally she wonders why she bothers to look good. She rarely goes out except for groceries and to work and to church. When Kathy lived at home and was old enough to babysit, Connie went to a movie now and then with her friends. Since Kathy moved out, Connie's friends drop in to see her because it's easier that way. Connie hosts a card game once a month on a Saturday night. That's as often as the women feel they can spend a Saturday night away from their husbands.

Connie used to invite them with their husbands, but being the only single woman in the group started to cause tensions, a flirty moment here, a little too much attention paid there, the hurt in a friend's eyes when a husband complimented Connie on her independence and coping skills, or on the cheese puffs she'd made. Connie needed her girlfriends more than she needed the attention of men, though she misses the men. Misses the smell of them, their muscled solidness, the way they seem so sure of their sometimes foolish opinions. She misses their non-judgmental generosities and the look of their fingernails, black-rimmed and nicked from factory work. Connie and her friends play euchre mostly, crib if the group is small, Rummoli if she has a crowd. But the fact is, no matter who she's around, she likes to look nice, so she does bother to take care of herself, and that's all there is to it.

"Are you listening, girls?" Connie tries again. "It says, and I quote, 'Cassius Clay, who now calls himself Muhammad Ali, continues his appeal of a possible five-year prison term for his 1967 conviction under the Selective Services Act.'

"Now listen up, because this is the part I really love," Connie calls out. "'Mr. Clay says boxing needs reviving: "There's no more poetry, no more shuffling, no more predicting rounds, they can't talk and they're ugly."'

"Gaw-damn that man's a hoot," she shouts. "'They can't talk and they're ugly.'" She repeats it for herself this time, and she laughs and shakes her head.

She leans back in her chair, half closes the paper, and continues to talk to herself. "He's right; there is no poetry without him. Not that I ever liked watching him fight, mind you. Can't stand the sound of a fist hitting flesh. But I do miss his mouthy backtalk, and all the jive in his interviews with Howard Cosell." She raises her voice and says, "Cassius Clay may be an underdog right now, losing his title and all, but he's no loser."

The picture window curtains are open, the cold late afternoon an arm's length away. Frost patterns like shatters form along the bottom of the window near the sill. On the other side of the glass, doily-sized snowflakes drift so slowly and fall so gently they appear to be pausing in the air before they make their way to the ground.

"There's a difference between underdogs and losers," she pronounces. She's using her French teacher "répétez-après-moi" tone now, the one she uses when she's really trying to get her daughters' attention. *Talking to you is like talking to stumps*, she tells them when she's particularly frustrated.

This time she's aiming her words at Kathy. Kathy's in another world these days, so preoccupied she doesn't notice Connie half the time. Or the rest of the world, for that matter. The other half of the time they'll be sitting together, talking, Kathy appearing to listen when suddenly her pupils will grow wide and dark, as if a cloud is passing before the sun. Her eyes lose their focus until they look like the eyes of a dead person. Connie knows that when Kathy shuts her out like that, she isn't listening to a word that she's saying either.

Now Shelly's a different story; Shelly has an excuse. She's autistic. Connie can talk and talk and she never knows if anything's going to stick in Shelly's mind. Shelly has never said an original sentence in her entire life; she only repeats fragments of information she hears. A single word, or a list of items. A simple rhyme, or a phrase from a book. Occasionally she remembers song lyrics, but never more than two or three lines.

Still, Connie's an optimist and thinks if she enunciates like a teacher giving a *dictée*, Shelly's odd and unfathomable mind will have a better chance of hearing particular words. Maybe she'll get their drift and possibly even put them together with some remembered image or thought and then turn them into an idea. Eleven years and counting and that's never happened.

Connie's general theory of talking to her kids—or to anyone's kids, for that matter—goes something like this: Kids' minds, even those of grown kids like Kathy, are like tape recorders. The machine is always on, always recording. Words go in and are entered on the loop of tape. Even if the brain doesn't seem to register the words, they're in there, stored for future use. And some day, maybe when the time is right, maybe when the words are needed, maybe when the mind is open to them, her daughters will unconsciously hit the play button at the right spot in the tape and they'll hear her words of praise, or advice, or some bit of wisdom inside their heads. Whatever it is they need to hear at the time.

So speaking to them is never a complete loss, because if she ever gave up and said nothing, then there would be nothing on the loop for them to hear in the future, and that, Connie's sure, would be a gaw-damned tragedy in any child's life.

"There's a difference between underdogs and losers," Connie repeats, trying a more conversational tone this time. She knows Kathy's nearby, heard her rummaging in the ironing board cupboard in the kitchen a minute ago, though she doesn't notice her standing behind her in the doorway between the kitchen and the dining area.

Connie lifts her head. It gets dark so early this time of year. She looks out the window at the dazzle of snowflakes illuminated by the porch light. They spiral past her on a swirl of wind. And now she can see Kathy reflected in the glass. She watches her daughter for a moment, then sighs, and folds back the newspaper to an article she read earlier and has decided to clip. She takes the tiny scissors she wears looped around her neck on a long, frayed, faded green ribbon and cuts the article out of the paper. She leans over the arm of her chair and slips it into a shoebox she keeps beside her on the floor for that purpose.

Connie saves newspaper articles to tape to her refrigerator door. She calls the fridge door her scrapbook. She started it a year ago on New Year's Day and she's been taping clipped news items to it ever since. Every time the door is opened or closed, the articles flap like the prayer flags Kathy strung in the backyard two summers ago when she was going through some hippie oo-ooming meditation craze. Tibetan prayer flags. Kathy showed her the image of a horse on one of them. Lung-ta, Kathy said it was called, and it meant Windhorse. Each time the wind blew, she told Connie, the fluttering flags sent blessings for happiness, long life, and prosperity to everyone in the neighbourhood.

Kathy moves into the dining room and takes the iron from the table. She's slighter than her mother, smaller breasted, fair where her mother is dark, but she has the same green eyes, the same strong shoulders and back and the same small waist. Where Connie's figure might be considered lush, Kathy's is muscular and chiseled, athletic.

Kathy set the iron to WARM and now she's testing it to see if it's ready. The cord swings down, taps against the wall beside her. She spits on her finger and touches it to the metal. The spit doesn't sizzle but it does slowly evaporate.

She watches the snow fall around her mother's reflection in the window. When Kathy arrived after work she asked her mother why she had curtains if she never bothered to use them. Winter dark falls early and when Kathy drove up around 4:30 Connie was backlit in the window so that each detail of her face and hands and clothes, each movement she made was entirely, vividly visible to the world outside.

Connie said, "I have nothing to hide. The neighbours know what I look like. They know every gaw-damned thing about me, so what the hell is there to worry about?"

The snow is falling harder now, swirling on a gust of wind, obscuring her mother's reflection for a moment.

"You don't have to shout," Kathy says, "I'm right behind you." She touches the warm iron to the sleeve of her shirt.

"The Boston Bruins used to be underdogs," Connie tells her, slightly less loudly. "Have you switched your allegiance to some other losing team now that they're winning? For all those years, Boston lost and lost, and you cheered for them. Your father cheered for them, too. Do you remember? But he was fickle. He cheered for any team that wasn't Montreal.

"God rest his soul," Connie says, and she crosses herself. "I hate saying anything about him when he isn't here to defend himself. But he was a bigot, Kathy, sure as shit, and who he loathed were the French. Not French from France, French from Canada. Whores-de-horses he used to call hors d'oeuvres. Remember that? Probably better if you don't.

"I miss him, I really do, but I don't miss that part of him one little bit. He was a card-carrying Liberal, your father was, all his too-short life. But Monsieur le Prime Minister, Pierre Elliott Trudeau, would have tested his loyalty to the limit.

"Now you, Kathy, you're not like your dad. As a kid you were always so quiet. So kind, and so …"

Connie pauses and Kathy waits to hear what she will say, wonders how her mother saw her as a child.

"… so receptive. You hardly said boo, and you went along with almost everything you were told. Never had a mean bone in your body, always loved everyone," Connie says. "Most especially underdogs. Like that retarded kid at school you were always getting in fights over?

Stevie what's-his-name? You were his very best friend. His only friend, if I remember correctly."

"Pocock," Kathy says, running the iron across her breasts and along her shoulders.

"Pocock? What the hell kind of name is that?" Connie says. "If I recall correctly, his mother had him late and he was never right. Didn't look mongoloid. Looked like Ichabod Crane when his hormones hit, tall and thin, though he had a chubby bum, poor soul. Didn't have those hands mongoloids have, either."

"Lordy, Kathy, will you look at these."

Kathy watches Connie flap her hands in the air. The newspaper slips from her lap onto the floor.

"They look like an old woman's," Connie says.

"Hazel!" Connie shouts, and she snaps her fingers.

Connie's fingernails are manicured and painted fuchsia and do not look like an old woman's.

"That's her name. Hazel Pocock. I remember now. I admired her. She forced the school to pass Stevie through every grade until grade eight. I never had the energy to fight the school for Shelly. But then, autistic retards are different from mongoloids. Stevie could talk. He liked to be around people.

"Hazel moved the family to North Tonawanda—you remember that kids' talent show you used to watch from there—so Stevie could go to a high school for special children. They had lots of money. I wonder what happened to him.

"Some people take in stray animals," Connie says as she leans over and pulls the newspaper back onto her lap. "You, my gentle-hearted and hopeless daughter, adopt losers."

Kathy switches the iron to her left hand and tries to press the sleeve on her right arm. Her mother is sitting with the paper in her lap, staring out at the snow that sifts past the window. One of the toilet paper rolls Connie uses to curl her dyed black hair slipped forward when she picked up the newspaper. Kathy watches Connie push the roll back into place and take the loosened bobby pin and shove it along her scalp, securing the roll to her head. Her mother shakes out the newspaper and begins to read again, but to herself this time.

There's a paper bag in the cupboard under the bathroom sink for old toilet paper rolls, overflowing last time Kathy checked. The empty rolls are the exact right size for the large glossy bouffant with an Annette Funicello curl-under that Connie likes to dry set and hairspray into place every night before she leaves for work at Smiles 'n Chuckles. Kathy wonders why Connie bothers, because her hair gets squished under a net every night anyway.

But that's her mother, every hair in place, nails manicured, lipstick on, eyebrows plucked to a thin black "Oh really!" line above her green eyes. She looks like a backup singer for some Motown girl group, for Aretha Franklin or Diana Ross. Except Connie's white and middle-aged. Still, Kathy can picture her in one of those tight Supremes dresses, short and sparkly, Connie all long-line panty-girdled curves with cross-your-heart breasts. Too bad about the Supremes break-up. Diana's going solo. Kathy wonders if she's scared about going out on her own.

"Stevie Pocock wasn't a loser," Kathy says. "He was slow."

She reaches the iron around her back and tries to run it up her backbone. She pushes it up as far as she can reach, which isn't very far.

"With a name like Pocock… oh, you know, everybody called him Poop-Cock."

"Now look at Boston," Connie interrupts. "From last to first. After they got Bobby Orr, they stopped losing, just like you said they would. One more Canadian Bob gone south for the big time. Like Bob Goulet and Bobby Curtola. So tell me why Mr. Smarty Pants Orr didn't sign with Toronto or Montreal? Keep the talent here in Canada for a change. Like our factories. Paper says they're being bought up by US companies every day. Pretty soon everything worth anything in Canada will be owned and run from the United States of America.

"Bet Boston takes the Stanley Cup this year because of him." Connie snaps the paper open and starts to read again. A loose piece drifts to the floor.

"Bobby never was—and never will be—a loser," Kathy says. "He signed with Boston because some idiot in Toronto wasn't smart enough to sign him."

Connie repeats what she reads in the sports section when Kathy's home, but she doesn't follow hockey on TV, has never gone to a live game. Her mother doesn't get her passion for hockey, why Kathy insisted on watching *Hockey Night in Canada* even after Charlie died.

At first she watched exactly because Charlie had died. Because it was something they'd done together, so she couldn't imagine not doing it. Then she watched because she wanted to learn, to improve her moves. Without her father to coach her on their backyard rink, without his running commentary at Junior A games at the Aud, she wasn't getting any better. And she wanted to get better because she wanted to think her father would be proud of her.

She watched to see how someone stickhandled or made a fast turn. See how a play formed on the ice. How a player on a breakaway skated down along the boards and after a quick turnaround flicked the puck in front of the goal where a rushing forward picked it up, shot, and scored.

She was learning technique. And she started to apply it when she skated after supper, whenever Connie let her go to the school rink. Practising abrupt turns. Practising backward starts and stops. She took her stick and skated with a puck, fast stops, restarts, caressing the puck with her stick, or deftly dropping the puck, an almost invisible move—she had it, then she didn't—for another player, one of those imaginary ones, the only ones she ever got to play with.

When she turned twelve, her mother let her take the bus to Junior A games on Saturday afternoons. She went alone and sat behind some regulars, men who had known Charlie, and who reminded her of her father. Working men who huffed warm breath into their callused bare hands and had weekend-stubbled cheeks. Who wore clean green cotton work pants with faded knees and baggy bums, school janitor pants. They called her Charlie's kid.

"Hey, it's Charlie's kid," one of them would say as she settled in her seat. Another would ask, "How're ya today?" Then another, usually the one with the Rangers toque—the one growing the Fu Manchu mustache that the other men kidded him about—would ask, "How's your mother doing these days?" Sometimes he'd add, "And that sister of yours, how's she getting along?"

Kathy said, fine and fine and fine. But once the game started it was all hockey talk. And she listened. Listened to their comments on who was good that day and who was having a hard time, and why. She listened to their commentary on the play. She brought her skates because after the games, after the ice was cleaned and smoothed, there was an hour-long free skate for the fans. Kathy practised what she'd learned from the men and combined it with what she saw on TV. And she improved, getting faster, stopping easier, turning on a dime.

When she got home, Connie would ask, "How was the game?"

"Good," Kathy told her, because that's all she wanted to hear. For a while Kathy tried to tell her what had really happened: a brilliant goal, an unfair penalty, a brutal drop-the-gloves fight. But Connie's hockey-talk stamina lasted about a minute before she'd tell Kathy there were leftover egg salad sandwiches in the fridge.

Then Bobby Orr joined the Bruins. If Connie came down to the rec room to watch a game with her, Kathy tried to explain what a good skater Bobby was. She'd use words she thought her mother liked. Dazzling, she said once. Like Cassius Clay dancing around the ring, evading opponents, making them look clumsy and slow. That was Bobby on the ice, she told her mother. An artist. She could watch him forever.

That night Connie called Kathy's enthusiasm for skating a hobby, like it was knitting or stamp collecting. Kathy had just told her mother that doing something with her skating was her dream, even though she had yet to figure out exactly what that dream could be. She was so excited she couldn't stop the words coming out of her mouth, even when she sensed she was going to get hammered.

She certainly wasn't going to get into the NHL, she told her mother. And she didn't figure skate, so that eliminated competitions. There didn't seem to be a job out there for a girl on hockey skates, who could skate circles around imaginary opponents, and stickhandle imaginary pucks into imaginary nets. Or none that she knew of. But she wasn't going to stop dreaming.

Her mother said, "Face it, Kathy, it's just a hobby."

Connie's turning from the window, and she's giving Kathy her I-don't-understand-you-I'll-never-understand-you look.

"Good Lord Jesus, Mary, and gaw-damned Joseph, Kathy. What are you doing?"

"Ironing my shirt."

"While you're wearing it?"

Kathy presses the cloth under her small breasts and across her flat abdomen. The shirt, shiny from the iron, is a psychedelic swirl of brown, turquoise, white and two shades of orange. The sleeves are long and tight, enormous cuffs balloon over her small wrists. The neck is a high wide band with a little zipper at the back. Her nipples are erect; she's not wearing a bra. The chemical scent of polyester sizing rises around her, almost, but not quite, obliterating the fine rich smell of the pot roast, smothered in carrots and potatoes and turnips, that is bubbling in the oven in Lipton onion soup mix gravy.

"The setting's low."

"You shouldn't have to iron polyester. Wash and wear, isn't that what the label says?" Connie looks down at her paper. "I can't watch," she says.

"So who's a loser if Boston's an underdog?" Kathy asks, wondering as she asks it if she really wants to know. She yanks the cord from the kitchen wall socket from where she's standing in the doorway.

"Don't yank the cord like that! You'll electrocute yourself," Connie says without looking up. "Doug. I'd say Doug's a big-time loser."

Doug still calls Connie trying to find out where Kathy is. Connie says she doesn't hang up, though she is tempted to, but she doesn't tell him anything, either. And Doug sends letters, mails them to her mother's address. Connie leaves them on the counter, where Kathy picks them up when she comes for supper.

"I could have put this in the garbage and you'd never have known it came," her mother had told her, waving that first letter in the air.

"But you didn't," was all Kathy said, and she grabbed the letter from her mother's hand and shoved it in her coat pocket.

Doug's still living in the communal house she shared with him and eight other hippies, up off Cambie on West 14th. The letters have intricate psychedelic drawings along the edges, and *I Love You* written over and over again in many scripts. He has calligraphy talent and he's persistent. But he's lying, because he doesn't love Kathy. He just doesn't like surprises. And he hates to lose.

He writes once a week, trying to get Kathy to come back to Vancouver, and back to him. She doesn't answer because she has no intention of going back to him. As far as she's concerned—and she's already told her mother this—it's over with Doug.

"I told you, he's history," Kathy says. "Why are you bringing him up again?"

"Maybe because I don't believe you. Maybe because every time you get a letter from him you look weepy," Connie says. "And like I said, it's a fine line between underdogs and losers. Underdogs have a chance. You're wasting your time on Doug. He's not a good man. You've said so yourself. Get over him.

"And while we're at it, while we're examining the life of Kathy Rausch, you're wasting time on that loser checkout job in a store that's on its last legs. You're smart, Kathy. All your teachers said you were smart. Go to college. Or at least get a job in a union shop.

"Look here," she says, and she shakes the newspaper, "the firemen are getting a 17% raise this year. Unionized job. And you remember Shirley Goetz from church? Promoted to line supervisor last week. Unionized job. That'll never happen in a grocery store. Women don't get to be managers in supermarkets. Even packers get promoted because they're boys, but women... never!"

"I order the cigarettes," Kathy interrupts.

Then she stops speaking because if she says more she will only get in deeper trouble. Cigarette ordering is a prestige position in Kathy's store, but it's just a bone they threw her when she threatened to quit when all the guys got a raise and Kathy's pay packet was exactly the same as always. Unmarried checkout girls are on the bottom of the grocery store food chain. Even Kathy knows this. And though her mother is right about wages and promotions, Kathy will never admit it, at least not to her.

"Yoo-hoo! Kathy-Kathy-Kathy! I'm talking to you. Do they pay you more for ordering cigarettes?" Connie calls.

Kathy very carefully and very slowly wraps the cord around the handle of the iron. She doesn't say anything because there's nothing to say.

"Do something with your life," Connie almost hisses. "You're going to be twenty soon."

Kathy leans on the door jamb. Holding the iron in one hand like a shield, she runs the fingers of her other hand up and down the thin strip of blond moulding along the edge of the walnut panelling her father installed in the dining area two weeks before he'd died in the car crash. Kathy had handed him nails and fetched cold beer. Her father told her she was a good carpenter's helper and she should consider becoming an apprentice when she grew up. Something to fall back on, he had said and winked, when she got too old to play hockey.

She sets the iron on the chrome dining table and turns into the kitchen, puts on a pair of oven mitts that are crusty with food stains and dotted with burn holes. The oven door squeals and a thick spicy steam rolls up out of the roasting pan when Kathy lifts the lid. Pot roast is one of her favourite winter meals and her mother is cooking it for her tonight as a special treat.

"You could at least move out of that house you're boarding in. Everyone knows it's a dope dealer's house," Connie yells from the living room.

"Go to hell," Kathy mouths as she bastes the meat and vegetables with the oniony gravy. "I can't hear you," she says out loud. She clatters the lid around to make noise, then sets it back on the pan and closes the oven door.

"There's been another hijacking," Connie shouts.

"What?" Kathy asks, as she walks back into the living room.

"Did you check that roast?" Connie says.

Kathy sits on the arm of her mother's chair.

"Um-hm," she nods. "What were you saying?"

"I said there's been another hijacking. Some Brazilians trying to get to Cuba. Here," Connie says, reaching under her chair for the box with the clipped-out article. She hands the clipping to Kathy. "Add this to my scrapbook, honey."

"Sure," Kathy says and slides off the chair.

Connie's fridge scrapbook has categories: Vietnam War. Labour News. Entertainment. Sports. Sports is for Kathy and it's mostly filled with tiny articles about their neighbour—and Kathy's best friend—Darlyn Smola, about Darlyn's baton twirling competitions. "*Twin City girl wins firsts in the senior fancy strut, senior flag twirling and senior two baton twirling,*" one article says. Darlyn is good. Really good. She almost always comes first in her category.

And there are hockey articles: *Leading Scorers: Orr (Bos) 54 Goyette (St L) 47 Esposito (Bos) 40 Tkaczuk (NY) 38* and *Goalie Gump Worsley says he'll retire rather than accept demotion to farm team.* Occasionally there's something about Cassius Clay, who Connie thinks is some kind of damn-fool nutcase hero for defying the United States draft.

Not that Connie doesn't believe in war. Maybe because she'd lived through World War II, she says, once she's on the topic. But she feels what Canada needs is a strong military that knows its arse from a hole in the ground (her words) and has leaders who have vision. And when she's really rolling she also tells Kathy, and anyone who's listening, that she believes there should be some kind of national service. Not like the US draft. That's just a way to kill off Negroes and the poor. Who are mostly Negroes, she adds.

No, she says, more like the community work the Company of Young Canadians does. Or the Mennonite Central Committee or some other church or volunteer group that does relief work. Give young people—all young people, no exceptions—a sense of civic duty, which seems to be sorely lacking since the last war. Kids have it too good, Connie likes to rant. They take too much for granted. They need something to help them get their lives in order, to figure out what really matters to them. "In my humble opinion, at least," she always adds.

Nine times out of ten this lecture is directed at Kathy. Especially the getting-lives-in-order part.

Kathy's unsure where she stands on the Vietnam War and the US draft, but she has been in bars and coffee houses and sat with boys running away from both the war and the draft, mostly working-class kids like herself who see no way out of going to Vietnam but to go into exile, who complain that university kids get exemptions and the rich boys' parents can afford to buy their way out of service.

Unlike Connie, who has the entire world and everything and everyone in it figured out, and knows the best way to do everything, Kathy can't figure out her own life, much less come up with ways that other people should be living. Still, she listens to Connie, tries to take in what she says, as long as she's not commenting too directly on her life. Then Kathy shuts her out, and every word Connie says is splintered almost to nothingness, into dust particles that drift away on the air.

If Kathy hears anything, it's the raw need in Connie's voice. (Connie calls this love—*I wouldn't say this if I didn't love you*, is her line.) Connie wants Kathy to be normal: have a reasonably good job with decent wages, preferably a union job with benefits and some security; have a stable relationship; live in a decent apartment; act like a responsible citizen.

In the kitchen Kathy notices a new sports article about a guy named Jerry Rahn, a bowler in Fergus who won three hundred dollars for getting a perfect score.

"Who's Jerry Rahn?" she calls to her mother as she tapes the hijacking article under *Reasons Not To Fly In Airplanes*.

"No idea," Connie yells back, "but it's an article that doesn't have to do with war or strikes or airplanes, and three hundred bucks is a lot of money. I was thinking maybe I should take up bowling."

That's how the hijacking section started. Connie thought she should take up flying. She'd never flown before. Still hasn't because she keeps developing theories about flying, or deterrents to flying, really. One of them has to do with the amount of worry it takes to hold an airplane in the sky.

Worry keeps airplanes from crashing, Connie's theory goes. Worry's a bit like prayer. Carries the same weight and has the same effect, which is sometimes none, depending on the moment. God—being arbitrary and not always up to the foolishness of mortals—listens or doesn't; acts or ignores. Worry's arbitrary too. You only know if worry works if you get a positive result.

The amount of worry necessary to keep an airplane flying is almost impossible to determine until a flight has successfully landed. Then there was enough worry. Everyone's done their part. So far, Connie hasn't found any newspaper articles to prove her worry theory, so *Hijackings* is a subcategory of *Reasons Not To Fly In Airplanes*, because extra worry is most surely required to keep a plane flying when it's been hijacked. And lately there have been hijackings almost every day.

"Tell me again what that article says, Kathy," Connie shouts.

"Four young men and a pretty woman landed the plane in Lima," Kathy shouts back. It's easier to indulge this passion of her mother's than it is to try to ignore it or to argue.

"Then they got stalled on the runway in Lima due to a dead airplane battery," she summarizes.

"Hear that?" Connie calls to her. "A dead battery saved them from crashing before they got to Cuba. Someone's mother had to do a lot of worrying to get that battery dead. They don't know how lucky they are."

"Where's Shelly?" Connie asks when Kathy comes back into the room.

"Lying between her mattress and the box spring," Kathy says.

"It's her comfort," Connie says shaking her head. "Will you go get her for supper, please?"

Before Kathy goes to get Shelly, she heads for the bathroom. She closes the door, locks it, steps into the tub and opens the window. Snowflakes sift through the screen; the wind lows through the crack. Kathy sucks cold air, holds it deep in her lungs. Sometimes she feels there's a weight on her chest and she can't catch her breath. Sometimes, when she's listening to her mother, hearing the sureness in her voice, hearing her theories and what she wants for her, Kathy's heart races and her muscles tense; she feels light-headed and breaks out in a sweat.

Kathy exhales slowly, watches her breath condense in the cold air. She steps out of the tub and pulls two plush rugs together and lies down. The air from the window cools her. She closes her eyes and breathes. In and out. Her heart slows.

The bathroom is extravagant, an oasis, because Connie likes to bathe. Long, hot, deep baths, with crackers and Velveeta and a thermos of coffee on a little moveable shelf Kathy bought her that extends across the tub. Wooden shelves, just outside the tub area but handy to it, hold bath salts and bubble stuff, expensive French milled soap, a Blue Mountain pottery ashtray, emollients and lotions. Magazines pack a wooden stand. Fluff: *Barbra and Pierre: Romance? Lose 15 Pounds in Ten Days. How To Tell if Your Husband is Cheating on You.* And, *6 Quick and Easy Casseroles for Leftover Turkey.* Thick lime-green towels hang from wooden racks, and the two plush bubblegum-pink mats—the ones Kathy's lying on—match the toilet seat cover.

As Kathy's body gentles, as her breathing slows, Connie's voice plays in her head: *Get a union job.*

She had a union job once, wrapping and soldering electrical coils. It didn't last long. Connie was so disappointed when she quit that Kathy doesn't bring it up. Now it's as if it never happened.

The work was demanding and varied and Kathy excelled at every assignment, so her supervisor made her a time setter. Kathy's speed and technique on each machine was monitored. At the end of a month, her averaged stats were posted as the new standard for each machine. When some girls cornered her in the parking lot after work one day, and threatened to beat the crap out of her if she didn't slow down, Kathy was only a little surprised. She knew that she'd been showing off and that her standards were making their work lives harder.

These dyed-blonde, big-haired girls had quit school when they'd turned sixteen and moved south to Varnum from Kapuskasing and

Temiscaming and Haileybury for the factory jobs and the big city life. They looked like they'd stepped out of old Elvis Presley movies: pouting rouged lips, innocent heavily made-up eyes, tiny waists cinched by wide belts, Jane Russell breasts in one-size-too-small blouses that strained their buttons. Kathy wondered if they were related, they looked so much alike.

They told Kathy they had no intention of meeting the pace she'd been setting. They had a plan, they said. They were going to stay in their jobs until some man rescued them from work, and no one, especially some hippie kid who thought she was special because she'd graduated from high school, was going to get them fired for working too slowly. No one was going to make them work harder than they had to until they reached their goal: a wedding.

"Kathy, what're you doing in there?" Connie calls from the living room.

"Nothing," Kathy calls back.

Kathy admired these girls, liked their spunk and humour, their blue eye shadow, black eyeliner and hairsprayed hair. She really didn't want to make their lives more difficult, she had just been bored with the repetition of the work and enjoyed the challenge her supervisor had set for her.

Kathy liked their French accents and their stories of small-town life. They were brave. They'd left their families and homes to find a different life in Varnum, a better life. That their lives wouldn't be very much different from what they'd find up north—a husband, a car, a mortgage, a department store charge card, some babies—never seemed to bother them. It was the city that made all the difference, and that seemed to be difference enough.

She got a kick out of the stories of their beer-drinking English boyfriends who thought French girls knew how to do sexual things with their tongues. How all they had to do was stick their tongues in a guy's mouth, move it around a bit, then lick his neck or his ear a little and he'd come, just like that. Right in his underpants, or in their hands. It was the thought of what might happen next that brought them off. It was so easy, practically all the girls were virgins. And they'd laughed, and Kathy had laughed with them, even though she knew she didn't want what they wanted. And without the variety of pace setting, her job became dull. So she quit wrapping and soldering electrical coils and that was the end of her union job.

"Are you getting Shelly or not?" Connie yells.

Kathy can hear her mother in the kitchen now, setting the table. Then she hears her walking up to the door.

"Kathy!"

Kathy straightens the rugs and grabs a magazine from the holder. On the cover is a woman with long blonde tresses. That's the only way you could describe the enormous amount of blonde hair that falls in thick waves and curls: tresses.

"This," she says, opening the door and flapping the magazine at her mother, "is engrossing."

She turns back into the bathroom and stuffs the magazine in the rack.

"Shelly," her mother says, and nods toward Shelly's room.

As Kathy walks to Shelly's room, she sees the set table, the steamed-up windows. On a platter in the middle of the chrome table is food for the gods: a slab of beef bursting its strings, surrounded by oven-browned carrots and onions and potatoes and turnips. Beside the platter, gravy congeals in a glass measuring cup, and the smell of it all, ambrosial.

SHELLY'S HAIR IS RED, BOWL CUT AND THICK. HER EYES ARE DARK grey, the colour of rain clouds just before a storm. They have silver crackles like lightning through them. Her complexion is porcelain and, like a doll, she has a high red blush on her cheeks, though this is from skin irritation rather than a mark of beauty. Shelly rubs her cheeks round and round with her hands. Constantly. Her cheeks are always chapped, and at their worst they have open sores on them.

"Supper," Kathy says, and with supreme care she takes Shelly's hands and pulls her from the sandwich of mattress and box spring. Shelly flops out onto the floor like a newborn, almost boneless. She is hardly ever this supple. The everyday Shelly is all stiff muscles and hard angles, sharp movements and jarring noises.

Shelly starts to rub.

"Gently, Shelly, gently," Kathy says and sits beside the bed. She takes Shelly's hands and places them on her own cheeks. Shelly doesn't pull away; she laughs, a horsy ha-ha-ha without a trace of happiness. She rubs Kathy's cheeks.

Shelly was born too fast, Connie says, popped right out of her after some indigestion and a few hard contractions. She didn't breathe right away, too shocked for breath, Connie says. It was a good thing Connie was already in the hospital with high blood pressure, the birth was so fast. Shelly didn't cry when she was born. Her clear grey eyes were wide open and they looked at the ceiling or the wall. Anywhere but at Connie. She was the prettiest baby imaginable. But no crying, not then.

Once Connie took her home, Shelly never stopped crying. That was the first clue Shelly was different. Nothing comforted her. If

Connie held her or tried to nurse her, Shelly resisted and cried harder. Kathy held her and she cried. Charlie held her and she cried the hardest.

Shelly didn't respond to cooing or smiles, she didn't look at people. In fact, she was almost aggressive in not looking at them. She hated to be held any time but particularly when she was fed. Connie took to propping her bottle on a towel. Only then would Shelly close her big grey eyes and fall not so much asleep as into a trance, making a rhythmical humming sound like a motor. The sound seemed to vibrate from her stomach like a cat's purr. It did not come from her throat like a normal baby.

When Connie took Shelly to the doctor, he said it was colic. Wait and it will go away. Then Charlie died in the accident and Connie stopped thinking about what was wrong with Shelly for a while, stopped thinking about anything or anyone. Kathy did what she could to help, but it was little enough. Mostly she kept Shelly away from Connie. Neighbours brought food, and a roster was set up to help with cleaning and other chores.

Connie's friends took turns sitting with her. They came in pairs. One would pull a chair up beside Connie's and talk in a low soothing voice; sometimes they held her hand, stroked it, while Connie stared out the window. The other was designated to hold Shelly, who would go silent in their arms. But it was a strange silence, stiff and formal and over-quiet, her little body rigid, her head turned away. It was as if she knew she had to get through this particular attention and she cooperated, but she wouldn't make anyone feel good. There was no cute in Shelly. When Kathy or Connie took her, Shelly reverted, and cried once again.

When Shelly was almost two and still cried more than a normal baby, and didn't talk and barely crawled, much less walked, Connie started taking her to the doctor so often that the doctor sent her to see a specialist. After months and months of tests, the specialist, a small man with a snowman shape who wore dull brown shoes and had nicotine stains on his fingers and on his teeth, told Connie that Shelly was mentally retarded, quite possibly a development problem called autism. He told her that Shelly was that way because Connie was a cold and distant mother. Connie never went back to see him.

"Do you want to skate tonight, Shelly?" Kathy asks her sister.

Shelly ha-ha-ha's her smileless laugh.

"Orr, Boston, 54. Goyette, St. Louis, 47. Esposito, Boston, 40. St. Marseille, St. Louis, 38. Tkaczuk, New York, 38." Shelly hums the hockey stats under her breath, a tuneless song.

"You're so smart," Kathy says. "You're the smartest girl I know."

"Ha-ha-ha," Shelly laughs and she rolls from side to side on the floor.

Shelly doesn't like toys or books, except for *Where the Wild Things Are*. "Let the wild rumpus start," Shelly yells when Kathy reaches that part of the story. The book is tattered, the pages thin and soft as old skin, the words nearly worn away because Shelly likes to rub them, too. It doesn't matter, because Connie and Kathy know the words by heart, the way Shelly knows hockey statistics by heart these days.

Connie reads Shelly hockey statistics from the newspaper because Shelly seems able to memorize them. Just like that. She has pockets of brilliance, but they don't add up to anything. She's fickle. She'll give up an interest in a flash and never repeat information she once knew by heart, not even when coaxed. Connie says Shelly has a bright light in one little part of her brain, and that light shines on only one tiny bit of knowledge at a time. When the light switches and shines on something new, all that was once known becomes lost in a deep impenetrable darkness.

"Up now, Shelly," Kathy says, and pulls her sister to her feet. She helps her wash up in the bathroom and they go to the table, where Connie is serving the pot roast.

"Bobby Orr, #4. Bobby Orr, #4," Shelly shouts as she rocks back and forth in her chair.

"Shush, Shelly. Eat," Connie says.

"Bobby Orr, #4," Shelly whispers while filling her mouth with food. Bits of pot roast and gravy spray across the table.

"I saw Ted Kennedy on TV yesterday," Connie says to Kathy. "Joan was with him. She has some tan, that woman, and she must wear sunglasses all the time because when she takes them off her eyes look raccoony. She did look relaxed, though. I don't know how she could be after that girl drowned. Mary Jo. The inquest has started, I guess.

"I wish the Kennedys weren't Catholic. It was so nice when Jack was elected; we were all so proud of him. It was a miracle. Then Robert. Now they're both dead, and that leaves the alcoholic philanderer. Now he's responsible for a girl's death. I suppose his brothers set a standard he couldn't meet. Could just be he's normal like the rest of us. Anyway, I wish he'd smarten up. His poor mother, what she must be going through."

A snowmobile drives by, a loud, screaming whirr. Shelly covers her ears and screams along with it.

"I hate those things," Connie says, getting up and going to Shelly. She takes Shelly's arms and holds them down at her sides, saying, shush-shush, until Shelly stops screaming.

"It's the Dietrich boy down the block," Connie continues, and she sits again. "Rides up and down the street making that horrible racket. He drives on people's lawns. It'll ruin the grass, doing that. I passed one tearing into the Lutheran Cemetery when I was driving to work, so I phoned the City. The guy said they're drafting a by-law to keep them off the streets."

"This is good, Mom," Kathy says, trying to deflect her mother from her snowmobile rant. "Blade roast's on sale. Want me to pick one up?"

"No thanks, honey. Al bought a side of frozen beef from some farmer he knows out near Heidelberg. Ended up selling me some roasts and hamburger for next to nothing."

They settle in to eat then, comfortably quiet, the clink of dinnerware on their plates. Al is Albert Smola, Connie's next-door neighbour, father to Kathy's best friend, Darlyn, baton twirling queen of North America. Al always has a friend, someone he knows who gets him cheap beef. Or flats of farm-fresh eggs, bushel baskets of peaches, grocery bags full of peas in the pod, and once a box filled with rhubarb roots, so that every house in the neighbourhood now has a rhubarb plant somewhere in their garden. Al always shares the bounty with his neighbours, but most especially with Connie.

Al sells insurance and Watkins products door-to-door to farmers. Likes to get out in the country, he says, so he works a rural route. One year he carried a line of dishes, Melmac, but it was too near the end of the Melmac craze and they didn't sell. Connie bought a set at a deep discount. Sky blue pine cones on white plastic, the plates now scored with knife marks and the pine cones worn away. They never look clean. Connie lets Shelly bang around with them in the sandbox.

For a while Al sold linens too, which he felt was a good complement to his main items, household cleaning and health care products. Recently he added a line of lingerie. Just testing the market, he told Connie when she asked him what was new. Connie told him she'd have nothing to do with lingerie; no self-respecting housewife would buy lingerie from a door-to-door salesman. And don't try to give me any samples, either. Since Charlie died, Al would do anything for Connie. Anything she asked. Connie never asks.

Connie pretends to ignore Al, says she doesn't want to encourage him, but she once called him debonair. Kathy had laughed and said, I think he looks like Elvis-getting-old. Like a greaser who's moved to the suburbs. Connie said, Al's not old. Kathy said, Mo-ther! He's older than you. Not giving up, Connie had asked, What's the matter with Elvis? And Kathy rolled her eyes and said, He's not Neil Young. Who? Connie asked. Exactly, Kathy said.

If Kathy accumulated all the things Connie has said about Al over the years, the list wouldn't be long, but it would add up to a positive image: He's dependable. He's a good father to Darlyn. He's a hard worker. He's a good neighbour. He's kind to Shelly, most particularly important. At least he's alive, she once joked. And he's debonair.

Al Brylcreems his dark brown hair—no grey yet—into a forward tilting shelf that juts above his brow, combed—tine marks showing in the grease—into a duck's ass at the back. His chore pants, old paint-speckled black Sunday trousers, are always pressed and clean. He wears thin beige dress socks, black pointy-toed shoes polished to a reflecting glow for work and dress-up. The same shoes, though battered and old, for at-home. His dress shirts are white. In winter he wears undershirts with short sleeves, a bit of chest hair curling above his crew neck collar, a grey wool car coat with wooden buttons done up with thick leather loops, zippered black galoshes stretched to a puckered rubber V in the front by his pointy-toed shoes.

"Do you want any more, honey?" Connie asks Kathy.

"No thanks," Kathy says and leans back from the table. "What are you working on these days?" she asks.

"Valentine stuff. Marshmallow hearts, your faves. Want me to bring some home?"

Kathy does love chocolate-coated marshmallow hearts. When Connie first started working at the candy factory, almost a year to the day after Charlie's accident, they ate themselves sick. She brought home tins of seconds and refilled each tin when it was emptied. Turkish delight, cream-filled chocolates, peppermint patties, toffees. Kathy got pimples, Shelly got diarrhea and two cavities in her baby teeth and had to be knocked out to have them filled, and Connie started getting fat. Soon enough they all became sick of the sweets, or Connie and Kathy did. Shelly had no control at all and would eat until the tins were empty. Connie only occasionally brings candy home now.

"Bobby Orr, #4," Shelly screams when Connie mentions marshmallow hearts. She flaps her hands in the air. "Bobby Orr, #4!"

"A couple would be nice. Thanks," Kathy says. "And some for Shelly. You like candy, don't you, Shelly?"

"Bobby Orr, #4," Shelly yells even louder.

After they clean up, Kathy helps Shelly dress. She'd checked the rink at the elementary school on her way over to supper. The ice was freshly flooded, a smooth silvery slab, seams rippled like soldered steel, but no deep cracks, no lines yet cut in the surface.

Tonight it's cold, but not bitter. No wind. The snow has stopped falling. As they walk down the path between the houses, they kick up snow like dust on a dry cornfield. The wind has blown most of the ice clear, drifts mound against the boards at one end. Laced up, Shelly takes off and skates circles along the boards, undeterred by the drifts, plowing through them. For such a stiff child she is graceful on ice, gliding steadily and rhythmically, turning with her left foot leading. Over, over, clack-clack-clack, three steps per turn, always the same. If she changes direction, she stumbles. Shelly can skate only one way, counter-clockwise, against the stream, but tonight there are only two other skaters so no one cares.

Kathy bought new hockey skates with her first paycheque from the store, boys' Bauers made right here in Varnum. They're a bit stiff still, but even so they feel like home. She moves to centre ice and skates backwards, imitates Bobby Orr's swishing hip movement, the technique he uses to block skaters, ramming them to stop a play, flinging them into the boards. Around the curve, foot behind foot, knees deeply bent, gliding back up the ice again. Her favourite sound, the slish of steel on ice.

Kathy used to try to get in on the shinny games guys played in the late evenings on school rinks. Fluid fast hockey, passes, a nod to a new player to let him know his team. She'd arrive early, warm up, wait for play to begin. But it was as if she were invisible. Few pucks were passed her way, play always shifting away from where she was on the ice to the other end or the other side of the rink. It wasn't aggressive, although she could have handled that; she was ready for action, for the odd check. She'd practised skating into the boards late at night, bouncing away while still stickhandling the puck. But no one checked her, no one told her to get off the ice. She could skate up and down, follow the play, once in a while tip a missed puck toward a nearby player, but for the most part, nothing. They sidelined her. She stopped going.

She'd never stop skating though. Nights when she was alone on the ice, she'd take a bag of pucks and stickhandle them, shoot them into the boards, skate to meet them, back into the boards, playing herself. Pick up a new puck, the nearest puck, when she missed one. Skate until she was sweating, steaming, adrenalin coursing, the thrill of it deep inside her body. Night, cold, stars, pretty moon—she didn't notice. There was only the thwack of her stick on a puck, the responding rumble from the boards.

Practising like Bobby, practising his flick of the wrist, almost invisible it was so casual. Backing away from an oncoming player, taking the puck to the side, up along the boards. Skating into another player, a deke to centre. Putting the puck in the net and starting over until her thighs ached.

Shelly bumps into Kathy. She grabs her jacket at the back and Kathy pulls her along, gently, slowly, a favourite game. Kathy turns and wraps her arms around her sister and they twirl together, the dervish twirl Connie taught Kathy when she was a little girl. Shelly's legs swing out and bob through the air and she screams her piercing almost-happiness into the night.

Kathy screams too, can't help it. It feels so good to be skating. She holds Shelly tight and twirls until she can hardly stand up, then she slows, lowers herself, Shelly still in her arms, until Shelly's skates touch the ice. They plunk down together, Shelly sitting quietly between Kathy's legs. When their dizziness passes, they slip cold feet into colder boots and clump home, almost touching but not quite.

KATHY'S CAR IS A 1966 VALIANT, SLANT SIX 225, FOUR-DOOR, monkey-shit brown automatic with just over 90,000 miles on it. A simple car renowned for reliability. A gas jockey anywhere could fix it with a bobby pin and some chewing gum. All the parts are straightforward, cheap and easy to get. Nothing fancy, but always ready to go. That's what Al told Kathy. Ever since Charlie died, Al has done his best to be the man around the house, for the most part outside it, shovelling snow, fixing broken eavestroughs, selling Kathy a car, mowing the lawn, doing car repairs, anything to be on the same property as Connie, to be able to look at her, maybe even have a conversation.

When Al sold Kathy his old Valiant he said, in his reassuring salesman voice, "I'd sell this car to your mother because I'd never have to worry about her when she was driving it." They stood on Al's black, perfectly sealed asphalt driveway, which was lined both sides like an airport runway with spotlights for Darlyn's night-time baton practice. Al rocked from foot to foot, looking over first one, then the other of Kathy's shoulders. Looking toward the house where Connie sat on the front porch on her aluminum chaise lounge with the white and turquoise plastic mesh. Connie faced away from them and toward the sun.

Connie was wearing faded brown short-shorts and a white halter top. Her skin was shiny with baby oil, her rolled-up hair covered with a black and white checkered kerchief tied round the back. A pair of faded yellow rubber thongs sat beside her on the cool grey concrete of the porch. She very deliberately read her newspaper, as deliberately as she ignored Kathy and Al.

It's not that Connie doesn't like Al, but he's married. And not just to anyone, but to Mah-gret. (The only way Connie can say Margaret's name the way it sounds when Margaret says it, is to hold her nose closed at the tip.) Margaret is Scottish, but has an English accent, acquired, she will tell anyone who will listen and Connie more than once, while attending St. Mary's School in Cambridge, England—a Catholic girls' boarding school—at the insistence of her maternal grandmother, who had enough money to have her way, and who loathed all things Protestant, and most particularly, all things Scottish and Protestant. It was her intention to school Scotland out of her granddaughter, come hell or high water, and reinforce all things British and Catholic.

Margaret calls herself a Pastonian, the name of her school alumnae. The Pastonians are hosting a tea this Friday, she once told Connie, who wondered if Margaret expected her to care. Margaret also told Connie that her one and only rebellion, her one rash act in life, other than getting pregnant, though she couldn't have been expected to know how rash that was going to be until she was in the middle of her labour, was to fall in love with a handsome Canadian soldier, Albert Smola, whom she met at a dance in Cambridge. She was married, like all the other English girls during the war, in a parachute-silk dress, just two months after meeting Albert and three days before he was sent to the front. He left, and she didn't see him for seven months, and if she hadn't had her wedding photo, she wasn't sure she would have recognized him when he returned. Then suddenly she was on a boat, throwing up every day, on her way to Canada.

"I guess you could say that was two rash acts," Margaret had said, "falling in love with a Canadian, and then actually marrying him. At least he was Catholic." And she added, "And he wasn't Scottish."

Margaret's accent—the entire Britishness of her—makes her seem distant and cold. She doesn't come out to have a coffee and a smoke, gather on someone's porch or picnic table, with the other women on the street. The neighbours call her the Queen. Queen Mah-gret this, the Queen that. On occasion Connie defends Margaret, telling her friends she thinks Margaret is lonely and has never really established herself since she moved to Canada. Just imagine, Connie'd say, moving to a new country and leaving your friends and family behind. Imagine landing in this neighbourhood, she'd say, raising her eyebrows. And they'd laugh together every time.

Margaret is curt to the point of rudeness, and she calls her bluntness honesty. She boldly told Connie (who stopped defending her for a time afterwards) that she was lucky Charlie had died because then she didn't have to share her bed with anyone. And more importantly, she'd added, Connie didn't have to have "relations." She confided to Connie that though they continued to share the same bed, she hadn't slept with Al "in that way" since Darlyn was born. The birth had been so hard, and so alarming, that Margaret never wanted another child ever again, and no sex ever was the only sure solution to that. As Darlyn is the same age as Kathy, that makes it nineteen, soon-to-be-twenty, sexless years.

As for Al, once when he came over to help Connie unplug her toilet and arrived drunk, he tried to convince Connie that he and Margaret really weren't married, not in the eyes of the Church, where sex must be a vital part of wedded Catholic life, he argued. "You're married as far as the Church of Connie Rausch is concerned," she told him, "so you're shit out of luck, Al. So to speak."

"I'm not a prude," she added, which made him secretly hopeful, "but I'd never knowingly sleep with a married man. Now you go on home and sober up and we'll pretend we didn't have this conversation. And thank you for unplugging my toilet. Tell Margaret I'm sorry I took you away from the family."

Considering that Connie hasn't had sex—other than masturbation—since Charlie died (although she's dated on and off over the years, she finds Shelly and serious dating, especially if it might involve sex, are incompatible), if you add Connie's sexless years to Al's, and then to Margaret's, that's one gaw-damned long sex-drought in only two of the houses on this one street. "Let's hope someone out there is making up for us," she told Margaret in a fit of reciprocal bluntness she liked to think was honesty and not provocation. Margaret had shuddered.

"And hopefully it's not our girls increasing the neighbourhood average," Connie added, to see if Margaret would shudder again.

Kathy bought the Valiant from Al two summers ago. She glued a plastic Jesus to the dashboard, strung purple whore-lure lights across the front and back windshields and set a nodding dog with glow-in-the-dark eyes on the shelf of the back window. But as the pièce de résistance, Kathy installed an 8-track tape player hooked up to a secondhand pair of walnut veneer household speakers that she sat on the floor in the back seat.

The house still smells like pot roast when Kathy pulls her jacket on and hugs Connie goodbye. Shelly's asleep, having gone to bed quietly for a change. The skating tired her out.

"Mary coming?" Kathy asks, knowing that she is, but it's neutral ground.

"As always," Connie says.

Mary's a retired nurse, a friend of the family now. She answered Connie's ad looking for an overnight babysitter. Connie started working nights when Shelly turned three. Charlie's life insurance company helped Connie set up a trust with an annuity that paid the household bills. But when Connie realized Shelly was a special child who would need help for the rest of her life, she also realized she was going to need more money than the annuity allowed. One of her friends got her a job at the candy factory, and though the shifts changed every three weeks—a day, evening, night rotation—Connie decided that nights worked best for her. She could work, and she could still be home for Shelly and Kathy.

That's when she placed the ad for overnight babysitting. Shelly takes a sleeping pill, so she seldom wakes up, but in case Shelly did wake up and needed help, Connie wanted someone intelligent and kind. And she wanted someone to keep an eye out for Kathy, who had too much of the burden of Shelly's care. Although Kathy protested, she was relieved, especially when she met Mary.

Mary's eyes and mouth have smile crinkles. When she arrives at night, white pincurls crisscrossed with black bobby pins cover her head. In the morning there's no sign of a curl, just cotton-ball tufts circling her kind face. There is no bullshit in her, not one tiny bit.

Mary had worked nights and liked the hours, she told Connie. And if Connie had a TV with good aerial reception, Mary said she'd take less than the going wage, to help out like. Mary was devoted to late-night television.

"Johnny Carson's my boyfriend," she told Connie at that first interview. "He makes me laugh. We have a date every weeknight, but I never have to clean up after him. Never have to smell his farts under the blanket in bed, or listen as he pees in the toilet. That's the way I like my men: on the other side of glass, with an 'off' switch available at all times."

Shelly met Mary and took to her right away, which was all Connie had to see. Mary came mornings for two weeks to get to know Shelly and the house, and it was hard at first to make Shelly go to bed when she knew Mary was coming to spend the night.

During the day Shelly goes to a special program started by Connie and the parents of six other retarded children, and run by a qualified special education teacher assisted by volunteers—do-gooders, Connie gratefully calls them—from Connie's church, Our Lady of Perpetual Hope. The parents pay a stipend for the teacher's salary, and for cleaning staff; the church gives them the space for free. One of the parents picks up and drops off Shelly. Connie goes to bed after Shelly leaves for school and sleeps until she arrives home around 3:30. For her part, Connie makes seven box lunches every morning after she gets off work, for Shelly to take for the children. They eat the healthy stuff, the fruit and raw vegetables and sandwiches, but they love the specially wrapped waxed paper packages of Easter eggs, or Valentine hearts, or hollow Santa Clauses.

"Are you going to stay to say hello to Mary?" Connie asks.

"I've got to get going," Kathy says. She leans over and sniffs her mother's uniform at the shoulder. "Smells like Turkish Delight," she says.

"You have a very sensitive sense of smell. Just like your father," Connie tells her. "It's all sugar to me."

"Right here," Kathy says, tapping her mother's uniform just above her heart. Then she licks the spot.

"Jesus wept, Kathy. Stop that." Connie pushes her away. "You're a strange one these days. Unhappy, I fear. I was serious before; you've got to figure out what you're going to do. Stop running away to places like Vancouver."

"I didn't run away," Kathy says, though in some respects that's what she and Doug had done. "I told you I was going, despite what you like to tell people. I lived in a nice house. I had a job. I had friends. Just like a regular person. Then one day I came back to Varnum. Now I'm living at Penny's."

"Boarding," Connie says. "With a snake. That ought to tell you something." Taking Kathy's hand, she pets it. "That's not a home. Come stay with us until you save some money to get a nice apartment."

"I've got money." Kathy pulls her hand away.

"Then do something with it. Take a typing course. Or hairdressing. You can open your own shop right here in our basement, like June up the street. Remember? You're all grown up, Kathy. It's time…"

"Mom." Kathy steps back just as Connie leans forward to kiss her.

"I'm talking to a stump," Connie says to the air in front of her, for Kathy has gone out the door.

Outside, the vast black sky is lavish with stars, the cold is endless. Runway lights flash on along the Smolas' driveway, an obsidian void between the now glittering snowbanks. Martial music blares. And there's Darlyn, red car coat done up to the neck with white bone buttons, white tights, white mid-calf boots with white tassels. Darlyn strutting down the runway, eyes ahead. She throws her baton into the air and it rises, disappears into darkness, gone, gone, gone. Flashes into sight, so fast. Darlyn marching in place, arm out, snatching the baton. Six high steps forward, up it goes again, no hint of exertion, no vapour from her perfect lips.

"Darlyn, you're the champion of the world!" Kathy shouts from the sidewalk.

Darlyn catches the baton and turns.

"Kathy," Darlyn shouts back. "Groovy." She smiles as she walks, twirling one hand to the other; the air is strobing.

"Do you have a cigarette?" she asks when she reaches Kathy.

Darlyn Smola could be "Baton Barbie." Full high breasts (less buoyant than Barbie's appear), spare waist, slim hips, slender legs, fine wrists, ankles and neck and all of it, every single bit of it, muscle. Brown eyes as depthless as milk chocolate. Red earmuffs over brown hair pulled back in a shiny ponytail. Perfect Darlyn, everything in proportion except her nose, which is not large so much as not small. Not a perky baton twirler's nose, nor even a formal Scottish nose. A Smola nose, her mother points out. From her paternal grandfather, Margaret says. Strong, long, foreign and entirely masculine.

Darlyn's nose always made her seem old and serious when she was little. More so because she was little and it wasn't. Looking at her friend, Kathy sees Darlyn has grown into her nose. She's taken it over, and she's become beautiful.

"You don't smoke," Kathy says.

"How do you know? You've been away for ages." Darlyn says. She shivers. "Can we sit in your car?"

"Be my guest," Kathy says.

Heat on, windows steaming and rolled down an inch so they won't be asphyxiated, Darlyn goes through Kathy's box of 8-tracks.

"I never listen to this stuff unless it's at a dance or something," she says. "Oh Leonard, sexy Leonard. Put him on."

They lean back in the seats while Leonard sings about the Sisters of Mercy.

"I love that line," Darlyn says, and she sings in a sweet un-Leonard-like voice, "It begins with your family, but soon it comes around to your soul."

"Can't twirl to it, though," she sighs.

"Have you tried?" Kathy asks.

"God, no. I still live at home, Kath. Get real. My mother listens to Gilbert and Sullivan and Gregorian chant, my father to polkas and Elvis. And to Bobby Curtola if he's being wild. There's only marching music for me. No, my friend, I haven't had a chance to twirl to Leonard. Don't think he'd appreciate it anyway."

"Bet he loves women in tights," Kathy says. She snaps Darlyn's stockings and dust drifts through a thin slice of light from the porch. Darlyn takes Kathy's hand and holds it.

"Why did you stop writing me?" she asks.

"Once I finished writing about the pretty mountains and the pretty ocean and the wild and wonderful characters in our communal house, I ran out of good things to say," Kathy tells her.

"Doug?" Darlyn asks.

"As I said, I ran out of good things to say."

"You could have called when you got home."

"I'm sorry," Kathy says.

"I missed you," Darlyn says. "I'm glad you're home.

"And I'm glad you came out to practise."

Leonard's singing about eyes soft with sorrow and they sing with him, "Hey that's no way to say goodbye." And they laugh.

"Remember when Mrs. Norris used to come out with the axe?" Darlyn says. "She'd walk beside George's car when we got home from a date. Then she'd linger in front of us, but she'd never look in the window, like she was pretending we weren't here. Like she just had this sudden urge to go for a little stroll with her trusty axe. She'd hold the axe down beside her leg, almost hidden. We could see the metal glint in the porch light every now and then. Scared George shitless. No making out with her around."

"Remember Mrs. Hauser, the Regal card lady?" It's Kathy's turn. "How she never left the house, not even to go to church. Mom sent me over there to get cards sometimes. Her hair was always perfect, in waves like chocolate icing on a bought cake. And Jake and Frankie— remember them?—they delivered the catalogues and orders when they did their paper route until their mom got uterine cancer and died. She used to tell Mom the tumour felt like a baby in there, floating around. Felt just like when she was pregnant with her boys.

"Did you know that Jake and Frankie bought cars with their paper route money?" Kathy says.

"Go away." Turning to look at Kathy, Darlyn adds, "My mother told me Mrs. Hauser was addicted to Valium."

"How would your mother know?"

"Because she's addicted to Valium." Darlyn laughs, but not very hard. "Did the boys really buy their cars with paper route money?"

"Yup. Jake and Frankie. We shoulda married us those rich paper boys. Frankie was in love with me in grade two. Remember? Used to follow me into the girls' washroom. Sister Ursula would head him off at the pass. She left the convent; did you know that? She came through my checkout at the store. I hardly recognized her; she's a middle-aged hippie with a long greying braid. Looks good, though. Still a do-gooder. A peacenik. She's going to Biafra because of the famine. She knew me right away," Kathy says.

"Where's Biafra?" Darlyn asks.

"Aren't you smart?" Kathy laughs. "That's the exact question Trudeau asked, according to the newspaper article my mother has pinned to her fridge scrapbook. Africa, west coast, broke away from Nigeria. That's all I know. What are you up to these days?"

"Doing some substitute teaching, twirling in between. Still winning the big prizes but it's not exciting anymore. I'm competing against sixteen-year-olds. I was named North York Twirling Queen for baton and two kinds of strutting. I also took a first in senior fling twirling and twirling with two batons last week.

"I love twirling, Kath. But I'm getting too old. Turning twenty, and who twirls at twenty? I don't know. Feeling kind of lost lately. Time to move out. Maybe I'll open a studio and teach. Twirling. Some dance. A wall of trophies to impress the Westmount types. What about you?"

"I'm a checkout girl again, same store as before, except now I'm at the bottom of the food chain again. When I left Vancouver, I somehow forgot to tell Doug I was going. Pretty funny, eh? If you're lost, Darlyn, then I'm so far off the path I'll never find it again. But don't tell my mother I admitted that.

"You know what I really want? I want to do something with skating, but I don't know what, except I want to be able to skate all the time. Maybe we can have a school together, you teach baton routines and I'll teach hockey moves, except I need a rink for that."

The runway lights flash off and on. Al's standing on the porch. They wave, and he waves and goes back inside.

"You still going with George?" Kathy asks.

"We fight and make up," Darlyn says. "I suppose I'll have to marry him one of these days."

The first time George asked Darlyn to marry him was in grade seven, on a school bus trip to Niagara Falls. Darlyn ignored him, so he said he'd let her off the hook if she'd go out with him instead. She ignored that too. George periodically asked her for dates until she consented in grade nine. They've been going out ever since.

In grade eleven Darlyn decided to have sex with George. She and Kathy found a doctor in Guelph who would give girls under twenty-one the birth control pill without permission from their parents. Kathy and Darlyn went to the doctor together and both got prescriptions, even though Kathy wasn't planning on sleeping with anyone at the time. They were sixteen-and-a-half and had borrowed Connie's car. Said they were going swimming at Elora to account for some of the miles.

It was a good thing they'd gone because Kathy decided that seventeen was the exact right age to have intercourse with Donny, her new boyfriend, who was exotic not only because he was Protestant, United Church of God, which was really like having no church at all, Connie told Kathy when Kathy told her, but also because he was old—almost twenty. And he could skate; all Kathy's boyfriends must be able to skate. Donny's dark eyebrows bushed over his cheerful chestnut eyes, his heart-shaped mouth nestled right in the centre of dimpled chipmunk cheeks.

He was ambitious, an apprentice drywaller. Drywallers are the up-and-coming tradesmen, he told Kathy. With all the new suburbs and shopping malls popping up, he'd never be out of work. He wanted to start his own contracting company; that was his goal. He was saving his money. Even after a shower, Donny's hair was chalky, his skin pale with residues of gypsum.

Older and working, a man with goals, a good skater, surely he was experienced at sex, Kathy thought. But Donny turned out to be a virgin, a hesitant one. And even though he told her he loved her, he loved somebody more than Kathy, but he didn't tell her that until later. The first time they tried, which turned out to be the last time, Donny stopped halfway between getting in and being out and rolled onto his back, his damp penis quickly wilting and flopping over on his naked leg.

"It's doesn't seem right," he finally said, after saying nothing for a long time.

By then they lay side by side on their backs looking at the poster of Jane Fonda as Barbarella, Queen of the Galaxy, tacked to Donny's bedroom ceiling. His parents had gone to their cottage, taking Donny's younger brother and sister, so the house was empty. Donny still lived at home so he could save money for his business. He took Kathy's hand, and lifting her fingers one by one he listed his reasons: What if Kathy got pregnant? I'm on the pill, Kathy said. He was too nervous (two); she was too young (three). I'm not too young if I say I'm not too young, she said, but the nervous part surprised her.

"Why are you nervous?" she asked him.

"I've never done this," he said.

"None of it?" she asked.

"The last part," he said.

"Coming?" she asked.

"No, before that, getting in there," he said.

"Shit," Kathy said. "I thought all boys knew how to do that. Don't you practise?"

"Maybe. Sometimes. Not on girls."

"Practise on me."

That's when Donny told her he loved her, but he loved somebody else more. And now that he was supposed to be having sex with Kathy, all he could think about was Janet Stuebing. So he thought he had better stop and tell Kathy.

"Janet Stuebing?" Kathy asked. "From the Chuckling Hen?" She had started to cry, but quietly.

Yes, that Janet Stuebing, he told her. Janet was his girlfriend before Kathy. He really loved Janet. He wanted to marry her. She broke up with him, and he was never sure why. Maybe because they didn't have sex, maybe that was it. Janet had nice breasts, he said. Her nipples were purple and there were little black hairs growing around them. Those little hairs made him horny, just the thought of them made him horny. But he never told Janet. He wished he'd told Janet.

Donny turned to Kathy and told her how sick he was after Janet left him. How every day his stomach hurt, and he couldn't eat. How lonely he'd been.

"Whoa, Donny," Kathy said, and she pulled the sheet up to cover herself. "I don't want to hear any more."

Donny looked surprised; he said Kathy was so easy to talk to. He'd never opened up like this before, and he began to cry. And Kathy cried harder. Bawled actually. Because her nipples were pink and hairless. Because she was only seventeen, and Janet Stuebing was nineteen and had a job at the Chuckling Hen where, it so happened, Kathy and her friends went for fries and gravy after school. She'd never be able to go back there because she'd know that under her uniform, Janet had little black hairs growing around her nipples. She cried because she was ready to have sex, had picked Donny, and now it wasn't going to happen.

After they stopped crying, they had showers. They decided Kathy should stay at Donny's house because she'd told Connie she was going with his family to their cottage. They brought blankets to the couch, and snuggled in together to watch TV. They talked and made popcorn. They smoked pot, and laughed, and listened to Neil Young. They talked some more. By Sunday afternoon, when they were still talking, they realized they were friends. Virginal friends, they said, and they laughed about that, too.

While Kathy was in Vancouver, Donny wrote and told her he was coming out to visit, hitchhiking. He was on a lay-off because the electricians were out on strike, and you couldn't drywall until a house was wired. He made it as far as Regina when he ran out of cash, so asked his parents wire him some so he could get home.

He brought a girl named Brenda Butt home with him. (Yes, indeed, that's her name, Donny told Kathy in a letter, so stop laughing.) Kathy got to meet her one night at the Rue, after she moved back to Varnum. A wisp of a woman with no butt to speak of, Brenda had a long neck and long thick wavy hair that made her look like the Lady of Shalott in the picture beside the poem Kathy studied in grade twelve.

Or when the moon was overhead,
Came two young lovers lately wed.
'I am half sick of shadows,' said
The Lady of Shalott.

Those were the words she remembered. Tennyson. About a girl sitting around waiting for something to happen in her life, sort of like Kathy's doing these days. In the picture, the Lady lies in a boat with her hair spread out around her head. Lilies float alongside, so of course she's dead; lilies are always a giveaway. She died because she was a bad girl; she gave up longing and did what she was told not to do: take life straight on.

Brenda Butt circles her eyes with kohl and draws a different black beauty spot on her face every day like Marilyn Monroe. She wears long skirts in layers and thin cotton peasant tops with no bra. The masses of silver bangles on her arms jingle like a tinker's cart when she moves. Kathy likes her. She smells earthy, like dust and dried flowers.

"The prairie," Brenda told her when Kathy mentioned how good she smelled. "Wheat and soil. Gets in the pores and you can never get it out."

Donny borrowed Kathy's room at the Lehmans' a couple of times when she was out, because he still lived at home. Though his mother, reluctantly, let Brenda sleep in his room, on a mattress on the floor she made up every day when she made Donny's bed, Donny found making love in his parents' house, with his mother and father in their bed one room away, more than a little trying.

Kathy's pillow smells like Brenda, her sweet dry scent. It fills Kathy with sadness, and a longing for something she can't pinpoint. Sometimes she places her face right into her pillow and draws Brenda's smell in. She breathes it out slowly. And then she cries for no reason she can figure out at all.

Leonard's finishing another song. Darlyn squeezes Kathy's hand.

"It really is good to have you home, Kath," she says. Then she asks, "Is Donny still around?"

Before Kathy met Doug, when Darlyn wasn't doing something with George, she sometimes hung out with Kathy and Donny, who hung out together when they weren't going out with anybody else. An off and on, copacetic threesome. That was Donny's favourite word, then. Copacetic, can you dig it, he'd say, and they'd laugh as if it was the funniest thing in the world.

When Kathy started dating Doug, everything changed. Though she still talked to Donny and Darlyn, she didn't see them often; it was all Doug, Doug, Doug. Doug was funny and could be charming, a muscular, compact, broodingly good-looking man who had played Junior A hockey. It was an irresistible combination.

They met at the Aud when Doug asked Kathy to skate to a couples-only song. ("Moon River." She never much liked it, but she hates it now.) Doug told her he'd been kicked off the Junior A team when he got caught smoking marijuana in the washroom of the team bus. He said he was going to quit hockey anyway. Too much like the military, regimented and no life of your own. The chicks were great, he said, he'd miss the chicks. But he'd get over it, especially if Kathy became his girlfriend.

They skated every chance they got. Doug said he gave up hockey, but not the rink. They'd toke up in the parking lot and go in. The high created a bubble around them in which every move they made was perfect, every word they said was witty. They were in love. So, at four minutes after midnight, January 1st, 1969, when Doug asked Kathy to take off to Vancouver with him, of course she said yes.

Connie was uncharacteristically quiet when Kathy told her she was going west, considering she had carried on a non-stop negative commentary about Doug until then. He was moody, she'd said. She didn't trust him because sometimes he was nice to her and sometimes he acted as if she didn't exist. Darlyn cried when Kathy called to tell her. Donny said, "Groovy, I'll come and visit."

Kathy's just about to tell Darlyn about Donny and Brenda Butt when the driveway lights flash on and off again. Kathy flashes the car lights; she presses the accelerator and makes the engine race, vroom-vroom. Again the girls wave to Al, who is silhouetted in the doorway. He waves and shuts the door.

"He's lonely," Darlyn says a bit wearily, "but he hates to be with my mother since she became a feminist. So he roams the house, going where she isn't.

"My mother says she doesn't want to spend time with one of the 'fascist prison guards,' as she calls all married men. She says the reason she's been on Valium all these years is because society likes to keep women drugged and quiet, not angry and asking questions and pissing people off.

"She's in a consciousness-raising group that meets twice a week at the university. They read women's poems and sing women's songs. They check in, everybody gets a chance, and that means they confess intimate stuff about their lives—'the personal is political' is Mom's mantra. Then they trash men and try to figure out how to overturn the government.

"Mom comes home and tells Dad, 'One is not born a woman; one becomes one.' She tells him he's part of a patriarchal conspiracy that says if you're female, you're not fully human. He asks, 'What's patriarchal? Who's not human?' She says, 'Read *The Second Sex*.' So he sits in his chair in the rec room at night trying to read Simone de Beauvoir. He sits there and he cries.

"Kathy, I can't stand it. That's why I came out to practise tonight. I had to get away from them. I'd move out right now, but I think it would kill Dad," Darlyn says.

"Who's Simone de Beauvoir?" Kathy asks.

"Some French women's libber," Darlyn says. "Dad doesn't get it. He asks her, 'Margaret, what I can do?' Mom tells him, 'It's not up to me to tell you, Al. You've got to figure it out for yourself.' So he brought her home a black corset with these red satin garters hanging from it. Mom tells me this stuff. I don't want to hear it, I tell her, but she says I need to hear so I don't get caught in the trap. I don't ask what trap, because I don't want to know that either. Mom said she didn't say a word to Dad about the corset, but walked to the garbage can, opened it, and threw it in."

The lights flick again and there's Al walking toward the car. He's holding his brown cardigan closed across his chest; he's wearing backless brown and green plaid slippers that flip away from his heels and make puffs of snow rise around his feet. He walks down his walkway, along the sidewalk in front of the house, and up Connie's driveway to the Valiant. He tilts sideways at the waist and places his mouth near the small opening of Darlyn's fogged up window. Steam from his breath comes into the car.

"Darlyn," says his voice, which Kathy always thought sounded like a funeral director's voice: deep, serious and terribly polite. "Darlyn, bring Kathy into the house instead of sitting out here in the cold."

As Darlyn rolls down her window he pulls his head back. Still tilted sideways, still holding his sweater in his fist, he nods towards Kathy.

"Kathy," he says. "How're you doing?"

"Fine, Mr. Smola. Thanks for the invite, but I have to get going. I have to work in the morning."

"As you wish," Al says. "Always good to see you, Kathy. You know you're always welcome in our house. How's your good mother doing these days?"

"Fine. Working too hard," Kathy says.

Al nods. "She's always been a hard worker," he says.

"Will I see you shortly?" he asks Darlyn, though it isn't really a question. Without waiting for an answer, he turns away. The tiny clouds of snow follow his feet back to the front door.

"Guess I'd better be going so you can go in," Kathy says. She squeezes Darlyn's hand. She's thinking: if Margaret Smola left Al, and Connie could see her way to marrying him, Darlyn would become her stepsister. She doesn't say this out loud.

"Don't be a stranger," Darlyn says. "Oh, by the way, I've got that corset if you ever need one. Rescued it from the garbage. I'm trying to figure out how to work it into a routine, but it hasn't come to me, yet. Not too much bordello baton twirling that I know of."

She leans over and brushes her lips along Kathy's cheek, then is out the door. She twirls her baton behind her back as she walks, flips it into the air, spins around and salutes. Kathy slips her car into gear. Darlyn catches the baton, turns and goose-steps into the house. The driveway lights go out. It is suddenly too dark, too quiet, a lesser world for the loss of Al's fine spotlights. And Darlyn.

THE ROAD IS ICY WHEN KATHY PULLS AWAY FROM HER MOTHER'S house. She bounces the rear end of the car off a snowbank, for fun, not hard enough to cause damage, just enough to glide sideways around the corner, a tap on the other side to straighten out, and she's away. The street is lined both sides with bungalows, each placed squarely in the centre of a 50 X 120-foot lot. About five variations on a theme, most a pinky-peach brick, the odd one a dusty grey with yellow tints.

Concrete porches, some with railings now, some still plain slabs, are built over fruit cellars with shelves lined with canning—summer peaches, mustard beans, eons-old dill pickles with brined-white lids, strawberry jam. There could be Christmas cake wrapped in brandy-soaked cheesecloth, soft drinks or extra beer for the weekend, leftover stew in the pot too big for the fridge. On hot days in the summer when Connie had to get some sleep before her night shift, she'd set up a camp cot in the fruit cellar, wrap a flannel sheet around herself, breathe in the cool damp air and sleep like a baby.

Some days, after Charlie had died, when Shelly was having a bad day, Connie took a chair into the fruit cellar and stood on it, closed her eyes and placed her face just in front of the tiny metal grille to the outside. Shelly's screams became a vague background noise then, while in front of her on a rush of cool air, there was the smell of grass, of damp concrete and earth; there was the sound of happy children playing in a sprinkler, the thick tarry suck of tires on hot asphalt.

Kathy found her there once, had gone looking for her mother because Shelly was crying. She looked in the fruit cellar only because the door was slightly ajar. It was a rule that the door be closed at all times to keep the cold air in. Kathy was about to close it when she sensed rather than heard someone inside. She looked through the crack and there was her mother standing on a chair, her face illuminated by a small pale rectangle of light coming in through the vent.

Kathy wanted to call out to her, but she didn't. She was not so much afraid as embarrassed, as if she had come upon her mother naked and not this ordinary woman dressed in brown slacks and a pink cotton blouse, standing on a kitchen chair with a paint-spattered seat and missing rungs. Standing absolutely still in the darkness, her face pressed to the light coming in from a frail bit of screening.

Tonight the sidewalks are cleared of snow, the driveways too. Germanic tidiness still influences these neighbourhoods that are a mix of immigrants now, no longer mostly German. They are still predominantly working class, though. In the summer there are neatly edged loamy gardens filled with annuals: petunias, geraniums, marigold, with some salvia and dusty miller and cosmos in the more adventurous plots. Or, in the few Portuguese gardens, there are flowering vegetables mixed in with more flamboyant groupings of annuals. All the gardens are set between neatly trimmed juniper or cedar shrubs that bookend the picture windows that look out on to the wide avenues. Snow covers the gardens now, except for the naked maples, one per boulevard. Red and green maples on alternating properties: artful city planning.

Kathy's parents had joined a Catholic housing co-operative chartered to buy suburban lots in an area called Pleasant View (flat as a pancake with no view at all, Connie liked to remind Charlie) to build affordable bungalows for its members. The lots were mapped and surveyed, the house designs drawn up, the project about to commence, when the deal fell through. Money problems, Connie told Kathy.

Affordability had brought them to the project and when the deal collapsed Connie was just as happy. She was a downtown girl. She liked a corner store to be on the corner, not ten long suburban blocks away. She liked to be able to walk to the pharmacy, the Capital or Starlight theatres, the Nut Shoppe for warm popcorn and fresh nuts, to the Palace for a tin roof sundae. Or wander out of their apartment on a warm summer evening, Gwen from upstairs keeping an ear out for Kathy. They might end up at the Varnum Hotel in the "Ladies and Escorts" beverage room having a draft. Or at Five Corners, where they'd buy an ice-cream bar and dawdle home.

Kathy's father liked Pleasant View and decided they should buy one of the bungalows being built a few blocks from their proposed co-op. He begged part of a down payment from his parents, who farmed near Meaford, and raised the rest himself. One Sunday afternoon in early fall of 1955, he borrowed a friend's car and brought Connie and Kathy through a wasteland to an almost finished house in the middle of a mound of mud and told them they'd be moving in after Remembrance Day.

They tiptoed across a two-by-six spanning the gulf between the mud in the driveway and the doorway. There was no porch yet, no fruit cellar. Kathy's father unlocked the door and swung it open, saying, *Ta-da*. Kathy ran through the house yelling, "Bedroom. Kitchen. Bathroom," her shouts echoing back to her from the pure white Gyproc walls. She flushed the toilet, turned on the taps, stuck her head into the milk box beside the back door, shouted, "Mud" at the mud in the backyard.

She ran down the open wooden stairs to the basement, which was enormous, one huge high-ceilinged concrete room. She could hear the click-click of her mother's two-toned high heels on the hardwood floors above her, the cul-umping of her father's Sunday browns as he followed her from room to room. Then, from a vent above her, Kathy heard her mother crying, her father speaking hushed words, a soothing sh-sh.

Kathy pressed her cheek to cool cement; she licked the concrete, tasted limestone, permanent and cold. Smelled fresh wood so sweet it was like being in a forest. She didn't care if her mother cried forever; she wanted to live here. "House," she whispered. "My house."

Aluminum doors, occasionally bearing the suburban coat of arms—the circled first initial of a family name—still predominate.

Many yards are fenced now, but when Kathy was growing up, the yards were one vast playground, big enough for games of scrub baseball, backyard rinks for figure skating and shinny, hide-and-seek that went on for hours, neighbourhood fireworks displays, the May 24th burning schoolhouse the kids' favourite. They cheered as it curled in on itself, charred and smoking. They played ball against the wall, the girls skipped in newly paved driveways, the boys zoomed Dinky Toys between their legs. They all played war or road hockey or touch football or Red Rover or Statues. Marbles in the spring, conkers in the fall.

The neighbourhood men lived outdoors in those yards, clearing snow after supper with heavy square metal shovels, working on the rinks, telling dirty jokes, their breath as hot and steamy on the cold air as the bad words slipping off their tongues. Kids sitting on sculpted snowbanks silently tying their skate laces strained to hear. "Bugger!" "Dummkopf!" they'd shout after their fathers had gone inside. "Pussy!" "Prick!" "Schweinehund!" "Boobies!"

In summer the men shared a beer while they built picnic tables, identical dimensions, regardless of family size, all painted the same dull red stain that rubbed off on clothing, bought in quantity for a good price at Mainway Market. They played horseshoes in the pits dug at the Rausches', the rhythmical clank and thud covering laughter, ohs and ahs, the swear words absorbed by the heat and lushness of summer. Played darts on a board Al Smola made and hung from cement hooks on his back wall.

They dug gardens for the women to plant the year's annuals, then weeded them, edged them, tidied them up in fall, covering new shrubs and the odd perennial, chrysanthemums maybe, with leaves from the maples. They mowed and raked lawns and drank more beer sitting on porches, or leaning against the sides of older model cars, which they had just washed and waxed, gleaming Fords and Chryslers and GMs, nothing foreign, for you had to support the local industry that made tires or springs or parts for American automobiles assembled by their union brothers in Windsor and Oakville. They dug worms for fishing, piled coolers and waders and fishing gear into cars and disappeared for long weekends up north—Lake Nipissing—to catch pike and pickerel and bass.

That's when the women came out to sit on the picnic tables in the shade, little kids playing at their feet. They smoked cigarettes, drank coffee and talked about sales at Foodmart and Loblaws, or how Ahrens had kids' canvas sneakers for a good price. They reminded each other that the public health nurse was coming to Our Lady of Perpetual Hope and Maple Avenue Public schools to give vaccinations to the children starting kindergarten. Talked about men, but only in the most general terms, an illness or a holiday or the possibility of a strike.

The Whites, second owners of their house, were the first to fence their yard, cutting it off from the others. They moved in after the lawns were well established, the gardens and trees beginning to look permanent. Foreign: British. Not snobs, but they had a dog. The only dog in the neighbourhood at that time, which made their ordinary spotted beagle named Flip seem extravagant, exotic even. Children begged to walk him, begged parents to get a Flip of their own.

The Whites didn't want Flip digging up anyone's garden or biting anyone's leg, didn't want him wandering away or getting hit by a car. That's what they said, anyway. So they built a ranch-style woven three-board fence that Flip dug under two days after it was finished so he could make his regular rounds of neighbourhood back doors, begging for treats. The Whites painted their fence the same dull red as the neighbourhood picnic tables.

Mr. White was the first grown-up Kathy knew who died who wasn't her grandfather or another really old person. Came home for lunch, ate a tuna salad sandwich (flaked premium tuna, Miracle Whip, finely chopped green onions, two washed pieces of iceberg lettuce overlapping—Mrs. White's usual) on lightly margarined pumpernickel delivered that morning to the door, with two home-canned gherkins on the side. For dessert, a cup of coffee, black, half a saccharin tablet, as Mr. White wanted to lose a bit of weight, and one butter tart, store-bought, on sale at Mainway Market at three packages (six in each) for a dollar. Washed his hands and wiped his mouth at the kitchen sink, dried them on a blue-checked terry tea towel, which he folded and placed on the counter. Smoked a Rothman's standing up while talking to Mrs. White about seeding the side yard, which was shaded, so the grass had become patchy. Tapped the ashes directly into the drain. Ran water over his cigarette butt, put the butt in the avocado green flip-top garbage can under the sink. He kissed Mrs. White goodbye on the lips, an everyday friendly kiss, nothing passionate, an I'll-see-you-later kiss.

Mr. White drove to work and was just about to sit at his desk, was lowering himself into his chair, talking to his secretary Bernice Clemmer about refilling the dye in the Gestetner machine. The mimeographs were getting a bit pale, he was telling her, when an artery blew up in his head.

He died, just like that. A little sigh, a look of shock in his eyes, then he fell rather gently, Bernice later said, like fainting in church, which she did on occasion if she fasted for Communion and went to 11:30 Mass. Crumpled in on himself first, then onto the floor. Blood all over, she said, coming from his mouth and nose and even from his ears.

These exact details of his last hour were discussed over and over by the women at the picnic tables, as if dissecting what had been eaten for lunch, or the kind of kiss that had been offered, could account for early mortality. Tuna with onions to be avoided at all costs, especially in combination with store-bought butter tarts. (Cigarettes couldn't matter—everyone smoked—it was agreed.) Children and husbands had to be kissed (and were pressed to kiss back, *just in case*) before leaving for school or work, the extreme import of the last kiss an essential feature in the pre-death drama.

But soon life became ordinary again and only when a husband came down with the flu and stayed home from work, or a child was having his tonsils out in hospital, only then was the spectre of early death reawakened and the rituals of kinds of kisses and forbidden combinations of food once again noted.

Kathy had flown up from Brownies to Girl Guides with Glenda White only the week before Mr. White's death, and her troop formed an honour guard for the funeral. The girls wore their blue uniforms, and poked each other while waiting for the hearse to arrive. Most of them had never been to a funeral and they wondered if the body would smell, if they would get to eat some of the triangular sandwiches with their crusts off, no tuna salad, no one in the Catholic Women's League had made tuna salad, and the funeral cookies, especially Connie's melt-in-your-mouth chocolate macaroons, which were famous throughout the Our Lady of Perpetual Hope parish. They wondered if Glenda's little brother would cry.

Everyone cried at the funeral mass, Glenda, Glenda's brother and all the Girl Guides. The men sniffed into clean, pressed handkerchiefs tucked into jacket pockets by wives, just in case. The women cried and cried, especially Mrs. White, who was now a widow. As if it were a disease they might catch, the women said the word "widow" tentatively, quietly, whispering it through their fingers into the ears of their friends. And true enough, before too long, Mrs. White was avoided like the plague by all except for a few brave, immune—or stupid, depending on how you looked at it—souls like Connie. Connie said it was scandalous the way women suddenly didn't invite Mrs. White to barbeques or potlucks or baby showers. As if she might steal away one of their lumpy, ill-tempered, balding, farting husbands.

Mrs. White learned to drive, found a job, lost some weight, bought some very nice new clothes and started to have her hair styled once a week in a classic Jackie Kennedy flip. Eventually she found a boyfriend, a gentle well-off bachelor, Basil Burkhardt, an engineer, whom she brought over to meet Connie. She moved with her children to California to be near him when he was hired to raise up by four feet the historic Bridgeport covered bridge in Nevada County to protect it from floodwaters. They never returned to Canada.

When Kathy's father died, Mrs. White sent Connie, Kathy and Shelly a lovely card that Connie kept on the windowsill above the kitchen sink for about three years. No doves or lilies or bleeding hands or burning hearts of Jesus, but a peaceful blue-green lake beneath a mountain and a bright sapphire sky, which eventually became covered with dried white potato spritz and warped with rain drops when the window didn't get closed fast enough during a storm. Or with tears every time Connie took it from the windowsill to reread it. (Kathy always felt it was very Californian to send a non-religious sympathy card.)

Inside, in neat feminine script, the card said: *I'm so sorry, Connie. I understand. It will take time, but you will stop hurting. Though not just yet, and not for a while. Call me if you want to talk. Love, Lizzy.* Then she printed her name, Elizabeth (White) Burkhardt, and her phone number in brackets at the bottom. It was the first they'd heard she'd married Basil.

Kathy drives down Maple Avenue. There's hardly any traffic, but there is an odour—faint tonight—of wieners. There's always some smell in Varnum, some worse than others. Rendered and processed meat of J.M. Schneider, Burns Foods, Hoffman Meats, Varnum Packers, Norstern Meat Packers. Hops from Labbatt's. Alcohol mash from Seagram's. Rubber from Uniroyal and BF Goodrich. Incinerators. Electroplating, metal product chemicals—General Springs, Budd Automotive, Kuntz Electric, Globe Stamping. Bread from Weston's. Cookies from Dares. Tanning chemicals from Robson-Lang. On any given day the city air exudes industry, is saturated with it, the smell of money going into some already-rich person's pocket. And these days that rich person likely lives in the States and not Canada. That's what the union folks are saying.

Charlie worked at Budd. A union man, he worked a press. He came home smelling of metal and grease and the no-water hand cleaner all the men used before they drove home after their shifts. He loved his job, loved being in the company of hard-working men. Believed in unions and their cause: fair play and fair pay for labour. He loved all things that had to do with cars, so was proud to be part of their manufacture, even from a distance.

"Your father loved to drive," Connie once told Kathy.

So it was a shock, but maybe not a surprise, that her father died in a car accident. On the stretch of 401 across from where Oakdale College now stands. Fell asleep at the wheel after a shift at the plant, the police report said, though what he was doing on the 401 heading west, no one knew. Not Connie, not his buddies, and certainly not the semi driver who saw him coming—tried to brake—but couldn't stop fast enough.

Charles (Charlie) Michael Rausch, born 1925, drove from his side of the road straight across the pretty wildflower-covered median, gaining speed as he went, dipping down into the culvert, rising up, tires churning the grass until they gained purchase on the blacktop again, accelerating full tilt right into the front end of the transport truck.

KATHY PULLS INTO THE LEHMANS' DRIVEWAY. PENNY'S LEFT FOR work, her tire tracks in the snow, the house dark except for Pete's room in the attic.

"Come up and see Teach," Pete shouts down as Kathy takes her boots off in the hallway.

Pete calls his part-time work maintaining the labs at Regent University supplemental income; his real money comes from drug-dealing. By working at the university, he maintains the appearance of a legitimate income. That's what he says, at least. Teach is a professor, and one of the research scientists Pete works for. Teach also buys lots of Pete's dope.

Harold Patrick Markham, Markham with an "h," Teach tells everyone when he first meets them. Who gives a flying fuck how it's spelled? Kathy wants to say. But she never does. Teach intimidates her. Most educated people intimidate her. And not only the people, but the broad manicured lawn in front of the university campus intimidates her. The Campus Centre, where kids her own age and probably no smarter than her hang out, intimidates her. Well, maybe they're smarter ambition-wise, but maybe not. Maybe they just perform better for their parents. Maybe they're obedient. Or maybe they have no imaginations. (Kathy doesn't want to probe that too deeply, because her imagination regarding her future in skating, or any future beyond checking out groceries, for that matter, isn't exactly working overtime.) The very word degree, as in university degree, is intimidating, because if you're talking degrees, there's got to be a scale with something higher and something lower.

And when it comes to degrees, Kathy feels lower these days, because no degree has to be lowest of all. It's the kind of stuff she and Donny talk about for hours when they smoke some dope. Semantics, my dear, they say in fake snooty voices, and they sniff and push up the ends of their noses with their fingertips. Then they laugh, because it makes them feel better to laugh. And because when you're stoned, laughing is what you do. Laughing and listening to music and eating and talking endlessly about nothing, and the degrees of nothing.

Marijuana's the best drug—the highest degree—for having sex, they've decided. Personal research proves it. Though they've preserved their virgin friendship, they have conducted marijuana and sex experiments with others. Grass is better than MDA because MDA is feel-good in the head. With grass, or hashish, especially if you eat it in brownies, every single inch of skin is a g-spot. The entire body anticipates touch, tingles with erotic sensation. No wonder it's illegal, they tell each other, because if it was legal, everybody'd buy it, and everybody'd be so busy making love they'd have no time for anything else, including getting degrees.

The only place Kathy doesn't feel intimidated around educated people is at the Rue, the bar where university kids drink alongside factory workers, people who collect pogey or deal drugs, people who hang Gyproc and work in grocery stores. Where Walton Emerson, a university English professor, sits at a corner table in a green suède jacket with fringed sleeves, a red or blue bandana around his thinning shoulder-length hair, and holds court with students and anyone else who'll listen to him talk while he gets pissed out of his tree on ten-cents-a-glass draft. He gives working-class kids—the proletariat, he calls them—ten-dollar bills. Or he tears the bills in half and uses them to roll joints that flare and taste like shit, but no one complains because the dope's free. Sometimes, if he's really drunk, he snorts a line of cocaine through a ten-dollar tube and hands the bill, still covered in powder, to some awed young woman, saying, *Wanna lick?*

Kathy feels fine at the Rue, thank you very much. She understands pubs and beer. Beer is a great leveler. Anyone can get a degree in beer drinking. Most of the people she grew up with and the ones who work at her store have advanced degrees in drinking beer, just like Walton Emerson and his students.

Teach is married but he practically lives at Pete and Penny's. Pete says he's never met Teach's wife, jokes there probably isn't one, that Teach made her up because he's actually a homo sexual. That's how Pete says it, as if it's two words. He says it in front of Teach, who doesn't say anything. Kathy thinks Pete's right; she thinks Teach is in love with Pete.

Teach wears his pants high at the waist and tight across the groin. He wears berets, or old green and khaki chapeaux—that's what Teach calls hats, my chapeau, he says—from army surplus stores. Crumpled things that look like camp hats for children. Throughout the winter, Pete and Teach smoke huge amounts of marijuana and drink brandy warmed over a candle flame from snifters the size of goldfish bowls. They play war games they've set up in the attic. In summer, they drink LSD-laced gin and tonic and play croquet tournaments in Pete's backyard. In between there are various drugs—a bit of speed, some MDA or mescaline, heroin once or twice, and reds when they can get them—to enhance the games of Monopoly and Risk, and the rounds of tiddlywinks and pick-up sticks they endlessly play.

"He's in love with you," Pete whispers as he greets Kathy on the landing. He's close to her. She smells the marijuana and brandy on his breath. She looks in his eyes as he speaks, but he's too close and her eyes cross. She looks down. He brushes her hand with his fingertips then leans away from her against the door jamb.

When Pete's near her, Kathy's both alert and relaxed. She never worries about what he thinks of her, yet she's entirely aware he watches her, and that he *does* think about her. His regard is sensual, but it doesn't feel sexual. Or that's what Kathy tells herself. It's as if he's a monk, conscious of everything about her—her soul and her body, her sexuality included—but he's above it all, just an observer.

Pete says Teach is in love with her to embarrass Kathy. He does that, gets people off balance, plays mind-fuck games, then sits back to see what happens.

"He likes your shimmering locks," he says.

Pete lifts her hair in his hand then lets it fall, strand by strand. Kathy's hair swishes into place, shines fluid gold even in the dim stairway light.

Pete and Teach play war games in the attic, *The Games Room*, pressed into a brass plate on the door, an old-fashioned skeleton-key lock above the brass handle. The lock is against Rhettbutler. True to his namesake, and much like his father, he thrives on chaos and excels at making messes that others have to clean up.

"Where's Rhettbutler?" Kathy asks as she moves through the doorway. The room reeks of marijuana.

"Chained to his bed," Pete says.

He might be. Pete enjoys telling stories on himself, about things he and Penny did to Rhettbutler when he was little. Embarrassing stories, because, Pete says, he likes to see Penny's blush, which starts in her ample cleavage and rises in irregular, scarlet blotches up her chest, into her face, and right on through to the part in the middle of her hair. When Rhettbutler was a baby, and Penny and Pete were new parents and very green, they masking-taped Rhettbutler's soother in his mouth so he couldn't spit it out. They put him in a harness attached to a pulley on the clothesline, and let him run back and forth to wear him out before his afternoon nap. Pete can go on and on about what they did to Rhettbutler when he was a little.

"Ah, lovely Kathy," Teach says. "My favourite Breck girl. Come kiss me."

Teach started kissing women on both cheeks after he came home from a conference, Animals in Laboratory Research, in Strasbourg. Friends kiss in Europe, he said the first time her tried to kiss Kathy. Kiss-kiss-kiss all the time, that's why he loved Europe, he said. He told Kathy he'd given a paper on how to de-scent skunks. It was an operation he'd performed on Fi-Fi, a baby skunk Pete had caught in his headlights, tiny and frightened, dancing a baby-skunk dance on the side of a dark back road. Its wildly smelly mother and four siblings were dead, run over by a car. Pete and Penny kept Fi-Fi as a pet until she became mean and bit Rhettbutler, around the time she was a year old.

It was sex that turned her mean, Teach said. All females become mean when they discover sex, he said. When Teach had de-scented her, he hadn't bothered to neuter her. After she bit Rhettbutler, Penny said enough's enough and asked Teach to put Fi-Fi down. They had a funeral and buried the skunk in the backyard. Her marker, a small limestone slab, like the old-fashioned cemetery markers used for dead babies, said *Our Beloved Fi-Fi, 1968-1969.*

"We're just about to commence battle," Pete says. He opens a box of cigars and offers one to Teach. Pete lights his, holds the match for Teach, sets his cigar in an ashtray and lights a joint, one of many in the cigar box. They pass it back and forth, offering some to Kathy, who takes one hit—for sleeping, she says—then shakes her head no when it's her turn again.

"Work tomorrow," she says as she lets out her breath.

Teach pours glasses of brandy, a tradition at the beginning of their battles. They're children, Kathy thinks, playing games. Happier doing the set-up, which has taken them over two weeks, and before that, months of painting soldiers and tanks and other artillery, than they are fighting the battle. Because they know how it is going to end; they know all the moves beforehand, have studied them while they prepared for the battle. It's like the dances you learn from books, with little feet and arrows. Move one step forward, quick-quick, slide, everything choreographed.

"Now this is a real battle, my spectacular Kathy," Teach says. He grins and waves his arm across the fake battlefield. Tonight Teach is wearing combat boots, khakis with many buttons and pockets and a safari shirt with a navy-blue ascot peeking out of one pocket and a rolled-up camp hat out of the other. His beige hair, wispy and fine, stands on end in the furnace-dried air. He looks as though he should wear glasses; he isn't, and he doesn't. But if anyone asked Kathy, she'd have to think, and then she'd likely say, yes, Teach wears glasses.

Teach has an ordinary forehead and nose, forgettable eyes, and pale grey lips as thin and wrinkled as used tinsel. Sometimes Kathy can't take her eyes off Teach's lips. She watches them now.

"Yes, real combat, not one of those impossible wars," Teach continues, still grinning, "like Vietnam, all jungle and guerilla action, and the bombing and total destruction of towns and villages full of civilians, and nobody knows who's good and who's bad so everybody has to die, civilian and soldier.

"Look, we have cannons. And rifles and horses and men in uniform who respect their uniform. We have rules of battle, rules for each engagement; we have honour and codes of conduct. Men will walk in a line directly into the bullets and cannon fire because their commanders tell them to. The first in line will get blown up and fall, and the men behind them will do the same. An egalitarian battle.

"There are no rules in Vietnam. There's chaos and carnage and dishonour. There's My Lai. Soldiers killing innocent people, sodomizing women, raping children, destroying everything in their sight, burning, mutilating, shooting bullets into the grass and into the trees just to kill, kill, kill."

Teach is spitting the words now, his grey lips pulled tight in a Tin Man smile. He holds an imaginary rifle; he shoots it. As he goes on and on, Kathy thinks of the boys who sit and drink coffee at the Ground Inn. Boys who have deserted active service, who have dodged the US draft, who come in off the streets because they've heard that the coffee house is a friendly place and someone will direct them to a church or an agency that will help them find a new life, in exile forever, in Canada.

Kathy remembers leaving Varnum for Vancouver, excited and happy, not sure if she'd return, hoping she wouldn't. But she could return if she wanted. Imagine if she'd left knowing she'd never be able to visit her mother or Shelly again, never see her friends. She wonders if she had to go to Vietnam—if she didn't choose to dodge the draft or desert—if she could say no to killing civilians. No to the men she trusted with her life, to her commanders, to the country she was fighting for. And she sees her potential for cowardice, and she's ashamed.

But here in this room, two stoned, cigar-smoking men drinking brandy from fishbowls are about to commence battle; they are about to play at war and she can take the high road.

"I'm going to bed," Kathy says.

"Can I join you?" asks Teach.

"Sorry, it's just me and the snake tonight," Kathy says, but she's not sorry at all.

"WE'RE GOING TO LIBERACE FRIDAY," DOUG SAYS OVER THE phone.

"Where are you?" Kathy asks.

"My mother's."

He's called her at work. Go to the office, you've got an urgent call, her manager told her when he came down to the floor to get her. It's noontime and busy, and she had to ask her customers to wait until someone took over her till.

"Is your mother OK?"

"She says for you to come watch hockey some night. They miss you."

Doug's mother, Blanche, cried, and his stepfather, Leon, gave her a big hug when Kathy visited them after she got back from Vancouver. Kathy told them that she'd left Doug, and she was sorry because Blanche and Leon had been so good to her. She promised to keep in touch, but she hadn't. It wasn't lost on Kathy that she'd told Blanche and Leon about the break-up when she never bothered to tell Doug.

"I'm not going," Kathy says.

"I'll pick you up around supper on Friday." He should be pleading, but he's not.

"You're not listening. I'm…"

"You owe me," he interrupts.

She knows that. She wants to ask, why Liberace? but she knows that too. It was one of their things, to dress up, to have a toke and go to concerts, whatever was playing. Chuck Berry, the Vienna Boys' Choir, Tiny Tim, Paul Butterfield, they'd been to them all.

Doug says, "We'll talk after, and you can tell me what a terrible person I am and all the terrible things I did to make you leave."

She doesn't say anything.

"I'll be there at six," he says.

Even before she hears the click she knows she'll go. Not because there's anything to talk about. They stopped talking long before she packed her bag and drove back to Varnum. And she'd worn out the terrible-person, terrible-things accusations before that. She'll go because when she heard his voice on the phone, she was relieved. They will go to the concert; when it's over they'll say goodbye to each other. And that will be the end of that, because she'll have said what she had failed to say.

She calls Donny to see if he and Brenda will come to the concert too. It's not like Kathy and Doug are going on a date. Donny says yes for him, and he'll check with Brenda and let Kathy know.

When Penny lets Doug in the door on Friday night, Kathy, Pete, Teach, Donny and Barry are sitting at the kitchen table.

"So, you're Doug," Penny says. "I can't believe we haven't met before, but I have heard a lot about you. Go in and have a seat. Pete's doing a party trick. He likes to pretend he's every mother's nightmare, but he's really a pussycat. And I've seen this one before, so if anyone asks, tell them Rhettbutler and I are slitting our wrists."

Doug doesn't go in; he leans on the door frame. The group at the table is talking, ignoring Pete, who's chewing mashed potatoes with his mouth open. He's also grinning, the potatoes a soggy, white wad between his teeth. As he chews and grins, the potatoes ooze over his lips and plop, bit by bit, onto his plate.

When the potatoes start to fall out of Pete's mouth onto his plate, Barry stops talking and watches. Like Penny, he's seen the trick before, but he can't believe an adult would do it, and why they'd do it more than once. It's so lame, so pre-teen boy, like snorting milk out your nostrils. When Barry asked, Pete said, "I don't explain; I do."

Pete picks up the regurgitated potatoes with his fork, and pops them into his mouth. He chews again. Without stopping talking,

Kathy reaches over and pulls Pete's plate from its place. The potatoes plop onto the table.

"Oh sorry," she says, "I thought you were done." She's seen the trick, too. In fact they all have. Except Doug.

"Lovely Kathy, so smart, so witty," Teach says.

From the doorway Doug says, "Hey, man, that's fucking nasty." He's smiling as he walks into the room. He says to Pete. "I'm Doug, Kathy's friend. I'm told you've heard a lot about me."

Donny, who has met Doug, nods in his direction. The rest *have* heard about him. But when Kathy told them Doug was coming she didn't mention the word friend; she said she had something to clear up. Pete keeps on chewing. He looks at Doug, looks at Kathy, looks back at Doug. Potatoes fall from his mouth. Doug backs away. Teach says, "Harold Markham, Markham with an 'h.' Any friend of Kathy's is an enemy of mine."

Barry, who stopped watching Pete to look at Doug, is now watching Teach. He'll tell Kathy later how much he loathes Teach, how condescending Teach is. Calls me "Ah, the Electrician," as if that's my name. Teach asks Barry to do things, like come to his house and install a stereo system, or rewire a light switch, and Barry's supposed to do it. Because Teach is smart and Barry isn't. If Teach is so smart, Barry will ask her, why doesn't he do his own wiring?

Every weekend when he arrives home, Barry asks Kathy if she's told anyone they're sleeping together.

"We're not sleeping together," she tells Barry.

"Sometimes we are," Barry says.

She hasn't told anyone, never would tell anyone, because she doesn't want anyone to know, but she doesn't tell Barry that. She likes to keep him on his toes. (Kathy does suspect Pete knows. There's something about the way he looks at her, dreamy and distant, but intimate, like he knows everything she's ever done, or ever will do. And none of it matters any more than the pile of twice-chewed potatoes growing cold on the table.)

"Sit down, Kathy's friend," Teach tells Doug. "Join the Kathy fan club."

"Don't you have a home?" Kathy says to Teach, and she gets up. "Didn't I hear somewhere you had a wife locked away in your basement?"

Pete gets up and stage-whispers in Kathy's ear, "I told you, he's is in love with you."

His breath is hot and potatoey. He licks some strands of her hair into his mouth and holds them between his teeth, pulling her along, tugging her slowly after him to where Teach is sitting. He lets the hair fall against her face. It's wet. Teach stands, a look of longing in his eyes. Barry stands and clenches his fists. Kathy quickly moves away from the table to the sink. She grabs a dishcloth and scoops the chewed potatoes from the table.

"Did you want to finish these?" she says to Pete, holding the cloth out to him.

"Kathy," he says, looking into her eyes.

Pete sits down, as do all of the men except Doug, who moves back to the doorway.

Doug asks, "Kathy, can we get out of here?" But it's not a question.

They turn then to look at him, really look. His coat is open, brown suede dissected into rectangles, shearling showing along the seams of each. Black jeans and a sky-blue silk shirt under an elaborately embroidered denim vest. His dark hair is parted in the middle and falls in wavy wedges onto his shoulders. He's grown a moustache; it's thin and weedy.

"Are you going out in that?" Doug asks Kathy.

The men look from him to Kathy. She wanted to make Liberace proud, not to out-dress him, but to be right there with him. She wanted a costume, something he'd wear if he was a girl. So that's what she shopped for when she went to the Sally Ann yesterday.

Kathy found a skirt so short—a mere band of crinkly black velvet—her pink underpants play peek-a-boo along the hem. She found white vinyl knee-high boots and black stockings. Her pink satin jacket, one size too small, fits like a skin and looks good over the translucent lime-green turtleneck she had in her closet.

Kathy looks down at herself. The cleft of her breasts is a dark shadow and her nipples, just visible under the green fabric, slip in and out of view as the jacket shifts. Her hair glistens on her shoulders; patchouli wafts from it when she moves. She can feel the slickness of her frosted lipstick, the weight of black mascara on her lashes.

"I said, Are you going out in that?"

"That's the plan, Doug," she says.

Donny looks from Kathy to Doug and back again. "Hubba-hubba," he says, "what a figure, two more legs you look like Trigger."

They all laugh. Except Doug.

"Thanks, Donny," Kathy says. And she whinnies and kisses him on the forehead, leaving a frosty set of lips.

Teach moves in for a kiss. Barry stands up and moves toward Teach. Penny comes down from Rhettbutler's room and walks between them. Pete sits and watches from his chair, leans back on two legs, teeters there.

"You look fab," Penny says, putting her hands on Kathy's shoulders and running them down her shiny arms. "Want to borrow my midi coat? You're gonna need it tonight if you don't want to freeze your pretty pink ass."

"Where's Brenda?" Penny asks Donny. Penny likes Brenda too, has told Kathy there's something open and innocent about her, like a Peter, Paul and Mary song, all harmony and sweetness with a little sadness at the edges.

"Teaching my mother how to crochet," Donny says.

"That's sweet," Penny says.

"Who wants some hash?" Pete says, and he plunks the chair legs on the floor and stands.

"Go up to the Games Room," Penny says to him. "Open the window. And be quiet, Rhettbutler's asleep." Penny never does drugs, doesn't like to be in the same room with people doing them. She occasionally has a drink, and if she does, it has to be something very pink and very sweet and frothy, umbrellas optional.

Pete winks at Penny. She walks over and stands before him, leans into him, her wonderful breasts pressed flat against his body.

She looks sexy even in her work uniform, a white plasticky tunic tucked into draw-string pants, spongy white shoes like nurses wear.

"Read my lips, Pete," she says, looking up at him. "Be. Quiet. Rhettbutler. Is. Asleep." She mouths each word, says it loudly. Pete grabs her around the waist and dips her over his arm, her hair brushing the floor. He leans, kisses her, and quick as that, she is up and walking away from him.

"Yes, my love," he says.

They are impossibly stoned when Teach says, "Dear Kathy, tell us about your love life. Tell us about your boyfriends."

Teach is just shit-disturbing, but Barry blanches. He can barely stand, but he gets up anyway and says he has to leave to pick up Rachel.

"Ah, the Electrician and the Virgin Goddess," Teach says, "on your way then." He dismisses Barry with a flap of his hand.

Pete draws dreamy circles along the grain of the hardwood floor. He looks at Kathy, smiles, and shrugs his shoulder slightly. They're sitting on cushions Penny made, beanbag chair knock-offs in bright shiny vinyl—reds and yellows and oranges—filled with Styrofoam pellets. But they're not filled full enough. The pellets separate and pile up on either side of their bums and they may as well be sitting on the wood.

"Tell them about the Frenchman," Donny says, "the revolutionary."

"Donny," Kathy warns.

"Donny, you tell us," Teach says.

"Donny," Kathy says again, but decides not to stop him. Maybe it's not such a bad thing to remind Doug she had a life before him. After all, when she asked Donny along, she told him it was to help keep a distance between her and Doug, and maybe this is exactly what he's doing.

Donny's lying on the floor, his arms crossed on his chest, his head sunk between two mounds of beanbag chair. They can't see his face. Doug and Teach are looking at Kathy. Pete's eyes are closed; he's humming under his breath.

"We hitchhiked to Quebec City a couple of summers ago, me and Kath," Donny says.

As Donny talks, Doug shifts in his chair toward Kathy. He places his hand over hers, as if by accident, and leans on it, as hard as he can. He presses Kathy's fingers into the floor. She doesn't look at him; she doesn't flinch. He takes his hand away from hers, casually, and she lifts it into her lap and cradles it there.

Donny's voice emerges from the vinyl chair, so detached that she could almost believe the story is about someone else.

"Not many rides, not great weather, but the people were far out..." Donny's voice says.

Kathy closes her eyes and remembers. She was supposed to go to Sauble Beach on a camping holiday with her then boyfriend. She'd booked vacation time from the store. The boyfriend changed his mind; he wanted to go camping with the guys, he needed some time on his own. She said going with the guys wasn't time on his own. He said she knew what he meant. She said he was selfish; he said she was. He said he was going anyway and she said if he went that was it. So the boyfriend became an ex. Kathy didn't want to waste a holiday sitting around crying, which was exactly what she was doing, so she talked Donny into taking off, hitchhiking. We'll go where the rides take us, she told him. The rides took them to Quebec City.

She fell in love with the city from the moment they drove off the highway and onto Pont de Québec, the newer Pont Frontenac almost complete beside it, metal over water. They were dropped off downtown near the Chateau, and she fell in love with it. She fell in love with the St. Lawrence River. Someday she'd go back to Quebec, and live somewhere along the river, she told Donny.

She fell in love with the boardwalk, with the milky coffee and the strong beer. The narrow streets that wound near the Chateau and down to Old Town. The smell of water and diesel from the port, the chugging and churning of the ferries, the wonderful impossible sounds of French being sung and laughed and shouted. She loved the artists selling paintings and carvings, the vendors selling Quebecois kitsch, the kids hanging out in the square selling dope, the transistor radios playing bilingual rock and roll.

She met a man by a fountain, Martin, who spoke a bit of English. He asked to share the joint she and Donny were smoking, and then offered an apartment for the night. It wasn't his, he said, it wasn't really anyone's, it belonged to an organization, but it was available and there were some mattresses and sometimes a bit of food.

They said, sure, and followed Martin to the apartment, which indeed had mattresses, five of them with three dingy pillows apiece, in a large living room that had little else except one shade-less lamp and an excellent stereo system. They drank cheap red wine, Yago, smoked rollies, talked about music, about hockey. They compared Bobby Orr and Maurice "the Rocket" Richard and agreed to disagree. They talked about unions and the wage controls Trudeau was talking about imposing, and they smoked more dope and talked about how good the dope was. People came and went, some speaking only French. Everyone was friendly; some shared a toke, most laughed. They listened to Jimi Hendrix. *There's too much confusion*, they sang with him, *we can't get no relief.*

Martin took her to a room with a bed that actually had sheets and blankets. Not mine, he said, but one they could share. If she wanted to, he added, and he shrugged his shoulders and smiled. Later he woke Kathy and drew patterns on her naked back with his finger. He kissed her neck, her shoulder blades, her buttocks and told her he had to go out. He had to find his brother. His brother was to have shown up that night and he hadn't. Martin was worried. He told her that if the police came to get the hell out. If they didn't get out in time, to tell the police nothing. No names, no numbers of people, not what anyone looked like, or how they came to be sleeping there. Nothing. Make something up. Make up names.

He whispered that he and his brother belonged to the organization that rented the apartment; he said that they didn't hate the English. They were nationalists, just like Trudeau. Except their nation was French, not English. They needed to protect all things French. Then he was gone. None of this worried Kathy. She kissed Martin and fell back to sleep.

There were no police. The apartment was empty when they got up. Kathy told Donny about Martin's brother while they drank black tea and ate Chinese oranges, the only food in they could find in the kitchen.

"Far out," Donny said, "terrorists."

They left that day and hitchhiked up to the Gaspé, then down to Fredericton where they pooled the last of their money for two stand-by tickets to Toronto. They hitchhiked home from there.

End of story.

She'd almost forgotten the trip. Donny's made it real again and when he finishes his version, the room is too quiet.

"Time to roll," Kathy says, and she hoists herself out of her chair and heads for the door. Donny gets up and follows her.

"Where are you going?" Doug asks him.

Donny says, "With you."

"I invited him," Kathy says as she leaves the room.

"Kathy," Doug begins, but she's gone. They can hear her going down the stairs, Donny following.

"See ya, Kathy's friend," Pete says without opening his eyes. Teach watches Doug walk out of the room.

"Bad, bad Kathy," he says.

Doug's driving Blanche's car, so they ride with him to the auditorium. They stand behind the arena in the cold and smoke another joint. Inside it's hot and packed and dark, except for one huge electric candelabra that illuminates the stage. Liberace's sitting at a Baldwin piano wearing a dazzling jacket of cascading colour; he makes Kathy look like a nun. A Burt Bacharach tune ushers them to their seats.

"Well, look me over. I didn't dress like this to go unnoticed," Liberace coos to the audience when the song is over. "I make the NBC peacock look like a plucked chicken."

He plays "Roll Out the Barrel." For all the Germans, he says, and for all the people of German descent, which is most of the audience, most of Varnum, for that matter. He plays "Lara's Theme" from *Dr.*

Zhivago, "Georgy Girl," some Liszt. His outfits become gaudier and gaudier: a black sequined tuxedo, a crimson suit. He plays his theme song, "I'll Be Seeing You."

They clap, Kathy and Doug and Donny and all the people around them. They stand and cheer and whistle; they sway back and forth; some hum, others sing along. For the finale the lights go down, the candelabra is turned off, and Liberace emerges onto the darkened stage flashing and twinkling, his jacket wired with tiny lights. The audience rises, screams a delight that only dies down when the Trinidad-Tripoli Steel Band, all twenty-seven pieces, fills the auditorium with sound. The last tune begins. Kathy cries laughing tears. She's in love with Liberace. She's in love with the world. And then it's over. The lights come on. They are a milling mass of bland coats and plain toques, schlepping along in black and brown galoshes through a cavern of cement, metal and industrial-green paint.

Kathy and Donny and Doug are squished in a shoulder-to-shoulder crowd, a press to the doors, when they bump into Darlyn and Al. Darlyn is Betty Anderson on *Father Knows Best*: wide skirt, matching sweater, swishy ponytail. Only her nose is un-Betty.

"Nice jacket," Al shouts above the noise. He's trying not to look at Kathy's nipples under her sheer turtleneck.

"We tried to get your mother to come," Darlyn shouts into Kathy's ear, "but she wouldn't take the night off work. Mary even said she'd babysit Shelly."

"Darlyn. Al," Kathy shouts back, pointing her thumb, "you remember Doug. He's here from Vancouver to visit his parents, and he invited me and Donny to the concert." Kathy raises her eyebrows at Darlyn, who rolls her eyes. Darlyn knows all about Doug's invitation. When Kathy called to tell her she was taking Donny along—for protection—Darlyn told her she was going with her father and they'd probably see each other. "And you remember Donny, don't you?"

"Oh, I remember Darlyn," Donny says. "How could I forget? But this Darlyn has no George, and she's all grown up."

Donny takes Darlyn's hand and holds it. He won't let go. The crowd tries to move around them. Darlyn turns red and lifts her hand in Donny's into the air. She nods toward their hands locked together. Donny lowers their hands, cups hers, then opens the palm and kisses it. He winks at her, theatrical. Then he lets her hand fall.

"Al," Donny says, and he turns toward Al and bows. "Nice to see you again."

Kathy and Darlyn look at each other and laugh.

Donny turns back to Darlyn. Watches her, transfixed and smiling. "Darlyn," he says, shaking his head. "Far out. Darlyn."

People mill around them. Kathy takes Donny by the elbow and steers him toward the doors. Doug follows. Donny strains backward on Kathy's arm, trying to see Darlyn and Al in the crowd.

"Oh my Darlyn, oh my Darlyn," Donny sings over his shoulder. "Oh my Darlyn-Clementine."

Donny pulls away from Kathy and turns. He throws out his arms and spreads his feet. Darlyn and Al have disappeared.

"You are lost and gone forever," he sings, "dreadful sorry, Clementine."

After the Liberace show she says goodbye. She tells Doug she's taking a taxi home.

"Don't be stupid," he says. "She's being stupid, isn't she, Donny?" It isn't a question. "I'll drop Donny off and drive you right home."

When they drop Donny off, she opens her door.

"I can walk from here," she says.

He takes her hand and pulls her back in.

"I told you I'd drive you home and I will," he says.

He gets out of the car and she tells him she's going straight to bed. She says she'd rather he didn't come in. He pushes past her and watches as she hangs up Penny's coat. She tells him to leave.

She sits at the kitchen table to smoke a cigarette. He sits across from her. He taps his fingers, ta-tum, ta-tum. She finishes the cigarette, butts it out on a plate littered with breadcrumbs and peanut butter smears. Using the cigarette butt, she makes patterns in the crumbs, then makes a pile of them in the centre of the plate. She sets the butt beside the pile. She puts her head down on her arms. She sniffs her fingers, the tarry smell of cigarette with a hint of patchouli. She closes her eyes and watches Doug through her eyelashes. Doug jiggles his leg.

"I'm going to bed," she says, and she gets up.

He gets up too.

"Alone," she says. "Goodbye, Doug."

That's what she wanted to say to him, just goodbye, but for the life of her she can't think why. It's not like he's listening, or would have listened had she said it before she left Vancouver. She walks to the stairs. He walks behind her to the landing and down the stairs into the basement. He follows her into her room.

"What are these?" He sits down on her bed and tips over a blue Mexican pottery bowl filled with spare change, a few pairs of earrings and two condoms. They spill onto the night table; some change falls to the floor. Kathy picks it up.

"My life savings," she says, jingling the coins in her hand.

"Let me rephrase, *who* are these for?" Doug asks, and he sets the condoms on the bed. He takes Kathy's wrist and pulls her, not hard but insistent, down beside him.

Kathy stands right back up and walks to the door. The condoms are in case, but in case of what is none of his business. She wishes Barry wasn't out with Rachel.

Doug slides the condoms into his pants pocket.

"I want you to go," she says.

She's leaning against the wall next to the cage where Freddy lies coiled, glossy muscle wound tightly. His eyes are open and he's testing the air with his tongue. He begins to unwind, coil by coil, and slides slowly toward Kathy, stretches his head up, flicks his tongue along the edges of the metal lattice of his breathing grille.

Doug notices Freddy. Kathy watches Doug watch Freddy.

"I asked you to go," she says again. Freddy bobs his head and flicks his tongue along the grate.

"We haven't had our talk yet," Doug says, still watching Freddy. He turns his attention to Kathy and says, "Did we?"

Doug's questions never sound like questions.

"You don't listen."

"You should have told me you were going."

"I was sorry about that but now I'm not."

"Why'd you come tonight?"

"Stupid, I guess," Kathy says. She can't stop herself.

Doug turns from her to watch Freddy again.

"Look at me," Kathy says. "I." She points to herself. "Want you." She points at Doug. "To go," she says, and points her thumb to the door.

"OK, OK," Doug says. He holds his hands up, surrendering. When he passes Kathy near the door, he grabs her forearms, and he kisses her. He presses her arms down at her sides and sticks his tongue in her mouth. Kathy bites down. She tastes blood.

"Mother-fucking-cock-sucking-cunt," he says. He holds her arms tighter. Flecks of blood hit her when he swears. He jerks her around and pushes her face down onto the bed. He flips her over roughly, crawls on top and pins her arms to the mattress. Kathy squirms. Doug spits on her. Blood.

"Bitch," he says.

She tries to pull her hands free. She wants to scratch him. She calls for Barry even though he isn't there. She wants to scare Doug. He hits her in the chest. It hurts enough to take her breath away. She lies still. He pulls the pillow from under her head and puts it over her face. He grabs her wrists and jerks her arms over her head. He pushes her hands into the wall. Her knuckles scrape against it. She lifts her body and turns. He wrenches her arms up harder, holds them at her wrists with one hand. He inches upward on the bed until he can hold the pillow in place with his knees.

She tries to breathe and can't. She kicks her legs. Kathy hears his fly unzip, can feel his hard penis hit the pillow. She wrenches her arms, not free, but the pillow loosens. She turns her head to the air.

Doug moves down her. One hand pulls her panties down, the other still holds her wrists. He rams himself into her, two-three-four-five times. He grunts. He gets up.

"This shouldn't have happened." His words come from above her. "I didn't mean it to."

She wills herself still, silent.

"I'm leaving now," he says.

She hears him go, hears him walk down the hall.

And now that it's quiet, she hears Freddy, realizes she's been hearing him all along. TAT. TAT. TAT. The pillow is loose now, hot and moist with her breath. TAT. TAT. TAT. Freddy's nose strikes the glass.

She doesn't want to see herself, so she reaches down, lifts her bum and pulls her panties up. Only then does she slip the pillow from her face and tuck it under her head. Her belly's cold. Her crotch is wet, semen leaking through her pink panties. She pulls the blanket up. "Shush, Freddy," she says. "Shush-shush."

Kathy stands up and strips off her clothes. She strips the bed, takes the bottom sheet and wipes between her legs. She throws the bedding in the corner, throws her Liberace clothes on top. She pulls on long johns, the fat, woolen tube socks Connie knit for her for skating. Pulls on jeans, an undershirt, a T-shirt and her warmest sweater. She picks up her skates, grabs her stick and her bag of pucks.

Freddy's still tapping his snake S-O-S. Kathy puts her face near the grille and whispers, "He's gone. It's OK, Freddy."

Freddy strikes TAT-TAT, and stops. His head bobs and weaves like a boxer's, then swiftly he rolls backwards, undulates into a thick coil and rests.

A thin layer of snow swirls and skids over the ice. Kathy laces up and leaves her stick and puck bag in the middle of the rink. Crouched like a speed skater, one arm pumping, leg over leg, she slices the ice until she's sweating and her thighs ache.

She grabs her stick and dumps her bag of pucks at centre ice. She slaps them one at a time against the boards, each shot a little higher. An ankle. A kneecap. His groin. His neck. His head. Another invisible opponent.

Out and around, she finds a puck, stickhandles it to centre ice, leaves it twirling and skates for the next. The pucks cleave to the blade of her stick, no shims, no shams, just goddamn perfection. She thinks there could be blood on them. She wishes there was blood on them.

She leaves the pucks, and she skates to the end of the rink, twirls there, holding her stick in front of her. It weaves it up and down, like Shelly's legs did when they twirled. When she lets it go, it flies forward, smashes onto the ice with a clap and skids into the boards. Without the balancing weight of it, she falls. Up in a second, she skates, propels herself into the boards. She turns and skates to the other end of the rink and slams into the boards again. Her shoulder hurts, the side of her face stings, her nose is wet with blood and snot.

"Fucker," she screams. "Fuck-er."

She plops on her bum, legs splayed forward, elbows behind her on the ice. Thin dry snowflakes fall on her face, melt, fall into her open mouth and onto her closed eyelids. They gather in her hair. Snow sifts past her on the wind; it covers her tracks.

Goddamn, she won't cry. If she keeps her eyes closed, she won't cry. But the tears want to come. She gets up; she will skate them away. Goddamn, goddamn, soon it will be spring.

Spring, 1970

Sometimes I lie awake at night and I ask, "Where have I gone wrong?" Then a voice says to me, "This is going to take more than one night."

— Charlie Brown

KATHY SHOULD BE GETTING UP BUT SHE DOESN'T WANT TO MOVE. If she moves she'll vomit. There's nothing in her stomach, but that doesn't mean she won't throw up, so she lies absolutely still in her bed with its new Marimekko rip-off sheets, happy stylized daisies splashed over a mosaic of blues and greens. Poly-cotton, wash and wear that she hopes won't pill like the nubbly sheets in the garbage bag in the corner of the room. She'd tied the bag shut against the vomit smell because it made her want to vomit more. The first morning she was sick, she threw up on the Liberace clothes and the bed linen she'd tossed on the floor after The Doug Incident.

That's what she calls it, "The Doug Incident." As if it was a nuclear accident, or a terrorist attack, or something. She wishes the Doug part of the incident could be hanged, like the cop-murderer, William Rosik, who's supposed to be executed on April 21st. Kathy taped a newspaper article about him to Connie's refrigerator under a new heading: *Worry (And Prayers)*.

Connie explained that she wasn't going to pray for the killer because he was alive, at least for now. He still had time to pray for himself. She did *worry*, though, but not for him, for us—for the country—because our antediluvian government was going to hang the poor bastard by the neck until he died. She said capital punishment was immoral; it was condoned revenge, an eye for an eye, and it didn't work as a deterrent. A calculated killer will murder a cop because he wants to, and one who is angry or desperate isn't going to stop and think, Oh dear, I had better not kill this policeman because then I'm going to be hanged. No time for that.

And she didn't think that by hanging, William Rosik would automatically be redeemed. Redemption by fire was hollow. Real redemption required an action. Rosik had to want to redeem himself, had to take responsibility for what he had done and try to make up for it. She believed he'd have the rest of his natural life to redeem himself because in the end, the death sentence would be remanded, and eventually Trudeau would do the right thing and repeal this last remnant of legalized barbarity.

Connie figured the dead policeman needed her prayers, and his widow needed both her prayers and worry. I pray for him, she told Kathy, because he likely didn't have time to pray for himself. He was living and breathing and just like that—and she snapped her fingers—he was dead. I also pray that his wife has lots of insurance, and that the police force doesn't leave her stranded in a few years, expecting her to remarry and have someone else look after her. Connie said she felt for all widows and their children. They needed all the help they could get.

That's when Kathy made the mistake of asking, "Why are you so upset about these people? You don't even know them."

"Just listen for a change," Connie told her. "Try to learn something."

"Like I have a choice," Kathy was murmuring when her mother started getting personal, which was a clear sign to shut up.

"I pray for the widow," Connie continued, "because I know what she's going through. One minute she has a certain kind of life. An ordinary life with smelly socks under the bed, and fights about how to make the g-d toast the right way, not burned every g-d time. About putting the cap back on the toothpaste or changing the toilet paper roll when it's empty.

"All worthy reasons for a fight," Connie added. "But the next thing she knows, her life is changed beyond anything she could have imagined, because her husband is dead."

And Connie knew, she told Kathy, what any widow wouldn't give to have a minute, just one, to say something pleasant, or perhaps to give that smile she'd withheld the morning her husband left for work.

"I pray she kissed her husband goodbye when he left that morning," Connie said, "or had sex with him the night before he went on shift. One final bit of kindness to be grateful to have given."

Connie started to cry.

"You know the last thing I said to your father when he left for work the day he died?" Connie asked Kathy, and by this time Kathy really didn't want to hear one more word.

"Nothing," Connie said. "He called out from the back door that he was leaving. He asked if I needed anything from the supermarket. I was sitting in this very chair. I was trying to feed Shelly. She was screaming and fighting me like always. I didn't bother to look up, didn't say a word. I thought, OK, you gaw-damned bastard, go to work and leave me with this screaming baby one more time. I thought other things as well and none of them were kind.

"Now I've forgiven myself for that lapse of kindness and for those harsh thoughts. They were true to the moment and I don't regret them. But I'm glad I didn't say anything. Saying nothing rather than speaking my mind turned out to be a bit of a blessing for me.

"So when some poor woman I don't happen to know personally becomes a widow when she had no idea it was going to be her turn, well, I believe she deserves my thoughts, and my prayers and worries both.

"Now put this article on the fridge," she ordered Kathy, waving her hand toward the kitchen. "Put it under *Worry (And Prayers)*."

Kathy can't lie here forever. She has to get up. It's Saturday, and she promised Connie she'd take Shelly skating at the Varnum Auditorium. She sits up slowly, wrapping her arms around her tummy and holding it tight, for comfort really. She situates her bum on the edge of the mattress and puts her head between her knees. She waits while her stomach settles.

These days, once she gets up, Kathy goes to work. She comes home and lies on her bed. She sleeps. Sometimes Barry leans in the doorway and watches her, but he never speaks, never crosses the threshold. She senses him there. He leaves little offerings on the floor:

a package of cigarettes, a Mars bar, an 8-track of *Déjà vu*. Kathy tosses the presents in the garbage bag, except for the tape, which she plays endlessly in the car.

She'd tied the sheets in the garbage bag after Pete came down one night to tell her she was supposed to call Connie. Kathy was curled on her side, her hands tucked between her knees. Though she was bitterly tired, she was awake, looking at patterns in the paint on her wall: faint bristle lines like veins, areas thickened by overlap where light flattened to nothingness.

"Kathy?" Pete said from the doorway.

"Hmm," she said. She wasn't moving then either.

"Are you all right?"

"Hmm?"

"I said, are you all right?"

"No," Kathy said to the wall.

"Do you want to smoke a joint?"

"Not really," Kathy said.

"Do you want to talk?"

"No," Kathy said.

"What's that smell?" Pete asked.

"Laundry," Kathy told him. She turned her head to look at him. "It's dirty, that's all." And she looked back at the wall.

Pete walked to the corner of the room. Kathy heard him there, heard him kick the sheets, heard his knees creak when he squatted down. She heard Pete whisper, *Shit*. When he got up, his knees creaked again.

He came and sat on the edge of Kathy's bed. Kathy didn't care that he was there until she felt him shift and suddenly he was curled up behind her. Then she wished herself away from him. She looked at the paint on the wall and willed herself part of it. He warmed her, though they weren't touching. Pete could be so quiet, so utterly still, especially when he was stoned, that his body seemed to disappear and his presence enhance. That's what she felt now, that the essence of Pete was touching her even if his body wasn't. She felt his breath on her hair and wished she'd washed it.

Soon she was breathing the same cool-warm rhythm as his breath, its absence and return. And she began to fall asleep. When she woke, Pete was gone, and she was sweating under a blanket that didn't belong to her. Pink wool with satin edging, it was grandmotherly and smelled of mothballs and marijuana.

After Pete's visit, she had a shower and washed her hair. She found a garbage bag and rolled the vomitty sheets and Liberace clothes into it. She threw in the letters Doug had sent her from Vancouver, and Barry's offerings. She tied the bag shut and tossed it into the corner. When she was ready, when the time was right, she'd know exactly what to do with it.

All winter, Kathy's life had been so flat she should have been able to see anything coming. But she didn't. Even the vomiting hadn't registered right away. Then it did, and she knew she was pregnant.

She bought a pregnancy test kit and confirmed it, and she made a doctor's appointment. The doctor warned her that getting past the abortion board at the hospital was a long shot; besides, he wasn't sure he could recommend her. She could go to the States—New York City or Boston, maybe Detroit. Or England, there was a clinic in England that did abortions on Canadian girls. He'd have to think about it, he said. He'd call her the next day with his decision.

But in the end he didn't call and she finally called him because the next day had turned into four. He said there would be no abortion, perhaps Kathy could keep the baby, or there was always adoption. When Kathy asked if he'd refer her to another doctor who might recommend an abortion, he said he didn't think so, no, he didn't think he could do that. He said he was sorry, and he hung up. But sorry wasn't the impression Kathy got. Dickless was more like it, because he wasn't even going to call to tell her he wasn't going to help.

She hadn't told him what Doug did, hadn't thought he'd believe her. She imagined all unmarried pregnant girls had elaborate stories to tell their doctors about why they were turning up in their offices pregnant and needing abortions.

After fretting and throwing up for another week, and trying to get through her work days without appearing to be sick or in distress,

Kathy drove to Guelph to see the doctor who'd given her and Darlyn their first birth control pills. He'd been sympathetic, but said he couldn't recommend her to the board at his hospital. He couldn't do that for a woman outside his practice. Birth control was one thing, but abortions were another. There were rules. But he did give her the number of the Women's Liberation Abortion Referral Service in Toronto. When she called, she was given the name of a doctor in Montreal listed in the Quebec medical register who might do an abortion.

The woman she spoke to asked Kathy to call her back and let her know if she was able to get an appointment in Montreal. Kathy never called her back. She was making her calls from a phone booth in the Beamer Street bus station, slipping change into the slot every time the operator told her to. Both her change and her patience were limited.

On her twentieth birthday, Kathy called Montreal and was told to come in two weeks to the day. She was asked how far along she thought she was and the date of her last menstrual period. She was asked if this was her first abortion. Her first pregnancy. She was asked if she had been using birth control at the time she became pregnant. (This was a routine question, the woman said, not a reason to say no to an abortion; mistakes happen.) She was asked if she was married. She'd have to have her husband's permission if she was married. She was asked if she was in good general health.

Kathy's answers were monosyllabic whenever possible. She glanced around the station waiting room hoping no one she knew came in. No one did. But there was a man with his long hair tied with a paisley bandana. He wore a red lumberjack coat, tight patched jeans with elaborate embroidery up the legs. He slouched on a wooden bench and smoked. He watched her, a look of deliberate inattention. A hippie, she thought, one of the dopers from Regent Park. He probably just needed a place to warm up.

Kathy was given instructions on how to get to the clinic. She was told to definitely not, under no circumstances, enter the clinic if she noticed a police car or anyone who might be a policeman in the vicinity. Err on the side of caution, she was told. She was to walk past the clinic and call from a payphone to get further instructions, or to rebook the appointment if she suspected anyone was watching her. She was to bring two sanitary napkin belts (in case one became bloody and needed washing), and it would be a good idea to bring a small box of maternity size napkins. She was to bring $200 cash, which she would pay in advance of the procedure, and for which she would not receive a receipt. She wasn't asked if she was able to afford $200. She would be booked under her first name, they didn't record last names, but could she please bring a piece of paper with her emergency contacts on it and have it in her pocket. Just in case.

Just in case of what Kathy didn't ask. She didn't want to know. Details were becoming overwhelming. Being accidentally pregnant was beginning to feel like an act of espionage, a betrayal of her country. She expected she'd have to eat the paper on which she wrote the name of her emergency contact once the abortion was over. Leave no traces; it would be as if nothing had ever occurred.

"Do you have any questions?" the woman asked.

"No," Kathy told her, though she had many questions, hundreds of questions.

"Is everything clear?" the woman asked. Her voice was gentle but firm, tinged with a French-Canadian accent.

"Yes," Kathy said, and there was a click on the line.

Kathy was lying. Nothing was clear. Everything was impossible to understand. Except that it was her birthday, and she was pregnant, and she felt horrible. What was most clear was that she needed not to be pregnant, and that she'd do whatever was necessary to achieve that. And she needed to tell someone.

"Darlyn?"

"Kathy. Happy birthday," Darlyn's cheerful voice said over the phone. "I was going to call you. Are you doing anything special? Do you want me and Donny to come over? We can take you out." After the Liberace concert Darlyn broke up with George, and Donny broke up with Brenda, and Darlyn and Donny began going out together.

"I think I'm pregnant," Kathy whispered to Darlyn, still unable to say that she was, whispering because the hippie was watching her again.

"You think you are?" smart friend Darlyn stage-whispered back. "Or you really are?"

"I'm pretty sure," Kathy said, speaking a little louder now that she didn't need to be specific.

"Did you have the test, Kathy?" wise Darlyn asked in her regular voice, her baton twirling champion confident voice.

"Yes," Kathy said.

"Did the bunny die?" coaxed patient, cool Darlyn.

Good old Darlyn. No oh-my-god, or who and how, or you slut, but right to the point. Kathy told her yes, the bunny died. That the bunny was so dead Kathy was waiting to go for an abortion. She said this out loud. Her voice echoed off the walls. She stared at the hippie. He closed his eyes and slowly lay back on the wooden bench.

"I have an appointment," she told Darlyn, her true friend, her fine friend, "in two weeks in Montreal."

"I'll come with you," Darlyn told her. "Don't worry. It'll be OK." As if she was holding Kathy in her arms, patting her on the back, saying there, there. As if by saying OK, it would be OK. And that's when Kathy cried. The hippie got up, took the bandana from his hair, handed it to Kathy, said good luck, and walked out of the bus station.

Kathy grabs a piece of cold, crispy toast from her bedside table. She makes the toast before she goes to bed, sliced white bread baked in a low oven until browned, like Melba toast. She breaks a piece, puts it on her tongue—she can't stand to have food touch her teeth these days—and lets it melt. Her mouth fills with saliva and she's sure she's going to throw up again, but she doesn't.

This is how she's staying alive: oven-dried bread or other soft white food: angel food cake, warm dinner rolls (no butter), toasted hot dog rolls (no hot dog), butterhorns and Chelsea buns (Kathy spits out the nuts and bits of dried fruit, but she swallows the raisins—for the iron), and toasted hot cross buns with a thin layer of raspberry jam. She's getting pimples, too much white flour and sugar and no meat or fruit or vegetables. Her face is as doughy and pale as the food she eats; her nipples are sore.

The Thursday of her birthday, the day she made the arrangements for the abortion, Connie had her over for supper. Kathy told her not to cook anything special because she'd had the flu and wasn't up to eating much. Connie made chicken noodle soup for her and Shelly, a hearty chicken broth for Kathy. She said she'd make a cake when Kathy felt better. After Kathy ate a few spoonfuls of soup, Connie came over to her and took Kathy's face in her hands. She looked into Kathy's eyes until Kathy coughed so she could turn her head away.

If her mother suspected, she didn't say. What she said was, "Come home and live with us."

Kathy tried to laugh; it sounded like a grunt.

"I told you, I had the flu. I'm not going to die or anything. And I'm not going to move back here," she said. And she hardened herself against the tears she saw welling in her mother's eyes.

SHELLY'S WRAPPED LIKE A MUMMY IN HER CARTOON QUILT. IT'S flannel and faded, frayed at the edges, threads hanging from the squares. And it's musty because it seldom gets washed. It's only a pieced quilt top, no batting and no backing, which Connie had started, using old pyjama material: pink bunnies on blue, blue bunnies on pink, bright spring flowers—pink on white, yellow on green, white on blue, red roses on yellow. Mickey Mouse and Donald Duck, brown puppies and white kittens and other bits of nighties or pyjamas Connie and Kathy and Shelly had owned.

Before Connie could stretch the top on the quilt frame, Shelly stole it from her ironing basket. She rolled herself in it and then lay on the floor to watch Saturday morning cartoons. When Connie tried to unwrap Shelly and convince her she could make the quilt prettier and softer by finishing it, Shelly closed her eyes, stiffened her body, knocked her head against the floor and screamed bloody murder. Connie let her have the quilt top.

Kathy and Shelly are watching Wile E. Coyote run past Road Runner over the edge of a cliff. Kathy's on the couch, Shelly's wrapped in her quilt on the floor, and Connie's in bed sleeping, her Saturday treat. Sun streams through the picture window. Prisms strung Pollyanna style along the top of the window frame beam rainbows across the walls and ceiling, across Shelly in her quilt. The furnace thrums alive, heat rises in a whoosh from the vents; the prisms turn gently on the moving air and the rainbows dance.

Wile E. Coyote hangs in the air and looks back at Road Runner, who has a puff of dust at his feet. Then Wile E. falls through a cartoon cloud and crashes flat as a pancake onto the road at the bottom of the mountain. Before the dust finishes rising, Road Runner zips into position beside Wile E. and waits for him to pop back into shape and take up the chase again.

Shelly laughs, "Ha-ha-ha!" Mirthless. Kathy laughs, too.

When the cartoon is over Kathy and Shelly are going to the auditorium for the Saturday morning public skate. Shelly's skates are by the door. Before she went to bed, Connie set them out for her. Then she tucked a two-dollar bill in Shelly's thin red leather wallet and tucked the wallet into the pocket of her jeans. In the pocket there's also a printed card with Shelly's name, Connie's name, Kathy's name and an address and phone number on it, in case Shelly gets lost.

Road Runner's feet twirl through the air, and then he's off. Wile E., revived and looking more like himself, is left in the dust again. When the commercial comes on, Kathy gets up and goes to Shelly. She sits down on the floor beside her cocooned sister and presses both her hands firmly on Shelly's cheeks. She rubs gently, the way Shelly likes her to.

"Time to get dressed, Shelly. We have to go or we'll miss skating," Kathy says. She holds Shelly's face still and looks into her eyes. Shelly grins; her breath smells like milk. Shelly wiggles out of the quilt and beams at Kathy because she's already dressed and ready to go. She laughs, and it almost sounds happy. It's a good joke, that's for sure, and Kathy laughs too, because sometimes Shelly's smarter than they give her credit for. And sometimes she's even dimmer than they could imagine, but it's always nice to be with Shelly on a good day.

While Kathy helps Shelly into her coat, she tells her about Charlie, and the rinks they used to make in the backyard. "Before you were born," she tells Shelly, "Dad made rinks as shiny as glass and he bought me a brand new pair of hockey skates. We skated at night under the stars and we had hot chocolate, just like we're going to have today. Even Mom skated. Imagine, Shelly—Mom. She was really good, a figure skater. I wish she'd skate with us. She hasn't skated once since Dad died."

Kathy tucks Shelly's mittens under her jacket sleeve. "He'd be so proud of you. You're such a good skater. You hardly ever fall."

She helps Shelly into her boots and Shelly sits on the floor while Kathy puts hers on. "You know what, Shelly? Some people actually get paid to skate, like Bobby Orr."

"Bobby Orr, #4," Shelly yells, "Bobby Orr, #4." She jumps, opens the door and runs outside. Kathy comes out after her.

"Maybe someday I will too," she says, and she catches up with Shelly and they get into the car.

It looks like she has no choice. Kathy's going to remember her abortion as The Day the Beatles Broke Up. The radio was filled with break-up chatter. Some DJs blamed Yoko Ono, who certainly didn't go out of her way to win hearts. Others said it was about money, or how the band lacked cohesion after Brian Epstein died. All the radio stations—French and English—played Beatles music.

"It's morbid, like they're dead," Darlyn said. "And it's really bringing me down."

Donny sang "Strawberry Fields" and soon they were singing all the tunes as they were played.

Kathy's lying on a double bed that's tucked under the sill of a dust-encrusted window. She's wrapped in a grey wool blanket, like the army surplus blankets her father used when he went fishing with "the boys." Camp blankets, the same ones she and Darlyn borrowed to build tents in their backyards.

Beside Kathy, Darlyn's asleep under a tattered bedspread and a yellowed sheet. Her arms are around Donny, who's smushed into the wall, snoring. Or not so much snoring as saying "HAGH" when he breathes out. For a time Kathy counted Donny's HAGHs, but stopped when she was distracted by the number of times someone dropped or clanged pots while preparing the breakfast she hoped to eat in the brasserie below their room. Forty-seven clangs and crashes so far. Before the snores and clangs, she counted drips from the bathroom showerhead as they hit the metal floor of the shower stall.

The bathroom holds a toilet on which it is impossible for a normal-sized person to sit without damaging their knees, and a much-dinged metal shower stall with a dripping showerhead, and a drain so clogged with variously-coloured hair that it didn't drain. Darlyn removed the wad with a piece of toilet paper. The sink is at the foot of the bed, not in the bathroom. Two dingy towels and a stiff dishcloth hang from an unbalanced metal rod, that when touched, clatters to the floor.

Darlyn and Donny drove with Kathy to Montreal. They left after work and drove through Friday night, arriving downtown on Saturday morning. They found a diner and had toast and café au lait, a coffee that was sweet and milky. They dunked their toast, holding floppy bites out to each other, laughing to cover their nervousness.

They had the morning to kill—Kathy's appointment was at two—so they walked through Old Montreal to a park. There a few musicians huddled—a bongo player, four acoustic guitarists, a girl on an autoharp, another playing a flute, a boy with a Jew's harp—sharing rhythms, jamming mostly, though occasionally a recognizable tune emerged and someone sang along until anarchy reigned again. It was exuberant, happy music. Listeners smoked cigarettes and joints, girls and boys, hippies mostly, danced. People talked. It wasn't really warm, about 55°, but the sun made it seem warmer, the way sun does in spring.

An office worker with a brown duffle coat over his suit, a pink button-down shirt and a paisley tie, offered Kathy a toke. She nodded no thanks. His curly hair was longish, dark brown, and he wore black horn-rimmed glasses over kind, blue-grey eyes. He said he was from Halifax. He'd moved to Montreal for the summer and decided not to go back to university in the Maritimes. His parents were pissed off, but he loved Montreal.

He came to the park to have lunch, to listen to the musicians if they were there, and to watch people. Writing programs, he said when Kathy asked what he did. In COBOL, he explained, and he told her how to spell it, all capitals. He worked for Northern Electric and his programs were transcribed onto punch cards that operators fed into computers. The computers were enormous, he told her, as big as a gymnasium, but the programmers weren't allowed in the computer room. When he smiled, his teeth were crooked and very white.

He said he was heading over to Phantasmagoria, a record shop, did she want to come? There was a balcony that ran around the upper level. He could listen to records and visit his friends there. She told him no, she had an appointment and he said, too bad, but she should go there some other time anyway. Maybe they'd run into each other.

"Another terrorist?" Donny asked when they walked back to the car.

"Pretty good disguise for a terrorist," Darlyn said.

"A computer programmer," Kathy told them.

"Way of the future," Donny said. "I think you should marry him."

They joked about Kathy living in the suburbs with a dope-smoking computer programmer, a nice station wagon instead of the shit-box Valiant they had come in, a dog, probably a retriever called Ringo. Kathy'd wear polyester pantsuits, a different colour every day, and there'd be a couple of kids. At the mention of kids they all stopped talking and headed back to the car.

"We'll be right here when it's over," Darlyn told Kathy as she got out of the car at the clinic. They'd circled the block to make sure there were no police. Darlyn got out and stood beside Kathy. Kathy took her hand.

"You're shaking," Darlyn said.

"Hmm," Kathy mumbled. Kathy squeezed, then let go of Darlyn's hand.

"Thanks," she said, and she started the walk to the clinic door. Halfway there she turned. Donny waved. Darlyn leaned into the car and came out with her baton. She twirled it, threw it in the air, spun around, dipped onto one knee and caught it. She threw both arms out and grinned, then stood and bowed. She lifted the baton in the air and shook it.

"It'll be this easy," Darlyn called, twirling the baton faster and faster. Kathy opened the clinic door and went in.

Kathy presses her fingers into her eyelids so that colours spark behind them. Sleep. Sleep. She needs to sleep. Donny is still snoring. While Kathy was at the clinic Darlyn and Donny found the room and decided they could share it. When they arrived after the abortion, Kathy could tell they'd had sex on the bed, which had the happy, rumpled look of lovemaking.

The room smells like cigarette butts and dead fish. And bleach. Kathy's lying on the outside edge of the bed in case she needs to get to the bathroom quickly. To pee, she told them, but really so she can check her pad. Small dense clots of blood slip like wee wet plums from between the lips of her vulva into the pad that lines her underwear.

She's bleeding only as much as she was told to expect, so she's not too alarmed. Not scared shitless or anything. She massages her fundus as instructed, or what she hopes is her fundus (she never knew she had a fundus until now) to keep her uterus firm and contracted to control the bleeding.

Yesterday she *was* scared shitless, but everyone was nice to her, the three nurses at the clinic so gentle and kind, though businesslike. No guilt trips. Kathy went from terror to something resembling calm once she was settled in a change room.

"Nobody gets pregnant on purpose just so they can have an abortion," one of the nurses said to her, then asked what Kathy intended to do for birth control when she left the clinic. She was given a brochure, in French and in English, with birth control options and information.

One of the nurses gave Kathy a routine physical—blood pressure, heart rate, listened to her lungs, prodded her abdomen, and asked some basic questions about her medical and menstrual history, and confirmed the dates of her last menstrual period. The doctor came in and asked why she wanted the abortion and why she hadn't been able to get one in her hometown. He asked who had referred her and nodded when she told him about the abortion referral line in Toronto. He asked for the money and she gave it to him, money she'd withdrawn from her bank in fifty dollar increments over the last two weeks, as if she was a criminal and was doing something wrong, something she had to hide. Which she was, of course.

"You understand you won't be getting a receipt?" he asked, and Kathy nodded.

The operating room was clean and well equipped. At least Kathy thought it was. She'd never had an abortion before. Except for having her tonsils out when she was five, she'd never been in an operating room. The nurse gave her a tour: here was the operating table covered in crisp clean white cotton; there were the stirrups where she'd place her feet. These were the stainless steel bowls and the wrapped gauze pads. And there on a stainless steel table was a parcel of sterilized instruments covered in green linen and tied closed with white string. This was the light they'd shine on Kathy's perineum. It was all so orderly and simple.

The room smelled faintly of Lysol, and a pleasant sweet smell that reminded her of the ether that had dripped through a strainer over gauze above her face before her tonsils were removed. Kathy had removed her jeans and underwear, washed her perineum the way the nurse had instructed, rinsed in a solution so cold it made her nipples erect. She wrapped a sheet around her waist, and walked into the operating room.

The doctor arrived in hospital scrubs and gloves. The nurse tied a mask over his face. The mask moved in and out with his breath. He told Kathy to get up on the table and the nurse helped her. The nurse placed her legs in the stirrups and her feet in sterile slippers. She told her they were going to wash her again, this time with disinfectant. Freezing solution flowed over her bottom into a basin. It made her anus contract and she was embarrassed that they should see it. They draped her legs and began.

"I'm inserting the speculum," the doctor told her.

"I'm dilating the cervix," he told her next.

"I'm cleaning the inside of the womb," he said after that. "It's called curettage."

It was painful, but bearable.

There was clanking and instructions to the nurse. Kathy stopped listening. She became aware only of her abdomen, the cramping, which was no worse at first than a period might be. She focused on it, needed to feel each twinge and scrape.

"Lie here for a few minutes," the doctor told her and he snapped off his gloves, then the overhead light, and he left. She never saw him again.

The nurse brought Kathy a warmed flannel blanket—it felt like heaven—and told her to rest while she cleaned up. When everything was tidied, she helped Kathy get her legs out of the stirrups and asked her to lift her bottom while she placed a clean pad between Kathy's legs. She helped Kathy sit up and bring her legs to the side of the table.

"Hold the pad," she told Kathy. "You can use the belt and one of the pads you brought when you get changed to go home."

Kathy rested, dozing for a time, shivering off and on—nerves, not cold, as they renewed the warmed blankets regularly. When she was told she could, she got dressed. The nurse gave her some pills, antibiotics, she said, and told her about her fundus. Then she told her she could go, and that her friends were waiting for her outside.

Darlyn and Donny met her at the door and held her elbows as she walked. She didn't need them to, but their touch calmed her and she suddenly felt so relaxed, so tired, she just wanted to sleep, which is what she did while they went out to sightsee Montreal. Kathy, bleeding and no longer pregnant, wrapped herself in a grey wool blanket and lay on the bed pushed under the dirt-caked window, and slept.

After Darlyn and Donny returned, a bit drunk, after they crawled into bed and fell directly to sleep, Kathy lay awake and listened to water drip from a leaky shower head, listened to pots and pans clang in the kitchen below, listened to Donny snore. Then finally, when despair at ever sleeping again had exhausted her, Kathy drifted off and dreamed of doctors in masks, and drummers making music. She dreamed a long-haired man in a brown duffle coat asked her to marry him. She dreamed that on the day the Beatles broke up she lay naked in a park. People milled around her, oblivious, which was a surprise, because lying between her legs was a pile of small, shiny red plums arranged in the shape of a baby.

KATHY'S MAKING FRENCH TOAST BEFORE SHE LEAVES FOR WORK. Only Rhettbutler's up so far, and he's eating toast as fast as Kathy can get it out of the pan.

"How come you're not fat?" Kathy asks.

He pours maple syrup until the toast swims. When he's finished eating, he licks the plate and starts over.

"A boy after my own heart," Penny says. She rumples his hair as she walks past him. "Just like his daddy, don't you think?" She's just out of the shower and her hair leaves drip trails down her blouse and the back of her jeans.

"Does he spit his food back on his plate?"

"Can I have the next batch?" Penny asks. Kathy slides two pieces of toast on a plate for her. Penny sits beside Rhettbutler and says, "You're much more mature than your daddy, aren't you, sweetie?"

"My ears are ringing," Pete says. He's standing in the doorway, pulling on a white T-shirt. Kathy notices his chest is nearly hairless except for the black silky ones that curl around his nipples, and a few that form a dark line that begins under his navel and disappears into his jeans. He kisses the top of Rhettbutler's head.

"Hey, buddy," he says. He takes Penny's long hair in his hands and shakes it; water droplets fly around the room.

"Peter Gerald Lehman!" Penny shouts.

While Penny's distracted, Pete steals her plate. She stabs the back of his hand with her fork. Five tine wounds puff up immediately; two bleed. Penny takes her plate back.

"Shit," Pete yells, and shakes his hand. He cups Penny's chin and tries to look into her eyes, but she's looking at her plate. She cuts a corner from her French toast. Before she gets it to her mouth, Pete leans down and kisses her. Penny looks at him then, wide eyes staring into his. She holds the fork at the ready and when Pete releases her chin, she pops the toast into her mouth and smacks her lips.

"You're sweetness and light this morning," he says and laughs.

Kathy hands Pete a plate and he sits on the other side of Rhettbutler.

He takes Rhettbutler's plate and pours the excess syrup from it onto his French toast. Rhettbutler screams and grabs the plate back. Syrup spills on the floor. Penny groans, but she keeps on eating.

"That's mine," Rhettbutler says. Pete growls at his son and pretends to bite his ear. Rhettbutler ignores him. Penny finishes her French toast.

"You guys are crazy," Kathy says. "And I have to leave soon."

"Isn't it early for you?" Penny asks.

"I'm on union duty," Kathy says. "A guy from the Retail Clerks Union is trying to help organize all the stores. I went to a meeting and volunteered to nab the people at my store in the break room before they punch in. Talk them into signing on. I give out pamphlets and say stuff like, 'united we stand.' Marvin says I'm a communist. His mother told him, if I'm doing union work, I'm a commie."

Marvin's a stock boy, whom Kathy's told them about before. He calls himself "third man" and technically he's right, because there are only four full-time grocery men in Kathy's store: the manager, the assistant manager, Marvin, and a never-ending stream of stock boys hired as "fourth man" who never last long because they realize fourth man means bottom of the rung, and that no one will ever get past Marvin in seniority.

Marvin started at the store when he was sixteen and boasts he's been working in the grocery business for twenty-two years. He's single and lives with his mother, with whom he fights. When they do, Marvin rages all day, telling anyone who will listen how he's going to get his own place. But by the end of the day he looks sheepish and wonders what his mother's making for supper, because she always makes a special meal after a fight.

Marvin has a round belly and freckled, pockmarked skin. His ties clip on, and he stores the tatty comb he uses to maintain his swirling pompadour in a pocket protector that says *Weston's Freshness Guaranteed*. His pants and cardigans are various browns; the pants have creases sewn in. His hands are big and red, often healing from some bruise or cut. Marvin will never join a union.

And other than Marvin there are only three full-time employees eligible for union status—managers, and produce and meat clerks are excluded—so Kathy knows the attempt is doomed. But union arguments are a switch from the routine of work, the coffee and cigarette and doughnut breaks, the noontime games of euchre for nickels or dimes, and the complaints about the smell of garbage near the loading dock, or the drafty doors, or whose turn it is to pack and carry out groceries for Kathy, especially when the weather is bad. Kathy's manager's been giving her the evil eye for days. He likes her, she knows, but he hates discord. And unions, he told Kathy, are a royal pain in the ass.

Kathy gathers the breakfast plates and starts washing them. When she turns around, Rhettbutler's climbing onto Penny's lap. His legs dangle outside hers; his bare feet almost touch the ground. He settles into her and hums. Penny turns his face to hers and licks the crumbs and syrup from around his mouth.

"You're yummy," she says. She tickles him, and he giggles and snuggles closer.

Sometimes since the abortion, when Kathy watches Rhettbutler and Penny, she wonders what kind of mother she'd have been. But she doesn't dwell on it, stops herself from dwelling on it. Pete and Penny tell funny stories about the mistakes they made when Rhettbutler was a baby, about how nervous they were and how little they knew about being parents. But as they gained experience they relaxed, and they realized a baby was a pretty hardy little being. That's when they began to enjoy Rhettbutler, they said. As Kathy turns back to the sink to finish the dishes, she wonders what kind of parents Penny and Pete would be if they didn't have each other.

Pete gets up and leans against the counter next to Kathy. His arm brushes hers. Ever since Pete lay behind her on her bed, the thought that he might touch her makes her edgy, a dangerous, sexual jitteriness that she knows means nothing good. Kathy gets the frying pan from the stove. She slides it into the dishwater. The pan sizzles.

"You're gonna get yourself fired," Pete says to her.

"They can't fire us for organizing," Kathy says. "But we have been told to be extra careful about being on time and not making any mistakes on cash, that kind of thing. If I get fired I'm going to get Alan Eagleson to be my agent and become the first ex-checkout girl in the NHL. Then I'll be in the Players Association and we'll negotiate me a big fat contract."

"We're in negotiations for our contract," Penny says. "It's not looking good. We might end up on strike."

"If you end up on strike, my lovely, and Kathy ends up fired, and The Eagle doesn't take her on as a client, then I'll be the only person bringing in a paycheque," Pete says. "I'll have to get some extra stock in."

"Little Barry," Penny says. "He makes enough to support us all."

"He spends every cent on women," Pete says. He's not looking at Kathy.

"Women?" Penny asks.

"Is there more than one woman, Kathy?" Pete asks. He still isn't looking at her. "You live down in the dungeon; you must know."

"Yes, there is," Kathy says to Penny. Pete must know that Barry spends nights in Kathy's bed. She turns to Pete and says, "I didn't want to tell you, Pete, but Freddy's a girl. And Little Barry's in love with her."

(She told Barry to go away. He was standing in her doorway and she was crying for no particular reason, as she had occasionally since the abortion. At the clinic they'd warned her it might happen. Fluctuating hormones, they said, that would settle after she'd had a couple of normal periods. But Barry didn't go; instead he sat and leaned his back against the doorframe and sang lullabies. "Hush-a-bye, don't you cry," he sang, "go to sleep my little baby." And one about a mucky kid, "dirty as a dust bin lid, when he finds out the things you did, you'll get a whack from your dad." She just cried harder, so Barry came in and lay beside her and held her, shushed her and they fell asleep.)

"Yup, Barry and Freddy have a weird thing going," Kathy says, and she smiles. "It's wild. You should see them. It's X-rated, man." She smiles harder.

(In the morning, she told Barry what had happened. About Doug having sex with her after the Liberace concert, how she didn't want him to. She told him about the pillow over her face, the scrapes on her knuckles. She told him about the morning sickness, and what it felt like to be pregnant, her breasts sore, a kind of tingly feeling under her skin, like anxiety, but nicer. And in the rare moments when she wasn't worrying about what to do about the baby, how she felt dreamy and content. How she hoped to feel that way again some day, when the time was right.)

"Freddy flicks his little tongue at Barry." Kathy demonstrates, turning toward Penny, stretching her neck out and flicking her tongue.

"Barry flicks his tongue at Freddy." She demonstrates again, this time for Rhettbutler.

Penny laughs. Rhettbutler yells, "Fre-ddy. Ba-rry."

(She told him everything; she lay on her side facing him; he lay on his side facing her. He listened and she fell asleep again. When she woke up he was gone. Like Pete had been gone, but different, a comfy gone that hadn't left her lonely. Barry slept beside her every night he was home and wasn't with Rachel. There had been no sex.)

"I'm sorry I have to break the news to you," Kathy says, "but Pete, your snake's an engagement wrecker."

She's grinning so hard her teeth have dried out. Pete grins back, like he's part of the game. He winks. Still grinning, she dries her hands on a dish towel. She grabs her jacket from a hook by the door and waves goodbye to them.

Kathy shivers as she walks to her car, not because it's cold, though it is a damp, low-sky day. She shivers because she's just dodged a bullet, and she feels ashamed for making fun of Barry.

The cool misty air and grey clouds are the right backdrop for mourning the students killed at Kent State University on Monday, shot by the Ohio National Guard while protesting the invasion of Cambodia. "An eerie quiet grips the campus after four are slain and seven wounded in rioting at Kent State University," the newscast begins. "Anxious parents came from hundreds of miles away to escort their children from the scarred campus." Closer to home, the announcer says, and goes on to describe another terrorist bomb blast in Montreal, the sixth in the last two weeks, and from there reports on rising concerns over the looming threat of rotating postal worker strikes at post offices throughout Canada.

"Enough already," Kathy says out loud and turns the radio off.

She pulls around the back of the grocery store, which is the oldest in the chain, dark and small in comparison to the bright, big stores being built in suburban malls. It has narrow, cramped aisles lined with wood and metal shelves on the verge of collapse and creaky hardwood floors sanded and refinished once a year that within two weeks look worn and defeated once again. Caulking lifts in slabs from the edges of the front window panes. whose storm coverings are now permanent, cemented into place. Dead flies, spiders, mice, and a sparrow—no one could figure out how it got there—are trapped between the windows. Their carcasses rest upon the sill.

Kathy parks beside Sally's car and heads inside. Sally's called an office girl even though she's forty-something. She has kiss-curls in front of her tiny ears and horn-rimmed glasses that magnify her kohl-lined eyes. She's smiling a big toothy smile as she unlocks the door for Kathy.

"Mornin', me trout," she says to Kathy.

Sally's kindness is legendary, as are her ruthless dealings with salesmen. She can laugh at herself, and says mistakes are just that, nothing monumental, nothing to stop you.

"Hi, Sally," Kathy says. "I smell fresh coffee."

"In my parlour," Sally says as they walk through the store to the break room.

Sally's husband, Roy, has a severe heart condition and hasn't worked in seven years. He cleans and cooks, and has a whiskey sour ready for Sally when she gets home. "He does his part," Sally once told Kathy, "and I keep us in rags and fags and hard tack." Kathy pours Sally a coffee and one for herself and they sit at the break room table.

"What's the world coming to?" Sally says when Kathy mentions Kent State. "Killing kids in university. Don't know how those men will live with themselves. Bad enough for soldiers in wars. But killing's killing, isn't it? Roy never got over the war. That's why his heart gave out. Part's physical, I know, but the war ground him down. He came back old. Not all of them, but Roy did. He was only twenty-two and already tuckered out.

"Here's the terrible part, ducky. Before the war, Roy was a butcher's apprentice. So when he came back, they wanted him right quick in the slaughterhouse. Day in, day out, carving sides of beef. Bleak, cold place. Even before he got sick, his heart wasn't in it.

"You know what we do? Once in a blue moon, remind ourselves we're alive. We make love real slow, even though the doctor told Roy to give it up. 'The kids have it right,' Roy tells me when I worry, 'make love, not war.' So we do, even if it'll be the death of him.

"Oh, hell," Sally adds, "give me one of those damn cards. You only live once. While I fill it out, you tell me what you're going to do about playing hockey this fall. I have to report back to Roy; he's taken an interest in you, girl."

Sally's the only person who takes Kathy seriously when she makes offhand remarks about her hockey career. Everyone knows Kathy can skate, but they think she's joking about making it her work, which is in fact what she prefers them to think. If they think it's a joke, then Kathy doesn't have to do anything about it. But Sally, who is honest to a fault and so takes people at their word, assumed Kathy meant what she said and asked Roy about girls and the NHL.

When Roy's not cooking and cleaning (and making love), he's reading hockey stats wherever he can find them, and player biographies, and team histories. He told Sally, who told Kathy, there wasn't girls' hockey at the NHL level, not even close. There were pretty active teams in Montreal, for sure, but Montreal's a long way from home and not very safe these days. If Kathy went to university, Queen's or Toronto or McMaster, say, they had teams and even some money to support them. There were teams scattered through the area, one in Guelph, he thought, used to be a good team in Preston. Season's over, he said, but come fall, practices would start again, and Kathy would be able to find someone to talk to. There wasn't an organized league for girls like there was for boys, so she'd have to do some legwork on her own.

Before Kathy can apologize and say she hasn't done any legwork, they're distracted by Marvin, who is letting himself in the front door. He stops near the first cash register, unzips his jacket and takes his comb out of his pocket protector. He fixes his hair, centre forward with a dangly bit in front, uplift on each side and curl over the centre, duck's ass in back.

"For being so pug-ugly," Sally says, "he's a vain one."

"He asked me out," Kathy says. As soon as the words pass her lips, she wishes she hadn't said them. "I'm not going, of course."

"Poor bastard," Sally says. "And I don't mean because he wants to go out with you. He's not the sharpest knife in the drawer, but he has a heart like anyone else, so it's natural enough for him to ask.

"What do you bet the guys put him up to it?" Sally asks. "They'd all like to ask you out. You're pretty, you're smart and you can out-hockey every one of them. They talk about you when you aren't around. I've been here for so long I'm invisible to them now, so they say stuff as if I'm not there, or don't count. Because I'm old.

"Even Brian would go out with you, and he's happily married," Sally adds.

"Do you think I should go out with Marvin?" Kathy asks, feeling sorry for him now that Sally's pointed out he has a heart.

"Never settle for second best," Sally says without hesitation.

On Monday morning, Kathy arrives early for work. It's her routine these days, to catch whoever is in the break room before they punch in, and give them her zis-boom-ba, rah-rah-rah, join-the-union lecture. She's just inside the back door when Howard Zell, the regional personnel supervisor, approaches her and tells her she is to go back outside and not return to the premises. Ever.

"As of this moment, you are no longer our employee, Miss Rausch," he says, "and you are not to set foot in this store again."

"Are you firing me, Mr. Zell?" Kathy asks. "Is it because I'm gathering signatures for a union?"

Howard tells her, yes, he's firing her, but it has nothing to do with her union work. The chain respects the right of employees to petition a union. We have nothing against unions, he says. Though, he adds, we prefer to work in good faith directly with our employees, not through intermediaries, to bring about satisfactory changes in workplace conditions. But really, he says, it has nothing to do with the union petition, it has to do with Kathy and the bare fact that her till regularly doesn't balance at the end of the day.

Kathy explains that she's not the only person who works on her till. That when she takes breaks, or goes to lunch, one or another of the stock boys takes over for her on her cash register. And when she places her cigarette orders, then later stocks them on the shelf, once again, someone else works on her till. Sometimes her manager, sometimes the office girl, whoever is available when she must be away from her cash register, works on her till because she is the only dedicated full-time checkout girl. We have a small staff, as you know, she explains, so practically every employee in the store is partly responsible if her till doesn't balance at the end of the day.

Howard Zell says, as far as her supervisors are concerned, her till doesn't balance, and it is *entirely* her responsibility. In discussion, he says, the issue of theft arose—sometimes her till is short—but he would like her to know right here and now that he was the one who suggested management not pursue a criminal investigation, for compassionate reasons, because a criminal record would have dire consequences and limit Kathy's ability to find another job.

Kathy says she is innocent until proven guilty, and asks Howard to please put in writing the reasons for her dismissal. He says he doesn't have to. It is his prerogative to fire her. But, he says, head office is way ahead of the game and has already sent the paperwork regarding the firing to the Labour Board; it is a legitimate case of termination due to incompetence. I repeat, he says, your firing has nothing to do with union recruitment. He tells her again the decision is final, and she should leave. There will be no reversal, Miss Rausch, he says, you should go home now.

Kathy doesn't go home. She gets in her car and drives straight to her mother's because she knows she has to tell Connie in person, and she wants to get it over with as quickly as possible. When Kathy arrives, Connie's making egg salad sandwiches and Shelly's trying to drown the strawberries left bobbing in her Cheerios milk.

"Day off, Kathy?" Connie asks. "Here, clean this out." She hands Kathy the egg salad bowl. Kathy automatically runs her finger along the inside of the bowl and is about to lick it when she realizes she can't eat it.

"I got fired," she says scraping the egg off her finger back into the bowl. She sets the bowl in the sink and washes her hands.

"The union," Connie says to Kathy's back.

"Howard Zell says not," Kathy says. She turns to face her mother as she dries her hands. Connie's eyes are floating, but the tears don't spill out.

"Howard says my till doesn't balance at the end of the day," Kathy says. "It's an excuse; of course it's the union. I'll call my organizer and we'll file an appeal. Don't worry, Mom, it'll be fine."

"Kathy," Connie says, and stops. She looks at Kathy. "It'll be fine," she echoes, but no one would believe her. "I have to go. I'm driving Shelly to school today."

"I'll take her," Kathy says, relieved to be able to get away so easily. "You go to bed. I'll call later."

Kathy does call, after a calming evening of road hockey. It was still light when she grabbed her stick and one of Rhettbutler's striped rubber balls and headed outside. She pinned an old blanket to a laundry rack she found in the basement and set it up as a goal. She danced the ball on the end of her stick, whacked it into the towel net and whooped. Within minutes Pete and Rhettbutler were out to see what was going on. They went back inside. Then Rhettbutler was beside her, a child's red-handled broom in his hands, and Pete had one of Kathy's old sticks. They tussled and turned, scuffled for the breakaway, laughed and shouted their way to the goal.

Kids came first, aluminum doors whapping behind them, and joined in the game. Fathers arrived to watch, then went inside and got their sticks. A small goalie net appeared and replaced Kathy's towel net; a second net arrived with a father-son team. Grunts and shouts, kids crying, cheers from the sidelines where women sat on lawn chairs smoking cigarettes and sipping coffee, dabbing at cuts and dirt with Kleenex and spit, gossiping. They played until the streetlights came on, until mothers called husbands and children in. Tomorrow, they said as they left. Tomorrow.

When Kathy finally called Connie, Mary answered the phone.

"She's putting her coat on," Mary told her, and she shouted away from the mouthpiece. "Connie, it's Kathy."

Kathy told her mother she'd be over on Sunday to cook supper for Mother's Day. And they could watch the Stanley Cup playoff, St. Louis and Boston, and the amazing Bobby Orr.

MARVIN'S SITTING ON CONNIE'S SAGGING REC ROOM COUCH. IT'S colonial, with varnish chipping from the arm rests, and covered wagons and grazing cattle fading into the landscape of its thinning upholstery. His right hand, bandaged across the knuckles, holds a beer and his feet are trying to avoid Shelly. Shelly lies on her side under the wagon wheel coffee table and picks at the threads of the unraveling braided rug. She looks like a piglet, her pale pink arms and soft pink tummy bulging out of a too-small T-shirt. Sitting in the middle of the coffee table is the huge white lily in its purple plastic planter that Marvin brought for Kathy.

Connie leans into the other end of the couch, her legs propped on the table—skin-tight, lime green pedal pushers, stop-sign-red toenails, dark green flip-flops.

"I'd love a beer right about now," she told Marvin when he offered her one, "but I can't. No rest for the weary, not even on Mother's Day. Unlike you, Marvin, and my unemployed daughter here, I have to work tonight. Maybe Kathy will have one with you."

Kathy would like to have a beer, many, in fact, but she thinks it would be a mistake now that Marvin's arrived. Kathy's sitting in the reproduction rocker to the left of Connie. Two milk-bucket lamps cast a low yellow light, while the blue-screen glow of the TV flickers across their faces.

Shelly stops picking at the rug and starts to rub her cheeks. Tiny beads of sweat dot her upper lip. The hair around her face is damp. She whispers, "Bobby Orr, #4, Bobby Orr, #4," under her breath, a monotone that's lost in the jangly, pre-game banter.

When a commercial comes on, Connie taps the purple planter with a red toenail and asks Marvin where he got the beautiful lily. She says she sure does wish it had been for her for Mother's Day considering nobody in her family got her flowers this year, though she didn't want to seem ungrateful for the cards from her daughters sitting there on the table. One is from Kathy and has a twenty-dollar bill in it, and the one from Shelly is painted entirely yellow, inside and out. It represents the sun, Shelly's teacher told Connie.

"At the store," Marvin says. "Left over," he adds. "From Easter." He's been talking in choppy, nervous sentences since he arrived.

"Oh," Connie drawls, "how very generous of you. Kathy's so lucky to have a workmate and friend like you."

"Everybody chipped in," Marvin says. "Wasn't just me."

"Well, then," Connie says, and she leans forward to give Marvin her full attention. "Kathy has many, many fine friends. And what an appropriate choice for a firing, an Easter lily. Perhaps Kathy will emerge from the tomb of joblessness alive and well and once again check out the groceries of the masses. Maybe she'll bodily ascend into checkout girl heaven and become the patron saint of workers who have attempted to start unions but failed. Maybe, Marvin. Or maybe she'll go hungry the rest of her days, stealing wilted lettuce leaves and rotting tomatoes from produce garbage bins.

"What do you think, Marvin?" Connie asks. "Do you have an opinion on Kathy's future?"

Kathy is staring at her mother. Her mother is staring at Marvin. Marvin looks at the TV. Shelly picks at the rug.

Because Marvin isn't looking at Connie, he doesn't see the smile that stretches like a tight, pink elastic across her face. Connie waits. Kathy watches to see what Marvin will do.

Marvin sets his beer on the end table and touches his hair. He reaches for the comb in his pocket protector. Mid-reach he thinks better of combing his hair and grabs the beer. He takes a swig and foam bubbles up over the top. He covers the foaming top with one hand and cups the dripping bottom with the other. Holding the bottle, top and bottom, in front of him, he watches the TV.

Without looking down, Marvin wipes one hand, and then the other, on his jeans. He furtively glances down at his damp jeans, then up from his jeans to the TV, then down again at Shelly, whose sweaty body is as close to his feet as is possible without actually touching them. Looking up again, Marvin leans forward and sets his beer on the table in front of him. While he's there he sniffs the lily. He jerks his head away, moves the plant a few inches closer to Connie's red toenails, thinks better of that and moves it to where it had been. He leans back then, hands on his thighs, and once and for all concentrates on the hockey players skating across the TV screen.

The Easter lily Marvin moved sideways, then moved back, is one tree-like leafy green stalk with seven enormous snow-white trumpets filled with anthers so laden, the pollen is dropping onto the table in little orange pyramids. It's in such full and fabulous bloom that it seems only seconds before it must collapse in upon itself and die. And it's smelly. Putrid and thick, like chicken that is turning, only sweeter.

The lily is a gift from the guys at the store, an embarrassed, guilty apology for Kathy's firing. There's also a card on the end table that Kathy put beside Connie's Mother's Day cards. On Kathy's card, a kitten stands beside a puddle of milk. Inside the card says, *Don't cry over spilled milk…* And to illustrate this optimism, the inside kitten is drinking from the milk puddle. Around the kitten are the signatures of the men from the store, with little notes saying, "Don't forget us!" and "Good luck!"

"That's mine," Marvin said when Kathy opened the card, pointing to an oversized, block-printed message that read, "Howard Zell—go to HELL!"

"It's for you, Kathy," Connie had called when Marvin arrived.

"Marvin?" Kathy had said as she neared the door.

Marvin had shuffled around the wet porch looking like he was going to bolt. Except Kathy knew he couldn't, because there at his feet was a case of twelve beer, and he'd never leave that behind. Marvin drank twenty-four beer every weekend, breaking them into even lots: eight for Friday, eight for Saturday and eight for Sunday.

"Marvin?" Kathy repeated.

"We picked straws," Marvin said. "I lost."

"Well," Kathy said. "Aren't you the lucky one? Let me take that plant from you."

"Hey, what happened?" she asked, balancing the plant on her hip and touching his bandaged knuckles. Marvin pulled his hand back.

"Hit an immoveable object at great speed," Marvin said. Sometimes Marvin said the most wonderful things, but Sally had already told Kathy what happened and this was her explanation:

Sally said they were in shock when they heard Kathy had been fired. She immediately called a florist and sent Kathy flowers, a dozen red roses, while the guys walked around swearing. We'll have a protest, a sit-in, they said. We'll picket the store, boycott the chain, slash Howard Zell's tires. It was crazy, Sally said, the ideas they came up with. Then Marvin smashed his fist through the fibreboard wall separating the bathroom stalls and ripped open his knuckles and Brian had to take him to the hospital for stitches. When they returned, and the accident report had been filed, Brian sent them all back to work, Sally said, so in the end, they did nothing for Kathy.

Until now.

"How'd you find me?" she asked.

"You a cop?" Marvin asked back.

Kathy laughed loudly. Maybe too loudly.

"Some little guy at your boarding house. Said his name was Barry Bender and he told me you'd be here." This last was his longest and fullest sentence yet.

Kathy motioned Marvin in.

"Mom, Marvin's coming in," she called, and then said to Marvin, "We're watching the Stanley Cup."

"Isn't everybody," he said as he grabbed his case of beer and moved past Kathy into the house.

Once Connie stops grilling Marvin and they settle into watching the pre-game warm-up, Kathy slips upstairs and calls Darlyn.

"Darlyn, guess who's here?" Kathy says without saying hello.

"Bobby Orr? Except he's supposed to be playing hockey, so I guess it can't be him."

"Marvin," Kathy says.

"Marvin? Who's…? Oh shit, Kathy, *the* Marvin? Pocket Protector Marvin?"

"The one and only."

"Can I come see?" Darlyn asks.

"Please," Kathy says. "I need you to rescue me. Mom's putting him through the wringer about me getting fired. And Shelly's scaring him by practically lying on his feet, but acting as if he isn't there."

"Can Donny come?"

"Of course," Kathy says.

"What about Dad?"

"More the merrier," Kathy says, hoping Connie won't be too put out about Al sitting around in their rec room.

"What about your mom? It's Mother's Day," Kathy asks.

"Mother will be happy to be rid of us," Darlyn says. "She now says Mother's Day is a *construct*—she uses words like that, Kathy—a capitalist *construct* of Hallmark Cards created for the specific reason of stealing money from the deluded. Besides which, she told us when we brought her breakfast in bed, Mother's Day is an insult to all women, not just mothers, as it doesn't honour the work women do all the other days of the year.

"And," Darlyn adds, "she'll be doubly happy to have us gone because she doesn't watch sports now. She thinks hockey is men being boys and the boys are play-acting war. She thinks all contact sports are deliberate and staged acts of belligerence that mimic war. That they're displays of patriarchal dominance put on for other men to see—pissing contests, she calls them. They're also reminders to women about who has the strength and power in the world.

"That's the way she talks now, Kathy," Darlyn sighs. "Those are the kinds of things she tells us. Dad looks confused and sad and goes into the basement. He pulls his chair right up to the TV screen and tries to keep the volume very, very low when he's watching *Wide World of Sports*, hoping Mom doesn't hear so he won't get another lecture. I'm not sure how long this can go on."

Darlyn cheers up and asks, "Should we bring beer? Donny brought a 2-4 with him. We can bring it if you like."

"Marvin brought a dozen," Kathy says, "but eight of them are for him so that leaves one each for you and Donny and Al and me. So, yes to beer. Bring lots and lots of beer."

Kathy gets back downstairs in time to watch the players line up on the ice for the national anthems. "Oh, Canada," Shelly yells. "Oh, Canada." It's the only part she knows.

The doorbell rings. Darlyn usually walks in, so Kathy gets up from the rocker to go upstairs. Connie double-steps up behind her, her flip-flops flip-flopping at double speed.

"Marvin's quite the loser," she huffs right into Kathy's ear. "You're gaw-damn lucky to get out of that place even if it does mean no job. Are they all like that?"

"Marvin's OK," Kathy says, more defensively than she'd like.

"Those flowers…"

Kathy's opening the front door; Connie's still hissing away.

"… are an insult."

"Barry," Kathy says. Connie peers over Kathy's shoulder.

"Another grocery boy?" Connie asks and gives Barry the once-over. Barry does the same to Connie.

"Mom, Barry Bender. Barry, this is my mother, Connie Rausch."

"Nice to meet you, Mrs. Rausch," Barry says in his best aspiring-to-Westmount way. "Happy Mother's Day," he says, and he reaches his hand around Kathy to shake Connie's.

Connie leans past Kathy, grabs his hand. Hard. Too hard. Barry winces. "I'm not your mother," Connie says.

"Barry's an electrician who works up at the Bruce," Kathy says.

"Ah, an electrician, not a grocery boy," Connie says. "Are you in the union?" she asks.

Loosening her grip a bit, but still holding Barry's hand, Connie tries to pull him past Kathy into the house. Kathy sticks her bum out and blocks Barry's way. She turns and scowls at her mother.

"Come in, Barry Bender. Come join our little party," Connie says. She's ignoring Kathy's scowl, but she does let go of Barry's hand.

Kathy mouths, *Go away*, to her mother, and turns back to Barry.

"That's if Kathy will let you in," Connie says. She shrugs her shoulders and twirls her finger beside her head. She mouths, *She's nuts*, to Barry.

Connie turns away then, and walks toward her bedroom. Barry leans past Kathy to watch her go, or more particularly to watch her bum inside the green pedal pushers. "I'm going to get changed for work. Get yourself a beer, Barry Bender. They're in the fridge."

Once Connie's bedroom door clicks shut, Kathy nudges Barry back outside.

"What're you doing here?" she asks.

"Your mom looks great for a…" Barry says.

"Stop," Kathy interrupts and holds up her hand. "Just tell me why you're here."

"Some weird guy with a bandaged fist came looking for you at Pete's and I told him where you were. Then I got worried I shouldn't have, so I came over to make sure he wasn't bugging you."

"Could have called," Kathy says.

"Yeah, well, I didn't. Are you watching the game?"

"Downstairs. Marvin's there now with Shelly."

"Marvin," Barry says and nods. "Who's Shelly?"

"My sister."

"You never told me you had a sister."

"I never told me lots of things."

"We could change that," Barry says.

"Oh lord." This is old territory and Kathy's tired of it. "Then what? You'll break up with Rachel and get engaged to me?"

"No," Barry says. He's hurt. He tries not to whine. "I did think we were friends."

"We are friends," Kathy says very gently.

Barry, when he comes home from weekend dates with Rachel, still crawls into Kathy's bed. He still wakes her up and they talk until they fall asleep. Barry tells her about Rachel: shopping for The Trousseau, renting a hall for The Wedding, picking out patterns for china and silver. Kathy tells him what Pete and Penny and Rhettbutler have been up to over the last week. On Friday night she stayed awake to tell him about getting fired. Usually, when Kathy wakes up in the morning, Barry's still there beside her.

"It's just that suddenly my life seems very complicated," Kathy says. "I got fired, and because I got fired Marvin's arrived bearing beer and flowers. It's Mother's Day and I'm trying really, really hard not to remember how close I recently came to becoming a mother. Darlyn's coming over with her boyfriend to get away from her mother who's turned into a fem-Nazi who thinks sports are pissing contests that governments use to keep men happy and women in their place. Darlyn's bringing her poor hurt and confused father who just happens to be in love with my mother. Now you, my engaged-to-Rachel-The-Virgin-Goddess sleeping buddy, have arrived to protect me from Marvin. And all I really want to do today is sit on my ass with my mom and my sister and watch Bobby Orr try to win the Stanley Cup.

"So forgive me, please, if I sound a little pissed off," Kathy says.

Barry watches Kathy. Kathy watches Barry right back. It's a watching contest to see who can watch the longest, and Kathy knows she can win. And if she wins, Barry will have to leave.

As she waits, this is what she sees: a very short, very tidy, very patient man with kind, watchful eyes, and small feet and hands. A man who, despite having a fiancée, sleeps in Kathy's bed, but who doesn't try to have sex with her. She sees a man who has come to her mother's house because he's worried about her. Because he's her friend.

"Of course we're friends," she sighs. There's no contest, no reason to make Barry leave. She leans over and kisses his cheek just as Darlyn crosses the driveway and walks up the porch steps to the door.

There's always been a quality to Darlyn that says "Baton Twirling Queen." Something to do with a swishy ponytail and erect posture. But more and more lately, the majorette looks like a hippie. Today it's the fringed buckskin vest she's wearing over her short-sleeved white blouse. Must be Donny's influence, because there he is, wearing a matching vest, though there's nothing but skin under his. Al, uninfluenced, looks decidedly and resolutely like himself.

"Don't want to disturb anything." Darlyn says. She laughs and comes right up behind Barry.

Barry turns to her.

"Darlyn Smola," she says.

"Barry Bender," he says, sticking his hand out to her.

"Barry," Darlyn says, smiling widely at Kathy while shaking Barry's hand.

"We've met," Donny says, leaning his head over Darlyn's shoulder and winking at Barry. Donny's got a 2-4 of beer lodged against his hip.

"Kathy," Al says. He ignores them all and squeezes past Kathy into the house. He looks around the living room, then turns to Kathy and asks, "Will we be graced with your mother's company this evening?"

"She's changing for work, Mr. Smola. I'm sure she'll join us when she's ready," Kathy says. The words are just out of her mouth when the bedroom door opens.

"Well then, the gang's all here," Connie says as she walks toward them. She's all white—skin, tunic, pants, apron, socks and shoes. All except for her perfect lips, which are candy-apple red. A smell like buttered toffee precedes her. As one, they turn to her and sniff the air. When she's finally standing in front of them, they sigh.

"Connie," Al whispers. He closes his eyes, cranes his head towards the scent of her and sniffs again. Connie leans as far from him as she can without moving her feet.

"Heavenly," Al says, and he shudders a little.

Darlyn looks at her father and groans. Connie rolls her eyes and laughs. From the basement they can hear Shelly yelling, *Bobby Orr, # 4. Bobby Orr, # 4.*

"Game time," Connie says. And when she turns and walks away, they follow her like ants on the trail of sugar.

OVERTIME IS ABOUT TO START. THE BOSTON BRUINS HAVE CRUISED through three games against St. Louis, but tonight the Blues are fighting back. The score's 3-3.

Only crumbs remain in the chip and pretzel bowls; a thin haze of cigarette smoke drifts past the TV screen, more hangs near the ceiling. Empty beer bottles lie on the floor beside chairs and cushions.

Donny's under the coffee table beside Shelly, who picks at a bit of rug near his hand and shoots him furtive glances. Even though she knows Donny, this is as close as they've ever been. Donny grins at her when she turns toward him and Shelly laughs ha-ha-ha. Donny laughs right back.

"Can't help it," he tells Darlyn.

Darlyn's sitting between Marvin and Kathy. She kicks Donny's ribs when he laughs. But then she laughs too.

"Hey, man, why'd you kick me then?"

"I know, I know," Darlyn says, and laughs some more.

"Stop kicking me." Donny grabs her foot, pulls off the sock and flubs farts on to the soft flesh of her arch. Darlyn screeches and Barry starts to laugh.

"What're you laughing at?" she says, turning to him.

"Fucked if I know," Barry says. Then quickly, "Sorry, sorry, I didn't mean to say it."

"Fuck, fuck, fuck," Shelly says softly, but they can hear her. Then she flubs fart noises on her arm. "Fuck, fuck, fuck," she says again.

"Barry!" Al scolds. It's the first time he's acknowledged Barry. He looks over at Connie. Connie's looking at the TV, ignoring them all.

Donny, looking at Shelly, who is trying not to look at him, flubs farts on his arm.

"Don't provoke her," Al says.

Donny says, "Shush," to Shelly. She looks right at him. She closes her eyes, puts her mouth on her arm, and makes more fart noises. "Fuck, fuck, fuck," she says when she's finished.

Donny grunts so as not to laugh. "Sh-sh-sh," he whispers, but he can't stop himself now.

"I'm so sorry, Mrs. Rausch," Barry says.

"What on earth for?" she says to the air, because she still isn't looking at anyone.

"Don't worry," Kathy says. She's nearly shouting to be heard. "Shelly learned the f-word ages ago. She'll get bored soon."

"We want Bobby Orr. We want # 4," Marvin shouts, surprising them all. Except for grunts and hoots when the play's been close, or a goal's been scored, he's been silent the entire game.

"Bobby Orr, # 4," Marvin shouts. Shelly stops making fart noises and looks up at him. She joins in. Soon they're all chanting, facing the TV, watching the gate open and the players come on the ice. The puck is dropped.

"Shut up!" Connie yells. "It's my day and I say shut up; I can't hear a thing."

They ignore her. She goes to the TV and turns up the volume. Sound booms.

"... *Westfall rolled it in front. Sanderson... tried a shot that was wide. Kennan cleared it but not out. Bobby Orr... behind the net to centre. And Orr... Bobby Orr... scores! And the Boston Bruins... have won the Stanley Cup...*"

They stand and scream. Al kisses Connie. Connie pushes him away. He steps on a beer bottle; his foot rolls forward, then back, and he loses his balance and thuds to his bum.

Donny tries to catch Al. The coffee table catches on his shoulder and tips sideways. Beer bottles, snack bowls, ashtrays and the Easter lily bounce around Shelly. Dirt flies across the carpet. Lily death-smell fills the room.

Shelly closes her eyes. She rubs her cheeks and screams louder than anyone. Marvin chants, Bobby Orr! Bobby Orr! Darlyn and Barry join in.

On TV, Bobby Orr is horizontal, flying through the air, mouth open, arms forward, legs out, launched into a dive.

"... *Orr putting it in....*"

"Bobby," Kathy cries. She walks forward and touches the screen.

"... *as Bobby Orr, the 22-year-old... sensation scores... after 40 seconds of overtime... and the... Boston Bruins win the Stanley Cup!*"

Summer, 1970

Inside the ring or out, ain't nothing wrong with going down. It's staying down that's wrong.
— Muhammad Ali

IT'S 8:00 A.M. AND ALREADY 80 DEGREES. THE AIR IN HER ROOM IS fusty. Kathy pushes Barry away, her skin slick where his touched it. She kicks the sheet from her feet; the blanket's already on the floor. Barry rolls on his back and groans. With his shoulder more off the bed than on, his forearm flops in the air, his hand brushes the floor. Kathy pulls herself up and leans against the wall, her back against it cool. She presses her cheek to the paint. Relief, then none.

It should seem strange that Barry sleeps in her bed whenever he's home, but it doesn't. They don't have sex; they talk instead. She said, he said: it balanced out. Last night Barry talked and Kathy listened, dozing off in the heat, waking to some change in his voice. His holidays start today, and he and Rachel are going with her parents to their cottage in Sauble Beach. Separate bedrooms, of course. They'll finalize their wedding plans: make up the guest list and pick invitations from a vast book Rachel borrowed from the printers; there are bridesmaids and best men to choose, a hall to rent, food, music, gifts, and all of it, every tiny detail, must pass the parent test. Barry said he just hopes they have plenty of beer to get him through the ordeal.

Last time Barry went to Rachel's cottage, he fell asleep on his back in the sun their first day at the beach. He couldn't put clothes on without crying, he was so badly burned. He won't do that again, he said. But it did provide a topic of conversation, because otherwise he and Rachel's parents have little to say. Every exchange for the rest of the holiday began, *Barry, how's the sunburn?* Even now when he sees Rachel's father, it's the first thing he says, then he laughs and says, just kidding. They're nice people, Barry said, though once, while

Rachel was helping him peel the blistered skin from his shoulders, her mother said, *Oh dear, don't take too much off. We don't want him to disappear.* And she giggled. Barry said he hoped he wasn't getting a mother-in-law who made short people jokes.

Kathy and Barry talk about anything, parents, work... well, maybe not hockey, because Barry isn't much interested in it, but anything else. About a month before she left him, Kathy remembers telling Doug she wanted to talk. A distance had grown between them and maybe it was just her, maybe it was because she was working and Doug wasn't. She was a bit jealous of all his free time. Or, she said, maybe it was all the drugs they were doing. (When she said *they* she meant *him*, because she had to be straight enough to go to work every day so other than smoking a bit of dope she wasn't doing many drugs.) But most of all, she wondered if he still loved her. Doug looked at her as if she were a Martian. He said to give him a minute, as he was trying to figure out what she wanted him to say.

It was after supper. They were sitting at the dining room table in their kitchen in Vancouver, a rare time when they were alone, their housemates at the park for an outdoor concert. They had smoked a joint before supper but they were no longer stoned. Doug set his empty coffee mug on his bread plate. He set the bread plate on his dinner plate. He placed his cutlery along the edge of his dinner plate and pushed this neat little stack to the right of his placemat.

Using her finger, Kathy played tic-tac-toe in the gravy congealing on her plate. Without looking up, she said she was lonely, but she didn't know why because there he was sitting across from her, not an arm's length away. She got up to clear the table. She put the ketchup in the fridge, and the butter, salt and pepper on the counter. She ran hot water into the sink and squirted in some dish detergent. She shook the placemats and put them in the drawer. She set the dirty dishes in the middle of the detergent suds, which funneled up around them. She wiped the table and the counter and began to wash, rinse and stack the dishes in the drying rack.

Doug got up from his chair and got his cigarettes, matches and an ashtray. He sat back down, this time in Kathy's chair, which faced the open window. A pigeon cooed. They both heard it. Pigeons were nesting in the rafters under the awning. Doug struck a match and lit his cigarette. He shook the match in the air and put it in the ashtray.

"Of course I love you," he said.

Kathy washed and rinsed the dirty pots, let the water out of the sink and swished it clean with fresh water.

"I said I love you," he said in the whoosh of his exhale.

"I heard," Kathy said. She folded the dishcloth and hung it over the water spout.

Doug sat at the table and smoked. Finally he asked, "Are you happy?"

"I don't know," she told him.

She should be happy, she said, so if she wasn't, the fault must be hers. Maybe she needed to find a place to skate, maybe that would make her happy. They hadn't been skating since they arrived in Vancouver eight months ago, she said. Maybe he'd like to skate with her again, maybe that would help. She was relieved to hear he loved her, she told him, because she hadn't been sure.

What she didn't say was that after hearing it she still felt lonely. She wanted more words than I-love-you-are-you-happy. She wanted an avalanche of words, enough to bury the sadness and unease in her heart. None of this had slipped off her tongue while she sat at the kitchen table in Vancouver. But the words Doug said that day were the exact right number for her to know she was going to leave him; it was just a matter of time.

Barry opens his eyes.

"Did you sleep well?" he asks Kathy. His breath smells like Limburger cheese.

"Too hot," Kathy says.

"I have to get moving," Barry says. "We're going to the farmers' market before we head out."

He rolls sideways off the bed onto his knees and hoists himself up; his wrinkled pyjama bottoms sag at the bum. He taps Freddy's window as he goes by but gets no response. Pete fed Freddy a lab rat the day before. Freddy retreats to digest, into a stillness like death.

Kathy stretches her arms and legs, exposing as much skin as she can to what little air circulates. Where Barry slept, the bed is damp. A breeze puffs the curtain on the window high up on the wall, but it doesn't make any difference. Kathy watches the curtain drift in and out. Mesmerized, she almost slips into sleep. She'll lie here a few minutes while Barry's in the shower.

She has an interview at Canadian Tire on Main Street at eleven o'clock. They have an employee share-buying policy, and Kathy likes the idea of owning part of the company she works for. She also has an application in at the post office. The money's great, but she's pretty sure nothing will come of it. They don't hire many women, not for the good jobs, and there have been rotating strikes across Ontario, seventy-eight so far, by Connie's count. Kathy told her mother her life must be pretty damn dull if she's counting the number of postal strikes reported in the newspaper. Connie told Kathy her life was far more full and productive than Kathy's seemed to be these days, so she'd best get a job, or shut up.

The strikes are a pressure tactic, to force the government to settle their contract. Last Friday the postal workers walked off the job at the Varnum plant. Kathy passed their picket line and stopped to chat with Harry Edmonds.

"Hey, Kath," he'd called, waving his On Strike placard at her, "long time no see."

Kathy wouldn't have recognized him; the last time she'd seen him was in grade eight. He told her he quit high school when he turned sixteen and worked nights in the warehouse at the Post Office, first as a temp, then permanent full-time. In the winter he delivered mail for guys who were sick or on holidays. He was getting his own route this summer, but contract talks soured and the rotating strikes began, and now everything was on hold.

"I'm getting on the gravy train," he said, "once this strike is over."

Harry said he married Margaret Ann Geisler, remember her, the smartest, prettiest girl in their class. They had a baby girl, Judith

Ann. Margaret Ann's gone back to her job as legal assistant to the judges at the courthouse and her mother babysits Judith Ann. When Harry gets his mail route, he said, and a nice fat raise, Margaret Ann can stay home.

(A housewife, Kathy thought. If Harry became a full-time postman, Margaret Ann could become a full-time housewife. At twenty. It made her want to cry, and she was immediately grateful she wasn't in that position.)

Harry told Kathy not to count on the post office; no one would be hired until the dispute was settled. He wondered if she was mistaken about the ad, perhaps what she saw was for casuals. That's what management called scabs, and scabs are not in unions. If it's a legitimate ad, she'll end up on strike anyway, Harry said. Kathy told him she wouldn't work as a scab.

Or get blown up. Connie says the mailbox bombings in Montreal have nothing to do with postal strikes anywhere else. It's the FLQ, she says. So far no one's been killed, but it's only a matter of time before someone dies, and it won't be a politician or terrorist, Connie told Kathy. It'll be some old lady mailing a birthday card to her grandson, or a mother with her newborn baby in a stroller sending a birth announcement to her friends and family. Or some poor bugger who happened to be walking by a mailbox while taking his dog to the park for a crap.

Kathy's glad Martin lives in Quebec City, not Montreal. Or she hopes he's still living there. She can imagine herself a separatist—what young working-class Catholic didn't have a teeny-tiny understanding of what it might be like to be French in Canada, in Quebec especially, and have to fight to keep your Frenchness? That's how she and Darlyn and Donny talk when they're having a beer or smoking a joint. But she can't imagine hurting people, and certainly not killing them. She hopes Martin is a pacifist separatist, though what members of the FLQ are being called these days is terrorists. Like the Arab guerillas in Lebanon who are killing Israelis.

Kathy has put in applications at other union plants as well— Schneiders, Marsland, Grebs, Weston's. Good money, good benefits and generous vacation pay. Then Connie might get off her back. Right now not much is available and most summer jobs have already been filled by university students, but Kathy isn't too worried. Her pogey will last until November.

Connie is worried. She calls every day to see if Kathy's found anything, or if she's had an interview. She told Kathy she put a word in for her at the candy factory. Kathy told her she wouldn't be caught dead working in the same place as her mother.

"I won't be provoked," Connie said. "This is serious, Kathy. You're twenty years old and you don't have a job."

And then the old saw. Kathy knew it was coming.

"In fact, you don't seem to have any direction right now," Connie said. "You could apply for days or afternoons when I'm not there."

"I'll find something on my own," Kathy said.

Connie didn't reply.

"Thanks anyway, Mom," Kathy said. She was groveling and she hated it.

"How's Barry?" Connie asked, changing the subject.

Since Stanley Cup night, Connie hasn't stopped pointing out how different Barry is from her other friends. Things like his manners (he called her Mrs. Rausch and said please and thank you), his clothes (clean and tidy and classy—Kathy didn't tell her that Rachel shopped for him and did his laundry at her parents' house every weekend, didn't tell Connie about Rachel at all) and his job (unionized electrician). Kathy sometimes wonders, if she married into a union job, married a union man, if Connie would be happy then. When Kathy complains that her mother's interfering, Connie says, "I just want you to be happy."

When Kathy was ten (and still happy) she told Connie she was going to marry someone just like her dad. Connie told her that a man like her father was exactly the wrong man to marry. But she didn't tell her why. Even when Kathy cried, Connie didn't explain or try to make her feel better. She said she wasn't going to explain, not because she was mean, but because she wanted Kathy to remember what she'd said. What do you remember about being happy, except that you were happy? Connie said. But when you cry, especially when your mother makes you cry, something sticks, some little bit of pain or anxiety stays in your mind, and you remember it.

Don't marry a man like your father, that's what I want to stick in there. That's what I want you to remember, Connie said. And here Kathy is, remembering. And hating that Connie is so often right.

Lately, in direct contradiction to her get-a-good-job-and-get-your-life-together routine, Connie's been telling Kathy, if she ever gets married, to go wild, to marry someone who makes her feel alive, not someone who makes her feel safe. But not someone like Doug, he's not a good man, there's something missing in him.

Charlie had been a good man, Connie said. But it would be better to marry someone so different from her father that she'd spend her entire marriage being surprised, discovering something she didn't know rather than putting up with what was familiar because it seemed comfortable. Marriage should be a rollicking and fearsome adventure, Connie said. It should never be boring. Boredom kills marriages. Calm is OK. Calm is not the same as boring, because calm doesn't last even if you want it to. But boredom can go on forever and ever. Boredom means the people lack imagination, or they lost it along the way.

Kathy asked her mother how she could be so sure about marriage when she'd been a widow for as long as she'd been married. After she stopped crying (it seems one or the other of them is crying or trying not to when they talk to each other these days) and asked Kathy where she got her cruel streak, Connie said it's exactly because she's a widow that she can be so sure. People in marriages aren't honest most of the time because they're trying to make things work and because they're afraid of what will happen if they don't work. Unless they're angry, they don't want to rock the boat, and they rarely say what they mean.

They don't talk about important stuff, like the fact that some days being a mother is so stifling or so difficult, that having a little car accident with a short stay in hospital can seem better than one more day of sitting on the floor building a fort with wooden alphabet blocks, or reading the same gaw-damned book over and over, or trying to make a perpetually unhappy child happy. They don't say that coming home to a needy, angry woman—a woman who won't or can't or doesn't know how to say she's needy or angry, and who thinks that having a car accident would be relief from being a mother—no, they don't say that it's a bit frightening walking in the door after work into a house where that woman waits for them.

They don't talk about those kinds of things. Instead, married people pick away at petty things like wet towels on the floor or the rotting lettuce in the crisper or how best to cook eggs—hard yolks or soft yolks—and they hope the other stuff, the real reason for the anger or the sadness, or the neediness will just blow over. And maybe, in a few weeks or months or years, it does blow over. But it doesn't go away. It stays in the marriage forever.

And young women are way too naïve and too hopeful about love and marriage, Connie said. Being in love is a sickness; it's madness, pure and simple. It's ups and downs and not eating or sleeping; it's waiting for someone to call or notice them. There's jealousy and distrust, or too much trust. Girls marry men who are dumb as posts and they still think romance will go on forever. They think their marriage will be perfect and completely different from their parents' marriage, which they consider sordid or disgusting.

Connie said she'd had years to think about her own marriage with no husband to distract her, no reason to lie about it anymore. And she'd been watching other married people and she'd rather have a marriage like Al and Margaret have right now, as confused and scary as it is, than the marriage they'd had for years where they were both like the walking dead. Now Margaret is coming alive and saying she's unhappy. And even if she's being a bit loopy spouting all those feminist ideas—that, by the way, have some merit, Connie added—at least Margaret's trying to be honest with Al.

So they're fighting now. Al's stopped accepting everything Margaret says, and they're having great big fights that Connie can hear through her windows. That's passion. That's trying at least, and not some g-d aren't-we-nice-people-living-together-in-this-nice-house façade. Connie can see the fear and anger in Margaret and Al, and it's exciting. It's like they've been underwater too long and they've come up for air, gasping. They'll either make a better marriage or they'll have no marriage, because there's no going back under for them. But either way, they won't have a dead marriage. Or a dead husband, Connie added, but that's as far as she'd go even when Kathy asked what she meant by that.

So according to Connie's rant, Barry, or someone like him—like Charlie, for instance, a safe man with nice clothes and good manners and a union job—is the last person Kathy should be thinking about marrying, which is good. Because a safe man is the absolute last man in the world Kathy thinks about these days, when she lets herself think about men at all.

Barry's standing above her, hair slicked back, a towel wrapped around his waist, sweat already beading along the curve of his backbone. He sits on the bed and Kathy runs her finger along his spine connecting the drops so they stream down the crack in his bum. He shivers and stands.

"Don't you have an interview?" he asks.

She closes her eyes and murmurs, "Too hot to move."

Barry leans over her and shakes his head. Droplets spray from his wet hair across Kathy's body, pinpricks of coolness. They last only a second. She laughs.

"Penny left for strike duty," Barry says. "Pete's taking Rhettbutler to Regent Park wading pool. You can get up now."

"Yes, Mom," Kathy says, smirking at Barry, but feeling a blush make her hotter than she already is.

Barry's too smart for his own good. Last night he mentioned Kathy seemed to be avoiding Pete and Penny, but mostly Pete. Kathy didn't say anything. And she isn't going to admit to herself, certainly not to her mother, that when she does think about a man, it's usually Pete Lehman who comes to mind.

PETE RAN OFF SIGNS FOR KATHY ON THE GESTETNER AT THE university. Kathy tacked them to utility poles in the neighbourhood, and posted one on the bulletin board at the Ground Inn.

Strong Reliable Honest
A Hard Worker at Good Rates
Indoors and Out
Call Kathy

There were a few calls, one from a heavy breather. "Kathy. Strong Kathy," the voice moaned, but after listening to a few grunts she hung up. It might have been Donny and Darlyn. Or Teach. He's been around a lot lately. Pete hosts an LSD-laced gin-and-tonic croquet tournament every Labour Day weekend—The Annual Stakes and Wicket Match—for friends and clients at the university. He sends out printed, embossed invitations. Dress code: pastel crimpolene for the women and polyester leisure suits for the men.

Teach helped Pete plan and mark various hazards on the course. Crib-notes, he called the drawings he made of their design, so he could set the course in his yard and practise every day. Isn't that cheating, Kathy asked him? I like to win, he told her. The prize was a specially wrapped grab bag of all the premium drugs Pete dealt.

Pete hired Kathy to reseed the backyard, layering measured amounts of grasses and fertilizers in the marked areas, and regularly watering and cutting them. Some sections are left long, the grass coarse and stringy so it snags croquet balls. Some areas are seeded to produce a dense, spongy surface, like moss, that slows the ball down and makes it harder to whack your opponent's ball. The centre wickets will be placed on a long oval strip of pale, thick grass seeded in sand and buzz-cut, on which balls move like lightning. Pete reads greenskeepers manuals, so he knows about grasses and how they function to speed up or slow down a ball. He said that seeded and maintained properly, the grass will grow toward the sun, and that the direction the blades of grass face will affect how a ball moves.

Kathy will string patio lanterns so players will be able to see after dark. She's setting up two rest stations, one near the house, and one in amongst Pete's three remaining leggy dope plants that are tucked in a sunny, pungent grotto along the back fence between the lilacs and the mock orange. There were a dozen plants, but the rest have mysteriously disappeared. Pete thinks Penny's pulling them out one by one, hoping he won't notice.

Penny says it's too overt, growing weed in the backyard. Selling it is one thing; it doesn't make her happy, but it pays the mortgage. And then some. Pete's buyers are well-off profs and stable PhD students at the university, who won't blow the whistle on him and jeopardize their own careers. But growing it in the backyard, that's dangerous, Penny says, that's asking for it. If Penny's not pulling the plants out, Pete doesn't want to know who it is. Paranoia's a no-no in this business, he told Kathy. It'll kill you if you let it. And life's already far too short.

Teach said he'd pay Kathy to serve the drinks at the match if she'd wear her see-through top and the little skirt with the high boots she wore to the Liberace concert.

"They're holy relics on the altar of Liberace," Kathy told him. "Only the chosen get to see them." Kathy didn't tell him the altar was a garbage bag in the corner of her room, stuffed with vomit-stiffened clothes and semen-encrusted bed sheets.

"Holy priestess, choose me," Teach said. He put his hands together and bowed.

Kathy gave him the finger. He grinned and said it didn't matter what she did or said, or even what she wore, it turned him on, every single thing about her made him hard. He grabbed his crotch and moved his hips back and forth and Kathy wondered if he did this in his classes, to his female students, or to the women who worked in his department. She wondered what his wife thought of him, if he really did have a wife.

"I'll wear the outfit if you bring your wife," Kathy told him. She made her voice sweet. Teach stopped smiling.

"You can't take a joke?" he asked.

"Hardy-ha-ha," Kathy cawed as she walked away from him. "You're a card, the funniest man alive. I should be paying to be in your hilarious presence. But hey, I'm broke, so I guess I'll leave because you're so funny and smart I can't afford you right now."

"Lippy Kathy," she heard Teach say as she walked away. "Come back."

Kathy is waiting for a call from the Tribal Liberation Store, a co-op that sells trinkets and crafts, where she'll work as a volunteer at first, then get a percentage of the profits. And she did get a couple of odd jobs, or not-so-odd jobs, with slightly odd people. She took down, re-puttied, washed and stored storm windows for a grateful old couple, Helen and Willie Szasz, wizened him-and-her apple dolls. They called her "dear" and said that for the first time in fifty-eight years, they thought they were going to have to leave the storm windows up all summer. Then they saw Kathy's ad on the utility pole. She was a lifesaver.

They made strong tea and put Carnation milk and two teaspoons of sugar in it without asking if that's what she wanted. They fed her sandwiches with a pink and green filling they called bologna salad. Willie wrote out the recipe while Helen dictated, so Kathy could try it at home: 1 coil ring bologna (skin off), minced, 1 heaping tablespoon Miracle Whip, 1 heaping tablespoon green relish. Mix together and spread on white bread. (A pretty contrast, the white and pink and green, Helen said.) Remove crusts, cut into triangles, and serve. (You can use butter, dear, but we don't; we're watching our waistlines, Helen said.) They took the bread from their freezer slice by slice, they told Kathy, so it was always fresh.

They served the bologna salad with very cold, wreath-shaped sugar cookies covered in damp red and green sprinkles. Leftovers, they said, from Christmas two years ago, when their son, Clarence, and his wife, Eleanor, came with their children. They'd stored the cookies in the freezer, too. Taste fresh-baked, they'd said. They didn't taste fresh-baked, they tasted freezer-burned.

"These are the best cookies I've had in ages," Kathy told them. She said how smart they were to keep them frozen. Not only fresh, but frugal, she added. Pensioners have to be frugal, they said.

They paid her extra. And they asked her to come back in the fall to put the windows back up. She said she would. They asked her to come for a visit anytime she wanted, to have more cookies, or maybe a piece of the birthday cake they'd saved from last summer when their daughter, Ginny, and her children came to visit. Yum, Kathy said, and she promised she would.

She had also been doing laundry for Mr. Vanderbergen, an elderly shut-in two doors down from Pete and Penny. He paid her more than the work was worth and fished for information about the Lehmans. You Hippies, he called Kathy, as if that was her name. You Hippies never have real jobs, he said, though Kathy had explained that her situation was temporary. He watched from his recliner as Kathy ironed his colourless dishcloths and worn tea towels, his old-man boxer shorts, faded shirts with fraying collars and yellowed cotton handkerchiefs. He'd nod off, then revive to ask, *How many people live in that house?*

His skin was taut, and his thick, white hair was clean, but when he breathed, one very long, very black hair moved in and out of his left nostril, and it was all Kathy could do not to watch. So she never looked at him unless she had to, and then only in glances that she realized must seem furtive, raising his suspicions that all You Hippies had something to hide and couldn't meet a fellow eye to eye.

Did Pete and Penny run a commune? he wanted to know. Kathy shook out then folded clean bath towels and facecloths, and stacked them in the wicker basket. *You Hippies always live in communes*, he said. *God knows what you get up to in them.* She paired socks and tucked the tops over the toes. *Who owns the Corvette? Why was it only there on weekends?* (The nose hair moved faster and faster as he got wound up.) *What did Pete do at the university? Why was he home so much? What did he do with his spare time?* Kathy set the ironed handkerchiefs and underwear in the basket with the towels and socks. *Did the Lehmans have a poisonous snake that roamed around the house? He'd heard a rumour, was it true?* She took the tea towels and dishcloths into the kitchen and slipped them in a drawer. *You Hippies never have ordinary pets,* he said, *like cats and dogs. Always has to be something exotic, something to scare the neighbours.* He was breathless.

He wouldn't change his mind no matter what she said, so Kathy told Mr. Vanderbergen that she was getting a full-time job and wouldn't be available any longer. You Hippies, he said, are unreliable. I should have known better than to let you in my house. Kathy wrapped the cord around the base of the cooled iron and stood it on the table. She folded the ironing board and hung it in the broom closet. She said goodbye and closed the door gently. She would miss the money.

She's also helping Pete and Penny in exchange for rent. Mowing the lawn, babysitting Rhettbutler, housecleaning, whatever they find for her. She doesn't declare any of the money on her UIC. Especially the drug money. That's the other thing she's doing: helping Pete with drug deals—deliveries and pickups, mostly grass, but some hashish and LSD now and then. She's not supposed to tell Penny, but Penny knows. Penny knows everything, just like Connie, something Kathy thinks must happen when you become a mother. You get pregnant and your hormones go crazy and suddenly you know everything there is to know in the world. Kathy figures she never got far enough along to experience the full effect.

When Pete pays her in kind, which he does on occasion, she prefers hashish. Then she carves off nickels and dimes to sell on her own, to Donny and Darlyn, to friends at the Rue, to kids at concerts, but only if she knows them. The proceeds (she loves that word, it sounds so hopeful, like she's moving in the right direction) go into a mason jar she's labeled: The Future. Under the words she pasted a picture she found in a magazine, a raggedy old hockey skate.

She's saved $275 already, most of it from selling grass at a Regent Park rock concert organized by the May Fourth Movement. *The Recorder* called the Movement "radical" because, as Connie pointed out the last time Kathy stopped by, the Movement urged kids to gate-crash Festival Express 1970 at the CNE. Connie also showed Kathy a photo in which Kathy, Donny, Darlyn and some friends sat on the grass in front of the stage where Copperpenny sang, "Stop (Wait a Minute)." Island Concert—*Hundreds of young people lounge on the grass in Regent Park*… the caption began. Kathy had no idea the photo had been taken, and was only grateful it hadn't caught her selling drugs.

Today, she and Pete are on their way to Toronto—to the airport, to be exact. Kathy only knows what Pete tells her, which is very little. Only what's necessary for business, that's the rule. Then yesterday he asked her to come along for company. If she wanted, he added. If she didn't have anything better to do, he said. This morning, he asked if they could take her car. He hated to ask, he said, hated to compromise her, but there was no way to call off the deal at the last minute and he had to get to Toronto. Penny needed their car, he said. She had picket duty, and she wasn't listening to reason.

Employees at the cookie factory went on strike at the end of May with a 100% vote to go out. Penny doesn't miss her picket shift and is consumed by the details of the strike; it's all she talks about. They want 80 cents an hour on a two-year contract. The company's offering 40 cents to men and 25 cents to women and women make up more than 70% of the strike vote. "If they think they're going to pit the men against the women," Penny had said, "they've got another thing coming. We're standing firm."

Police were brought in to escort non-union workers, who were roundly jeered, across the picket line. Penny read them *The Recorder* article while they were eating breakfast. "Roundly jeered," she repeated and laughed. "Those little shits! We'll show them. They're not getting in there without a fight."

"There were 350 of us yelling," she said. "A huge turnout, and a bigger racket. Most of the strike-breakers are university students. They'll be making twice as much as us in a year or two anyway."

"Little shits," Penny repeated as she closed the paper, "Who do they think they are, taking jobs away from working people?"

Car windows open, Kathy and Pete head down the 401, cut hay perfuming the humid air. Pete knows where they're going, so he's driving, and Kathy gets to be a passenger in her own car. They pass the escarpment, the swimming hole beneath it and soon the Schneiders sign looms on the other side of the highway. Kathy turns to see it. *Famous for Quality Meats* it says, and tells them it's 79° at—wait for it—10:37.

When she was young, on summer days like this, her father took them for drives on Sundays after Mass, quests for locally made ice cream in villages off the beaten track. Mission accomplished, they'd speed home along the 401 because they'd dawdled an entire day away. When they passed the Schneiders sign, her father always said—every single time—that it should have *Welcome to Varnum* on it. It was the city sign, as far as he was concerned, and he figured there were lots of Varnumites who felt the same way.

Then Connie—every single time—said the airline pilots who landed at Malton called the sign the Wiener Beacon because it stood along one of their approach paths. It didn't bore Kathy that her parents said the same thing every time; she couldn't wait to hear their voices. And if they forgot, she'd remind them and they'd look at each other and laugh, then say the words she wanted to hear. Next to skating on their backyard rink, Kathy's best memories were family car rides, her mother and father in the front seat while she roamed the back.

After Shelly, the excursions ended. Her father said a car was too small a space for a baby who never stopped crying. Instead, Charlie drove by himself on Sundays, bringing home a generic tub of runny ice cream, if he remembered at all. Kathy begged him to take her along, but he told her to stay with her mother, who needed her.

Kathy was too young to say, it's you she needs, but she thinks it now. Driving along the 401 with Pete, she understands why her father took off every Sunday without them, but she wishes he hadn't. She remembers standing beside the car as he slowly pulled away, watching the car move down the street, watching it turn the corner. Waiting in case he changed his mind just this one time and came back to get her.

It wasn't fair to Connie, and particularly to Kathy. She longed to be with him, for relief from Shelly's crying and her mother's distress at not being able to stop it, and for the possibility of happiness.

Sundays became the emblem of how their lives had changed. Connie went by herself to early Mass, hoping Shelly would sleep until she got back. Then Charlie and Kathy went to Mass, the only time they spent alone after Shelly. Kathy sat in the front seat where the sweet spice of her father's aftershave and the chemical astringency of their freshly polished shoes mingled. She looked at his hands on the wheel, ragged fingernails, a healing scrape across his knuckles, or she looked sideways out the window. They drove in silence, because the drive was so short, because the quiet was so blessed. They shared that.

The drive after Mass was also gorgeously silent. At breakfast together they ate quickly, to get the meal over with. For a time Connie tried to draw Charlie out, but when he talked, Shelly screamed, for the sound of his voice made Shelly cry harder. He would stop talking, carry his dishes to the sink, rinse them and stack them in the drainer. He'd sit on the steps near the back door and put on his shoes. He'd grab his jacket and call to them, "I won't be long."

It was a lie. It was always long.

Though everyone calls it Malton, it's now officially the Toronto International Airport. And when Yorkdale Shopping Centre opened, it seemed as though Toronto would engulf the countryside, stretch right out to Mississauga and then on to Varnum. But it hasn't. Horses still graze in lush pasture, twitching flies away, and corn still grows bright green against the dark earth. Neglected apple trees form leafy parasols over encroaching vetch and clover. The orange and yellow heads of day lilies float on their stems and old lilacs bushes shimmer beside tumble-down summer kitchens and the foundations of old barns. Fat Holsteins stand motionless but for their swishing tails. Giant elms line laneways.

The air is hotter near the airport. Kathy's back is stuck to the car seat and her waistband is soaked with sweat. She leans her head out the window; the wind whips her hair, pounds her skin, but it isn't cooling.

She's dressed simply: blue jeans, a pale blue peasant blouse with white embroidery across the yoke, leather sandals. She'd changed a dozen times before they left, wanting to look good without appearing to be trying. Pete's wearing what he always wears, blue jeans and a white T-shirt. He's driving barefoot, a pair of dusty plastic thongs, the imprint of his feet worn into them, on the floor near the brake pedal. His hair is tousled, his cheeks smooth, his fingernails white on dark summer-tanned hands. Her stomach churns when she's near him; she's sure she'd faint if he touched her, a swoon. Like a swathed Victorian lady having tea with her betrothed whom she isn't allowed to touch. Brush a sleeve, swoon. Scent of tobacco and sweat, swoon. Fingertips meet, faint dead away.

It's erotic, not touching Pete, an aphrodisiac. The slightest possibility of contact, skin to skin, and her groin aches. So she avoids him, is never alone with him if she can help it. Until now. A car is a very small space. Kathy presses herself against her door, keeping the maximum distance between them. When she thinks about touching Pete, she thinks about Penny and Rhettbutler, and what comes after. She hates it, of course, hates how helpless she feels to the attraction, and she's ashamed before the fact. But at her most honest, she wants Pete and the anything-can-happen danger of his touch.

"You're positive we're nowhere near the crash site?" Kathy asks.

A week ago, on its approach to the airport, an engine fell off a DC-8 and the pilot had tried to land without it. The plane crashed, killing 108 people. They're squeamish, so many people dead, but they're more afraid the area will be teeming with police, investigators and reporters. The plane went down in a farmer's garden, not right at the airport, but the proximity of so many officials has them edgy.

"I checked," Pete says. "It's on another approach."

Reassured, she turns up the radio because she doesn't want to talk. When "Ohio" comes on, they both begin to hum. They look at each other, smile, and sing along.

"Kathy," Pete says when the song is over, "turn the radio off."

Kathy does.

"Give me your hand," he says, glancing at the road then at her.

Kathy looks at Pete. They both look forward at the road. Kathy closes her eyes and slides her hand over the hot seat. She stops moving her hand when Pete covers it with his. He slips his thumb into her palm and strokes the top of her hand with his fingers.

It lasts only a minute or two, until they exit the highway and Pete simply slides his hand from hers. When she opens her eyes, they're on a gravel road along the perimeter of the airport. They pull onto a grassy shoulder and Pete turns off the motor. The air is still, the quiet, sudden; the engine ticks in the heat.

There are several parked cars, small knots of people talking near them. A couple sits in folding chairs on the edge of the grass, drinking Coke. All watch the runway.

Beside Kathy and Pete, a man and girl sit on a plaid blanket spread over the hood of their car. The binoculars the girl wears around her neck are so heavy they make her slouch; her head sticks out like a turtle's.

She has dandelion-fluff hair that lifts on the breeze, a halo of down that settles when the wind does. The man takes the binoculars but doesn't remove the strap from her neck. When pulled sideways, the girl leans her elbow on his thigh and holds her head in her hand. The man checks his watch, and after looking through the binoculars, he sets them gently in the girl's lap again, and she straightens and resumes her turtle stance.

"Any second now," he tells her.

As if on cue, an enormous rumbling approaches. Getting louder and closer, the crush of pulsating noise instinctively makes them duck. The jet looms above them, huge, thundering. It is pure shuddering noise, and then it is gone. They turn to watch it rise and disappear in the distance.

Kathy turns to tell Pete what a thrill it was, when a man who has been leaning on the door of his car pushes himself away from it and walks toward them. A lunch box—black metal with a rounded top—swings in his hand. His stride is so measured, so precise, his arms move in such long graceful rhythmical arcs, that it is like watching a dance.

"Glad you could make it," the man says to Pete. "It's a busy place since the crash." He shrugs towards the people. "Half of them are vultures."

Pete doesn't say anything. Kathy notices he's holding a large brown paper bag. She can't remember seeing it in the car. She also notices how handsome the man talking to Pete is.

"I brought lunch. Might not be enough for your girlfriend." The man nods towards Kathy, then turns to look at her, really look at her. His eyes give nothing away. He turns back to Pete and says, "I wasn't expecting this."

A blush rises from Kathy's chest, up her neck and onto her cheeks. The man holds the lunch box out to Pete.

"Hey, man, it's cool. She's cool," Pete says. He holds the bag out. "Look, I brought lunch, too. Do you want to trade? I love a surprise."

The words are cordial, but there's no friendliness in their tone or delivery. The men's bodies force relaxation. Motors turn over, dust kicks up from wheels as the other plane watchers drive away. The white-haired girl slides off the hood of the car, binoculars bumping when she lands. The man vaults forward. He grabs the blanket, squarely folds it and tucks it in the back seat. The girl looks sideways at Kathy as they drive way. Kathy smiles, but the girl doesn't. She holds Kathy's eyes, blinks and abruptly turns away.

Lunch Box Man's white T-shirt shows off the muscles of his taut abdomen. He's wearing black jeans and black leather shoes. The shoes have rounded toes and thick brown soles, unexpectedly comfortable looking. He's a head taller than Pete, and aggressively handsome. There's a shock of white in his otherwise black hair. Noticing it, Kathy sees his skin is pockmarked, and this one imperfection is what makes him seem perfect. Pete takes the lunch box and hands him the paper bag.

"Thanks, man," Pete says. "No peanut butter, I hope. I hate peanut butter."

"Naw," the man says. "Tuna salad. I believe it's your favourite."

"Great," Pete says, grinning. "You believe right, love that tuna salad."

"I'll save this for later," the man says holding up the paper bag. "I have to get back to work. See you next week?"

"Anything you say," Pete says. "Hey, man, enjoy," he calls. The man is already walking away.

"Oh, I will," he says, but he doesn't turn to them. As he gets in his car, a jet thumps them with noise and wind. They duck, he doesn't.

"Who was that?" Kathy asks when they can be heard.

"I have no idea," Pete says. "Never asked; don't want to know."

"Shit," Kathy says. "It's like Clint Eastwood. A bit more dust, a serape or two, some sinister music."

A car drives up and parks in front of them. A man in a business suit gets out. He's holding opera glasses.

"Let's get out of here. Too many eyes; the crash has me spooked," Pete says. "It's bringing out the weirdos, the ones who want to be first on the scene and get their pictures in the paper. Usually it's only us regulars, the guy with the little girl, they're here every week. And the Coke drinkers with the lawn chairs. Too many new faces today, freaks me out."

"Hey," the man in the suit calls to them. "Were you here when the jet crashed?"

Pete puts his hand up, a gesture first defensive, then dismissive. "No, man," he says, and he gets into the car.

"Get in now," he says to Kathy very quietly. She's standing next to his door. Then loudly, out the window, he yells, "Didn't see it, man."

By the time Kathy's in the car, Pete has it started and in gear. The man steps forward and walks parallel to the car as they drive past. Kathy turns to see what will happen. He follows them, stops, and then shrugs his shoulders and goes back to his car. When they turn onto the main road, Pete picks up the lunch box that's been sitting on the seat between them and hands it to Kathy.

"Open it," he says. She opens it and there's a sandwich neatly wrapped in waxed paper. She unwraps it.

"Tuna salad," she says sniffing, and holds it out to Pete.

"Yeah, I know," Pete says and he takes an enormous bite. "My favourite," he mumbles through the food. "What's under the sandwich?" Kathy puts the sandwich back in the paper and sets it on the seat.

"Cigarettes; they're open." Kathy holds the package out to him, Player's plain, and he puts it in his shirt pocket.

"What else?" Pete asks.

"Dessert maybe?" She lifts another waxed paper parcel out of the box, this one heavier than the first, and opens it. Wrapped in clear plastic and taped with Scotch tape is an enormous chuck of hashish.

"Fuck me gently," she whispers. She rewraps the hash, tucks it back in the lunch box, and closes the clasp. "If this is your lunch, what's his?"

"Chicken salad." Pete's eating the tuna salad. "On cracked wheat. That's what he likes, that's what I make," Pete says. "Here, have some of this." He hands Kathy the sandwich. "Puts black olives and green peppers and red onions in it, like a Greek salad. Look inside; it's beautiful. He's a fucking sandwich artist."

"What else was in that bag?"

"For his dessert," Pete says, "carefully wrapped in foil to preserve its freshness, there's dough. Lots and lots of well-kneaded dough packaged in various combinations though it all tastes the same, like paper. But that's just the way Mr. Muscle likes it, and I always aim to please."

Pete pulls into a truck stop so Kathy can go to the bathroom. When she gets back the lunch box is gone.

"Where is it?" she asks.

"Trunk," Pete says. He takes the pack of Player's plain out of his pocket. Inside are two rows of rollies, neat little twists at the top.

"My dessert," Pete says. He pulls a joint from the pack, lights it, takes a hit and hands it off to Kathy. She tokes and chokes, the tobacco-hash combo scorching, but a spicy taste lingers, peppery-sweet hashish.

And there it is, the buttery feel of the skin, heartbeat slowed to what's necessary, breath sighing from the lungs, the world an elemental, shimmering, dreamy place.

"Mellow," she says. The word is all her mouth can hold.

Heading to the highway, the car seems to be going ten miles an hour, though they're traveling the speed limit. Kathy checks and makes Pete laugh. Turning onto the ramp, the tilt of the grade feels extreme. Kathy leans into the turn, leans into the door, leans so hard she thinks she'll pass right through the metal and fall onto the pavement. The tilt seems more extreme as they gain speed. Finally they greet the highway.

"Let's do that again," Pete says. The exit ramp immediately appears and they round the upward turn, leaning the other way now, leaning and laughing. At the top of the turn, Pete checks traffic and heads down the ramp. "Last time," he yells and they scream and lean and laugh and howl and just like that, they're on the highway heading home, sitting straight, normal as any Mr. and Mrs. Smith.

She wakes to water droplets pinging against the car, the sprinkler throwing lazy circles over the lawn. Occasional drops come through the window. Kathy rolls it up and slides across the seat to the dry side. She heads for the bathroom. She needs a drink, her mouth is wooly and rank, and she needs to pee.

From the basement, she can hear Penny tell Pete about the strike. It's over, Penny says. They had a vote. They're getting a 19.7% annual wage hike. And she laughs. She says she's working for two weeks and then she's taking her summer holidays. She's going to Sauble Beach with her parents and she'll take Rhettbutler with her. Pete can come if he wants, if he can get the time. Kathy can bring in the mail and the newspaper. Or he can come up on weekends.

Kathy flushes the toilet and washes her hands. She fills a glass with water, downs it and walks to her room. Freddy's coiled in the back of his cage. He's been quiet lately. Kathy wonders if he's sick and reminds herself to ask Pete to check him.

The bag in the corner doesn't smell any more, but she knows she has to deal with it. Have a bonfire and burn the damn things. She resolves to call Darlyn and Donny and ask them to come, somewhere, she'll think of a place. Blue Springs, maybe. Or Varnum Park. They could have a swim, roast some wieners, burn some clothes.

Kathy strips to her underwear and lies on the bed. If she burns the clothes, Doug will go up in flames too, symbolically, of course. Another reason to deal with them. She wishes she didn't know that Penny was going away. It's too complicated. Maybe she should move.

She closes her eyes. She can almost feel Pete's hand on hers. Freddy moves in his cage, a slur of snake flesh over newspaper and sawdust. She's glad he's alive. A lawn mower buzzes, clanks a protest when the blade strikes something solid. It roars alive again and becomes a steady drone. Kathy turns on her side, tucks her hands between her thighs and soon hears nothing at all.

AL'S BIRTHDAY IS TODAY AND CONNIE'S HAVING A BARBEQUE for him. Since she's hosting, she told Al, she wanted Margaret to be invited. Margaret's been living with her feminist friends in a co-op house downtown for the last month and Al and Connie have noticed the co-op gals have helped loosen her up. She's no less prickly, but she's happier. Gals. Al has to stop using words like gals and girls. I'm a woman, Margaret says. Call us women.

Al told Connie the women versus gals story, and Connie said she agreed with Margaret semantically, but she didn't care what she was called as long as no one called her late for supper. And she laughed and said that's what Charlie used to say when they had arguments and Connie called him a bugger or an asshole. "'Well, Connie,' he'd say, 'I agree with you semantically, but just don't call me late for supper.'"

Sometimes a joke was needed to make them see the silliness of their fight. But when Connie felt justified in her argument, she wanted to win and not be diverted by laughter, which she felt trivialized what she was saying. And this is the irony, she told Al, "I never got to use that punch line, because I did all the cooking, and all of the calling to supper, too."

At this point in the conversation, Al wondered how they got to the gender division of domestic chores. To change the subject, he asked Connie what kind of cake she was going to make him. He told her that his favourite was spice cake with penuche icing. But that a chocolate cake with boiled icing would be fine too.

With that, Connie said, "See? Here we are, right back to who's serving, and who's being served."

Al said, "Don't have the party then."

And Connie said, "Maybe I won't."

And Al said, "I'll bring my own cake if it makes you feel better."

And Connie said, "Oh, for Christ's sake, Al, don't be a child, I'm having the party and I'll bake the cake. But you better bake me a cake on my birthday or this will be the last one you ever get."

Then Connie told Al, "Since Margaret moved in with the feminists, you can have a real rip-roaring conversation with her. Just like we're having now. Margaret's new life has spilled over into ours. Makes you think, doesn't it, Al? All your life you live a certain way and then one person changes and every blessed little thing that used to be a habit or a truth changes right along with them. Or that's the way it seems.

"Happened after Charlie died. I had to rethink my life. Just like that." And Connie snapped her fingers.

"I wasn't a wife; I was a widow. I still had two kids, and one of them was never going to be able live on her own. I had the same house to look after, with furniture that likely wouldn't change for decades. I had the same bills to pay, and suppers to make and floors to scrub and toilets to clean and PTA to attend. It all looked the same from the outside, every single gaw-damned detail exactly as it was, but everything had changed. It was so confusing. And it made me feel trapped. The house in the suburbs I never wanted. The second child he desperately wanted. Skating on hockey skates and rules for making rinks and looking for ice cream, it was all Charlie.

"As soon as I got over being sad, or even before," Connie said, "I was pissed off. There's energy to anger, Al. It fuels you; it keeps you going. It's the fire that makes you burn with life when you feel like you're dead, it keeps your heart beating when you think it's too broken to tick or tock, it forces you to make decisions when you think your brain has turned to mush. It keeps your muscles moving when you're sure you couldn't lift a finger, much less get your whole body up and out of bed to tend to a baby who never takes comfort from you. Being pissed off helped me get a job and pay the bills and find help for Shelly.

"I wish Kathy could have been a little pissed off back then. Or even now," Connie mused. "She still misses her father; she always was a serious child, but she became more serious after he died and I had a hand in that, I suppose. I needed her too much. Charlie was nicer to her than I was; he loved her without reserve. And with Shelly to look after, I didn't have time for Kathy, hardly a minute to say anything to her except to set the table or ask did she have her homework done. But that's another story.

"Every day I read the paper, Al, and every day there were stories of people whose lives had changed in a second. Like mine did. Those stories kept me going. They kept the fires stoked and reminded me to never, ever to let my guard down again."

Connie snorted then and said, "But here I am planning a party for the husband of my next-door neighbour because she left him and moved into a women's commune. And because she left, everything has changed. Your life, and now my life. We have to be careful, Al. We have to take our time and think about what we're doing."

Al has to agree, Margaret's changed. She's a bit frightening when she launches one of her radical feminist rants about men (read Al) oppressing women (read Margaret) and how the personal (which she says includes their married life) is political (to be used for public—and publication, Al fears—fodder). But she's happier, and for the most part nicer, too. Now she and Connie are becoming friends, so Connie's happy. And because they're happy, Al's happiest of all. At least he thinks he is.

The birthday will be the first time Al will be in the same place with both Connie and Margaret since Margaret and Al turned into Al and Connie. He's a little uncomfortable. More than a little, really. He tries not to, tries to be modern, but he worries about what people think: The neighbours and people at church, but mostly he worries about Darlyn.

When he told her a minute ago that he was in love with Connie, she said she knew and she didn't mind. They—Al and Darlyn and Donny—are sitting in the kitchen where the walls are painted eggshell, the colour Margaret chose when they changed their newly married carnival of primaries—yellows and blues and greens—into a single, tasteful middle-aged off-white. We can't afford new furniture, Margaret said, but we can make our walls look classy. The fresh paint made their old furniture look tawdry. Even Al, who never noticed décor, as Margaret used to call it, noticed that. Now Margaret's décor includes concrete-block-and-salvaged-board bookcases, and a mattress on the floor.

Horizontal shafts of sunlight stream through windows set high on the wall. Bungalow windows. Someday Al will ask Connie why she thinks they build windows so high up on bungalow walls. Windows you have to stand up to see out of. No doubt she'll have a theory. A breeze pushes Margaret's gauzy curtains out and sucks them back against the screen again. Al and Darlyn sit on chrome chairs with turquoise vinyl covers, bum prints worn into them, their pleated corners cracked.

It's an ordinary summer morning, in an ordinary kitchen, the kind Al sits in every day selling his wares to housewives. It's so ordinary he can't believe he's talking to his mostly grown-up daughter about her now-absent mother, and the next-door neighbour he's dating. They lean their elbows on the speckled, turquoise Arborite. Al stirs sugar into his coffee and Darlyn butters her toast. Donny lies on the floor and rubs Darlyn's foot.

Donny. Yes, well, Donny isn't ordinary. He's shirtless, sockless, shoeless, in fact all he's wearing are very short, very tight cut-off blue jeans with legs so wildly uneven and frayed the threads dangle and catch on the hairs on his thighs. There are holes under the seams of the back pockets. Donny's underwearless, so when he moves, hairy pink bum flesh peaks through the shredded denim. At least while Donny's lying on his back, Al doesn't have to try *not* to look at the small amount of shredded material covering his rear end.

Donny's pulled an all-nighter. He won the Gyproc contract in the new subdivision past Bridge Street, and as fast as he and his crew finish a house, a contracted painting crew moves in to lay down undercoating, then paint the walls and ceilings. It's the new way,

Donny says. Like line work in a factory, each house has a plan and a timetable. Subcontracted crews come in, perform their magic and move on the next house. The next crew moves into the house, and so on and so on. If one crew gets behind, it affects the whole line. When the electricians staged a one-day labour walkout in solidarity with the striking workers at the cookie factory a couple of weeks ago, they blew the timetable. To catch up, Donny's crew has been working nights, and this morning they finished sanding their catch-up house.

Donny arrived while Al and Darlyn were making breakfast. He gave Darlyn a dusty kiss and offered Al one, too. Al declined. Donny went down to his room—he's been renting from Al since Margaret moved out—washed up in the laundry tub and changed into his shorts. He had a quick toke off the roach he keeps with his cigarettes, and blew the smoke out the open basement window. Then he came up and lay down under the table—cooler there, he said—by Darlyn's feet.

Donny's long frizzy hair is almost white with dust. He'd washed his face and hands, but not his ears and neck and wrists. He looks like a made-up cadaver, Al realizes, and shivers.

"It's not just a foot rub, Al," Donny's telling him. "It's reflexology. You massage a certain part of the foot and it affects a specific part of the body. It's all mapped out like a star chart. Really. I heard about it on the radio, so I got a book out of the library. Oh, shit, Darlyn, remind me I have to take it back. I think it's overdue. So, Al, let's say you massage part of the big toe. If you hit the right spot, it will help clear up your sinuses, or something like that. It's not sex, or getting into some chick's pants—no offence intended, Al—it's therapeutic. Want me to do yours when I'm finished Darlyn's?"

"No, that's all right," Al says. "But thanks, anyway."

"It's not like it hasn't been obvious for years," Darlyn's saying. Al just told her he was going to take Connie out on a date. "It's all right, Dad. Don't worry about it. Kathy and I figured it out ages ago."

"Groovy. I like Connie," Donny says. "How does that feel, my darlin' Darlyn? I'm working on your heart. Are you falling even more in love with me?"

"No, but my right arm is going to sleep," Darlyn says and she shakes out her lifeless arm. To Al she says, "Since she moved out, Mom's happier than I've seen her in years. No offence, Dad. So you're happy. Mom's happy. Mrs. Rausch is happy. Kathy and I are happy. Even Shelly seems to like you, so we think she's happy. It's always hard to tell with Shelly. So everything's cool."

"Yeah, man, cool," Donny says, and giggles. "Happy, happy, happy." Darlyn pulls her bare foot out of Donny's hand and rubs it on his stomach. Donny groans.

Al forgets and glances down. He looks away. His daughter's rubbing her foot on a man's stomach under his kitchen table. He's trying to keep an open mind about Donny. He likes him for the most part, but Darlyn's old boyfriend George was an easier go. A little more…ah…normal.

"And if you marry Connie, then Kathy and I will be stepsisters," Darlyn says.

"Far out," Donny says. He takes Darlyn's foot and nibbles the insole. She laughs out loud.

"On second thought," he mumbles, his mouth still on Darlyn's foot, "that's heavy." He closes his eyes and rocks his head back and forth, his lips brushing the bottom of Darlyn's foot. He whispers "heavy" until it becomes a hum. Darlyn gently withdraws her foot and tucks it up under her bum. Donny rolls over on his belly, puts his dusty head on his folded arms, and falls asleep.

"I never mentioned marriage, Darlyn," Al says. He walks to the door. As he opens it to leave, he turns to Darlyn and says, "Don't get your hopes up. No one ever talked about marriage."

But they have talked about it, he and Connie. And in his heart of hearts, that's exactly what he wants. To be married to Connie. Connie said she isn't sure she wants to be married again. Men leave; they up and die, she told Al. She's been alone for a long time and she's doing just fine, thank you very much. She doesn't think she's a feminist, she told Al, but she knows what she knows, and marriage hasn't been a sure deal for her. And look at Margaret, she said, and her voice trailed off.

Al isn't getting used to the women in his life telling him how he's an oppressor, but he's no longer surprised by it. He says what he needs to, knowing he's going to have to take his licks. But he knows better than to try to argue too much, because there is some truth to what they're saying, even he can see that. But he doesn't know how to change something like marriage. How do you change an institution that's been around for thousands of years? That's what he wants to know.

Once Connie even flapped a magazine in his face and told him to listen up. Then she read: "Radical feminists say, 'marriage is the primary instrument of women's psychological and economic subjugation. Women are naïve signatories to a bad deal, enslaving themselves in perpetuity for a man's pledge of protection and support in a cozy, cloistered, soul-destroying security.'

"Unquote," Connie said.

"I don't want to subjugate you." It was the only word he understood.

What he wanted was to wake up in the morning in a house that Connie lived in too, to lay his head on a pillow that carried her scent. He wanted to make breakfast for her when she got home from her shift, and to help get Shelly ready for her school. To lie down with Connie before she fell asleep, to talk about her night at work and his coming day on the road. To sit the way they were sitting, two easy chairs before a picture window, magazines and newspapers scattered about, two cups of coffee steaming on the end table.

"It's too early for us to talk about marriage, Al. Margaret's only been gone a month. And no one's said anything about divorce yet, not to mention annulment." Connie had smoothed the pages of the magazine.

"We could live together," Al suggested. "Like kids do these days."

"A-l," Connie said stretching the letters of his name into two syllables. It was her way of warning him.

"I'm going to give this to Kathy to read," she said, changing the subject. "You know what she told me the other day? She said she's waiting to hear about a job in the Tribal Liberation Shop. It's some kind of hippie co-op that sells trinkets and crafts. She says she'll be working one day a week for free to support the communal effort, but when the shop starts to make some money, she'll start to get paid a percentage of the profits. I don't know, Al.

"The other thing she wants, is to get a job skating. Hockey skating, Al. She's a girl. Not that she can't skate, but it's a hobby, not a career. She got the notion from Charlie that girls can play hockey, and I thought it was cute when she was little. Then he died and left her high and dry. She's living in a dream world, Al, only I don't know if it's her dream or Charlie's.

"She seems so confused these days. Am I wrong, do you think?"

Al hadn't told Connie this yet—it takes a certain energy and preparedness to talk to Connie about serious subjects—but ever since Margaret left, he's confused. Margaret's living in a communal house with women from her collective. Four are single, two married with young kids, two are Margaret's age, late forties, and one is in her sixties and has finally left an abusive husband. He can understand that, but the ones with kids he doesn't get. Taking children from their fathers to live in what will likely be poverty. He wonders how they got that desperate.

They were starting a magazine, Margaret told him. She was going to devote all of her energy and talent—she has a talent for writing, she said—into making it a successful magazine. She apologized for all the years she was a wet rag. They were wasted years for both of them, she said, and she was sorry. She wasn't exonerating him, but with the help of consciousness-raising she'd moved beyond anger at Al per se, to understanding it was patriarchal institutions that were oppressive.

She was never meant for marriage, Margaret said, had never liked sex (at least not with men, she said, but she didn't elaborate, and Al didn't ask) so it had been unfair to stay married. Al was a decent enough person. For a man, she added. (She didn't elaborate on that either, and Al certainly didn't want to hear any more about his male privilege and what pigs most men were.) She said it was perfectly legitimate for a woman to be single, and she'd work with Al to get an annulment from their marriage, if that's what he wanted.

Margaret also told Al that she wasn't blind; she knew he'd been in love with Connie for a long time. She thanked him for not doing anything about it (he didn't tell Margaret that Connie would have nothing to do with him as long as he was married), and said if he wanted to date Connie, Margaret would understand. In fact, she'd be happy for him, and for Connie, if Connie decided she wanted to go out with him.

Margaret had gone to Connie and said that when the scales fell from her eyes and she saw how women were treated, she realized that Connie had been living a free and independent life as a widow, while she, Margaret, had lived in married bondage. She said she had a lot to learn from a woman like Connie, who hadn't immediately married again.

Connie didn't point out that very few men wanted to marry a woman with two children, one autistic and difficult to handle, who would never grow up and move away, the other a dreamer with no apparent ambition except skating, and even that seemed to be unrealizable. She told Margaret she was happy for her, and any time she wanted to talk about marriage and its advantages and disadvantages, Connie would welcome the chance. She invited Margaret to join her card club where they could chew the fat on a regular basis.

When Margaret mentioned dating Al, with her blessing, Connie acted surprised. But when Al asked to take her and Shelly to the drive-in, she said yes. They'd had a good enough time. The movies, a double bill, were nothing special. Shelly sat between them, sharing popcorn and Orange Crush. After the first feature, she had her sleeping pill and crawled into the back seat, wrapped herself in her cartoon quilt, and slept.

Al took Connie bowling once (she hadn't met Jerry Rahn and she hadn't won $300) and they went out to supper a couple of times, but most evenings Al came over and they drank instant coffee and read the newspaper together before Connie left for work. Al taped Connie's clippings to the refrigerator door, the latest about Arab terrorists, who hijacked a plane from Greece and were getting what they demanded: the release of their imprisoned compatriots.

Connie ranted about that, said politicians shouldn't give in to thugs, it made flying unsafe for everyone. Connie said even if Greece expelled all the Arabs, as they said they might, it meant nothing now. Terrorists knew they could get their way by hijacking planes, so the precedent was set and the world was less safe as a consequence.

These days, although Al's rattled and confused, he's happy. To be able to sit in Connie's living room and listen to her particular views on life, to look at her perfect black hair and her beautiful red lips. (Lips she lets him kiss, but that's all until the annulment.) To be going next door to the first birthday party anyone's had for him since he was a child. Even though he doesn't understand what's going on half the time, life isn't so bad.

"Happy birthday to you, happy birthday to you. Happy birthday, dear Da-ad. Happy birth…"

Whump! A ball of fire explodes from the hibachi. Flames leap toward Al and Darlyn, who is singing to her father.

"…day to Mother-of-Christ-what-the-ahhhhh…"

Darlyn's eyebrows are smoking. The rainbow-coloured ribbons dangling from the ends of her pigtails are smouldering. Al's holding a can of lighter fluid in one hand and a lit match in the other. His eyebrows are smoking, too. Steam rises from his hair.

"Oh-my-god," he says. He reaches for Darlyn's braids. Darlyn sees the match and lighter fluid coming her way and she screams. Al backs away. He looks down at his hands.

"Oh-my-god," he says again, and tosses the match into the barbeque. It flares again but not catastrophically.

Shelly's standing beside Al. She puts her arms down at her sides, turns her face skyward and screams along with Darlyn, an ear-piercing mix of terror and delight. Donny's drying a beer for Margaret from the water-and-ice-filled wading pool with a tea towel. Margaret grabs the towel and runs to Darlyn. She flaps the towel at her and the smouldering ribbons flare.

"Jee-zus, Mom," Darlyn yells. She grabs the towel from Margaret and beats at her braids, but the smouldering continues to rise up the ribbons. She drops the towel and beats with her hands. She screams again.

Shelly, who stopped screaming when Darlyn did, resumes, vigorously and joyously. Margaret steps backwards until she bumps into the wading pool. The inflated edge squishes under her weight and she loses her balance and plunks onto her bum. Water and ice swoosh over the edge of the pool, over Donny's feet.

"Damn," he yells when the ice water hits his feet. He lifts one, then the other.

"Christ Almighty!" Margaret shouts, floundering in the pool. Floating bottles rattle against her, clink together. She gets on her hands and knees and Donny helps her out.

"Sh-sh-sh-it," she says, her teeth chattering.

Darlyn stops screaming to watch her mother. Margaret's hair drips, her shorts and shirt stick to her skin, her breasts, which have been bra-less since she moved into the women's commune, look like two vacuum-packed pork roasts attached to her chest. Darlyn laughs. She can't help it. Even though the smouldering ribbons are scorching her braids and the air begins to smell of burnt hair, she laughs.

Kathy's laughing too, so hard she's snorting. She empties her beer glass on the grass, scoops ice water from the pool and dunks each end of Darlyn's braids. The smouldering ribbons fizzle out, once and for all. The smell of burnt hair mingles with the smell of lighter fluid emanating from the hibachi, which, despite the whoosh of flame that caused all the trouble, isn't going. No sparks, no embers, no coals, only one thin line of smoke snaking up from the spent match.

"Give me that." Connie's taking charge. She grabs the lighter fluid from Al and shoos him away. "I told you that was too much starter."

She tells Kathy, "Stop that stupid snorting and go help your sister." Shelly's now screeching ha-ha-ha in big hoarse gulps.

She turns to Darlyn and says, "At least you're not burned."

"What do you call this?" Darlyn waves her singed, wet pigtails in Connie's face.

Squishing over to Darlyn, Margaret says, "Sweetie." Her wet shorts are bunched in her crotch, underwear lines show along the tops of her round thighs. She hugs Darlyn.

"You're wet," Darlyn says.

"Welcome to the suburban barbeque," a voice says, and Pete Lehman rounds the corner. Barry and Rachel follow behind him.

Connie had suggested Kathy invite her friends. I'd like to meet them, she'd said.

"What a pleasure to have been invited," Pete says.

They turn to see who's speaking. Pete walks toward them unbuttoning his shirt. His skin is tanned, silky black hair shines in a line from his navel to the belt buckle at the top of his fly. He walks to Margaret and swings his clean, white shirt smooth-as-butter-chivalrous over her shoulders.

Shelly's ha-ha's stop and she stares at Pete.

"How gallant," Margaret says, pronouncing it *gal-lont*. She plucks her shorts from her crotch and holds out her hand. "Margaret Smola," she says. Like Shelly, she can't take her eyes off Pete.

"Charmed," Pete says, taking her hand. "Pete Lehman. I'm Kathy's friend."

He turns Margaret's wet hand over in his, draws it to his lips, and kisses the palm. Margaret blushes, but doesn't take her hand away. Pete puts his hand over hers, then draws both of his away from Margaret's, slowly, until only their fingertips touch. He holds the pose a second, then steps back. Margaret's hand floats in the air in front of her. Pete turns full circle and winks at them all.

"Is that sausage I smell?" he asks. His grin invites them to smile.

Darlyn laughs. Kathy has never really stopped. And soon they're all smiling and laughing, except Shelly, who just stares. And Al, whose expression is pained and apologetic.

It doesn't smell like sausage; it smells like burnt hair, beer and lighter fluid-doused charcoal. It smells like devilled egg, coleslaw, raw onions, raw meat and coconut suntan oil. And above all, there is the smell of aftershave. Al seems to have bathed in it today. Aqua Velva, because Connie said she liked it. When he arrived, they—each of them separately—suggested he take a dip in Shelly's wading pool to wash it off. He ignored them, of course, but when Connie said he stank, he looked particularly hurt.

"Aqua Velva," Pete says, shaking Al's hand. "My dad used to wear it, too."

Pete turns to Connie. "You must be Connie," he says. Connie nods. "Thanks so much for inviting me. I'm sorry Penny and Rhettbutler can't be here, but they're visiting with Penny's parents."

"Pete Lehman," she says. She looks him up and down. "Good to meet you, at last." She turns, and though Pete has already spoken to each of them, Connie says to her guests, "Pete Lehman, everyone. Kathy's friend and landlord."

Pete turns and bows. Then he goes to Shelly.

"And you must be Shelly," Pete says. He kneels in front of her.

"What pretty hair," he tells her. He doesn't touch her but with his hands makes a halo in the air around her head. She looks at his face, levelly and unafraid. She reaches out and makes a halo in the air around Pete's head. She puts her hands down at her sides and leans forward ever so slightly and sniffs Pete.

"Pete, Pete, Pete," she yells, and runs away from him, her arms windmilling, propelling her in circles around the yard.

By the time Rachel and Barry are introduced, beer is being opened, and everyone is talking. Darlyn and Margaret go next door to change into dry clothes. They bring back a portable radio and tune it to a soft rock station. Glowing coals have miraculously appeared in the hibachi.

Al grills hamburgers and Connie hands them to Kathy. Kathy ladles potato salad and coleslaw onto plates and encourages people to eat. Shelly's floating her hamburger on a paper plate in the pool; she keeps her eye on Pete at all times. Darlyn and Donny and Rachel and Barry dance until someone calls out, switch partners, and they do as they are told before they drift over to the picnic table for food.

When Al is almost finished his food, Connie nods to Darlyn and they disappear into the house. Connie comes out first, carrying a huge rectangular cake covered in penuche icing. Lettering in blue frosting says, *Happy Birthday, Al*. Forty-eight blue-and-white-striped candles blaze and dip, then blaze again.

"Happy birthday to you," Connie warbles as she walks down the steps onto the lawn. As their voices join hers, they warble too, but quickly harmonize, except Shelly's, which bellows.

Darlyn slips behind Connie. As Connie nears the picnic table, she begins to twirl two batons, a deft routine of throws and spins as sparkly as the candles on Al's cake. When she reaches her father she kneels before him and tosses her batons into the air. She stands and catches them over his head, twirls them there, whirling like helicopter blades. She slowly moves them alongside Al's arms and brings them in to her sides and stops. The sudden shift in the air makes the candles on the cake flicker, but they hold.

As they sing the last *to yo-ou*, Al blushes and grins. He claps his hands, and they all clap with him. Then Al leans over the cake and in one big breath blows out the candles, splattering bits of blue wax over the icing and onto the plastic tablecloth.

Kathy sings too, sings loud and strong. But she's not thinking about Al; she's thinking about tonight. Two things are happening after the party. Kathy and Darlyn and Donny and Barry and Rachel and Pete are going to Varnum Park for a bonfire. Kathy's invited them to come with her to get rid of a few things that need getting rid of, she told them. Just a bag of old stuff.

After the bonfire, Donny and Darlyn are going home to sleep at the Smolas'. Rachel and Barry are driving back up to Rachel's parents' cottage and they will sleep there. Pete and Kathy are going home; sleep may or may not be what they do.

PETE HAS TO MEET UP WITH A FRIEND AT HIS HOUSE. BARRY AND Rachel are dropping him off, and Pete's friend will give him a ride to the park later. But not too late, he told Kathy as he was leaving Al's party. I promise, he said, and he smiled his winning smile and gave her hand a squeeze. Darlyn and Donny will help Al carry his birthday loot home before they leave. Kathy double-checked to make sure their plans were solid, that they'd all make it to the park at some point in the night.

It's after ten as Kathy drives down Regent Street, windows open, street lights sparking through the leaves of the mature maples and elms that line the road. A summer-soft night breeze slips over her, tickles her neck, makes her shiver. The radio's playing and Kathy wails along with Janis.

Janis is getting lots of airplay, since the Festival Express tour. The tour opened at the CNE in Toronto after the Montreal concert was cancelled by city officials. They were afraid of riots, they said, because the concert was being held on St. Jean-Baptiste Day. Huge crowds fuelled by alcohol and drugs, free love and rock music, and separation politics— nine bombings in a two-week period—seemed too volatile a mix.

Some day Kathy will go to Montreal for St. Jean-Baptiste Day, see what it's all about. It has to be more fun than an abortion. She wonders if Janis has had an abortion. Can't imagine that she hasn't; she's renowned for her sexual exploits. And whether or not the stories are sensationalized, fragments are probably true. One mistake, one drunken or stoned night without a diaphragm or a condom, just one indiscretion, that's all.

People talk about free love, they talk about what birth control they use, but no one ever talks about their abortions; certainly celebrities don't. Kathy told Darlyn and Donny and Barry, but none of them mention it any more. If she brought it up they'd talk about it, because they're her friends, but she doesn't bring it up. More than the abortion, for which she only feels relief, the secrecy makes her sad.

Kathy reads *The Recorder* and *Chatelaine*, every article that mentions abortion. It's the "issue" of abortion that's discussed, how women should have access to it or not, depending on a writer's slant. In the articles, no one says, "I had an abortion and this is my story." They don't even tell you what you can expect, before, during or after. Margaret's consciousness-raising group might talk about particulars. Kathy should ask, but then Margaret will want to know why she's asking, and Kathy doesn't think she wants her best friend's mother, and lately a friend to Connie, wondering whether Kathy had an abortion.

Connie didn't ask, but Kathy's pretty sure she suspected the pregnancy. If she had asked, Kathy would have lied. But if pressed, or if something had happened and she had to, she would have said, yes, but she had a miscarriage. Miscarriages are legitimate. And Kathy thinks that sometimes, like D and Cs, miscarriages are a euphemism for abortion. Connie would have an opinion—some righteous socio-political theory—on the subject, that's for sure. And though in her heart Kathy knows her mother would be kind and say all the right things, the last person she'd tell about the abortion is her mother.

If Kathy did tell Connie, she wouldn't want her to say anything. Not one word. She'd want her mother to lead her to Connie's big double bed, where Kathy and Shelly slept with their mother when they were sick. She'd want to lie down on the bed with her mother, have her mother hold her, spooned around her back, no sound but the whispers of their breath.

Hold her and not let her go, not ease the pressure for one second, until Kathy slipped from her mother's arms and walked out of the room because she'd been held enough. That's what she'd do if she had a daughter who had to have an abortion.

She doesn't think about the baby often, but when she does, she's not happy, and she's not sad. Sometimes she wonders what her life would have been like. She'd be big, almost seven months by now, unemployed except for odd jobs and drug deals, boarding in a room with a boa constrictor, warding off her mother, and about to sleep with her landlord, who is married and a father.

The baby would have no father, or none that Kathy would admit to. Doug went back to Vancouver and no one has heard from him. Not Blanche, not Connie, and certainly not Kathy. If she'd had the baby she'd lie and says its absent father was a sweet young man who had come to Varnum under an assumed name because he was a draft dodger, but he decided, because his exile from America was breaking his mother's heart, to go to Vietnam. After he left Canada, Kathy never heard from him again. Or he was a brilliant mathematician, theirs love at first sight. But he died in a car accident. Or a tender, altruistic fellow who went off to help the poor people in Biafra before he ever knew he was going to be a father. No forwarding address. But none of these is a good enough story for a real baby, only an imaginary one.

She wonders if Shelly notices she doesn't have a father. When Shelly was a baby, Charlie was seldom home. And when he was, his unhappiness was palpable, yet he was so withdrawn, it was like being haunted by a father rather than having one. So if she did notice, what would she miss, unlike Kathy, who misses Charlie in invisible, mostly unconscious ways every single day?

At the campsite, she stops the car and turns off the ignition. Silence overwhelms, and Janis and the imaginary-baby stories are replaced by small sounds: the tick-tick of the car engine, crickets chirupping, and a rustle of leaves as the breeze passes through them. In the distance there's the lilt of conversation, but nothing she can make out.

Saplings and low dense bushes grow beneath the beech and maple that surround the site. A thick cedar hedge beside the parking spot ensures privacy. On one side is a grassy tent site, on the other, a picnic table. In the middle is the firepit, a red brick patio circling it. Kathy walks to a nearby tap to fill the pail she's brought, just in case.

She digs a hole in the firepit with a trowel, and wedges a cross—a body with arms she made from a broken rake—long end down, as far into the ash and ground as she can. She piles stones around it and makes sure it's sturdy. She doesn't want it to tip over. Not right away.

The air is warm still, the night humid though not sticky. The sky is bright enough to see by, a dazzle, really, the moon a thick silvery wedge, stars flickering through thin wisps of quickly passing cloud. She sits back and watches. Laughter drifts on a breeze.

She gives the cross a shake—solid enough—and gets the garbage bag from the trunk of the car. The clothes are clean. She'd scraped away the vomit cemented to the material, and washed everything. Kathy slips the transparent green turtleneck over the stake, stretches the armholes to fit over the crossbar. She threads the sleeves of the pink satin jacket over the top. She shakes out the tiny black velvet skirt and pins it, with the safety pins she has in her pocket, to the bottom of the green shirt. Before coming, she'd sewed the pink satin underpants to the skirt so they dangle beneath its hem. She wraps the textured stockings around the base of the cross, lets the ends dangle.

She left the vinyl boots at home—they would melt rather than burn—and she took the sheets to the Sally Ann. Someone could use them. She builds a Girl Guide teepee around the stake: crumpled newspaper around the dangling ends of the stockings, dead twigs over the paper, kindling leaning over the twigs, and four dry sticks of firewood tipped up and resting on the stake. The fire is set.

Kathy rings the effigy with lawn chairs and sits down to have a cigarette. She waits. Car lights brush past her, past the site. Donny's car backs up and parks beside hers. And as Max says in *Where the Wild Things Are*, *Let the wild rumpus start*.

"I recognize these," Darlyn says as she circles the effigy.

"Liberace night," Donny says. "Oh my darlin', oh my darlin'…" he sings, and gives Darlyn a big kiss on the cheek. "That's the night I fell in love with my Darlyn."

"I get it," Darlyn says.

"Do I get it?" Donny asks. He looks at Darlyn. "What don't I get?"

Darlyn and Kathy look at him, look at the effigy.

"Oh," he says. "Are you all right?" he asks Kathy.

"Right as rain." It's the first thing she's said since they arrived.

They sit and pass a joint while they wait for Barry and Rachel and Pete.

"Rachel's pretty nice," Darlyn says, sucking in some smoke. She hands the joint to Kathy and sits back in her chair. On the exhale she adds, "For a Westmount girl."

Kathy snorts in the middle of her toke. Smoke shoots from her nostrils. She coughs.

"Gimme that," Donny says. He leans over in his chair, almost tips, rights himself, and grabs the joint from Kathy. He takes a long drag, exhales a tiny smoke ring and sips in a few little tokes. He passes the joint back to Kathy, who takes a quick toke and passes it to Darlyn.

"Why do you keep saying 'for a Westmount girl'?" Donny asks. He's holding his breath so the words sound like little oinks coming from his throat. "Is she nice? Or isn't she?"

"She's got perfect hair," Kathy says.

"She's got perfect clothes," Darlyn says and tokes. "This is good." She exhales and sighs. "Where'd you get it?"

"Pete." Kathy's holding smoke in, so it comes out, "Bleat."

"She's got a perfect boyfriend," Darlyn says.

Kathy mouths, *Barry*, and lifts her eyebrows, and she and Darlyn begin to bray.

"She's going to have the perfect wedding," Kathy says, catching her breath.

"And she's the perfect virgin," Darlyn hoots.

"No, she's not," Kathy says. "Barry introduced her to marijuana." She leans forward in her chair and stares at her effigy. "And one thing led to another and they're sleeping together now."

"Far out," says Darlyn, and she leans forward.

"Far fucking out," says Donny, and he leans forward, too.

As one, they sit back in their chairs, and they laugh.

"Look at the moon," Donny says. They look up.

"She lives in a great big fucking house," Darlyn says, watching the sky.

Mansions, they call the houses of rich kids, whose parties they've attended in Westmount and Forest Hills. Houses at least twice the size of the blue-collar bungalows they grew up in, though Donny admits he grew up in a split level. A very small split level, he wants them to know. The kind of house Connie has always aspired to, Kathy tells them, a split level with a sunken living room and wall-to-wall shag carpet.

In dreamy voices they describe rooms they've been in, most of them, like Connie's dream house, carpeted wall-to-wall with broadloom or shag so thick you could sleep on it. They try to outdo each other: Kitchens with islands and breakfast nooks and dishwashers and maids. Zillions of appliances in pink or avocado or harvest gold and sound systems built into the walls. Formal dining rooms with more furniture in one room than they had in their entire houses, stacked with sets of dishes and crystal and real silver. Some even had fireplaces. In fact, fireplaces all over, upstairs and down, in dens and in master bedrooms. Libraries with desks and bookcases built in. Toilets with spray jets that washed your bum. Showers separate from the bathtub. Bathrooms with heated towel racks. Separate sinks for the husband and the wife. Some bathrooms were attached to master bedrooms, some to guest rooms where no one ever slept. Beds had more pillows than heads.

And not only that, rich people owned cottages right on the water, at Sauble Beach and Southampton and Port Elgin; they owned whole islands in Honey Harbour and the Muskokas. They had motorboats to get them to their islands. They had water skis and canoes and sailboats and houses to house them. Some even had cabins and chalets at Blue Mountain where they went to ski. None of them—Donny or Kathy or Darlyn—had ever skied. Skiing was for rich people.

They light another joint and are warming up to how Sand Hills thinks it's so good compared to Varnum, Sand Hills having the university and Varnum most of the heavy industry, when Barry and Rachel arrive. They can hardly stand, they're so stoned. Barry reaches for the joint and Rachel tells them about Pete's friend.

"He's gorgeous," Rachel says.

She takes the joint from Barry and draws in hard and holds. Kathy waits to hear what she'll say next.

Rachel waves her hand in front of her face, the joint glows. Barry takes it from her. "He doesn't have it now, but he has lots of old acne scars, so you wouldn't think he'd be handsome. But he is." She uses her hands to square her face. "You know how they say chiselled features? Well, that's him." She stands on tiptoe and puts her hand in the air. "He's this tall, and bulging with muscles."

"Lunch Box Man," Kathy whispers.

"Pardon me?" Rachel says, but she doesn't wait for an answer. "Give me that," she says, and grabs the joint again. "Did you get his name?" she asks Barry.

"Didn't say," Barry says. He turns to Kathy. "So what's the agenda? Pete said to start without him. He'll get here when he can."

Kathy nods towards the firepit.

"Oh, man," Barry says, staring at the ur-Kathy rising on the stake. "How did I miss that?"

Kathy pulls a Zippo from her pocket. She flicks it as she walks to the car for lighter fluid. She sprays some fluid on the clothes and wood, then she lights the kindling. The fire licks up and catches on the stockings in a whoosh. The effigy is a conflagration. Bits of burning cloth float in the air.

"Get them!" Darlyn yells. They whoop and chase the cinders, beating them until they're out, running to the next one. When the fire calms, and there are no more flying sparks, they sit in the lawn chairs. They smoke joints and cigarettes, and they drink the beer Barry brought. They roast marshmallows on sticks until the bag is empty.

It's almost dawn when Kathy sends everyone home. She wants to clean the site alone. She wants to say a last goodbye to her old self, she tells them, the one that had anything to do with Doug. She stirs up the ashes. Dulled safety pins, bits of melted buttons and sequins are all that's left.

"That'll do," Kathy says to the air. By the time she starts her car, the black sky is turning grey.

Pete never showed and Kathy's ashamed for wanting him so badly when he clearly didn't want her. Her eyes ache with unshed tears, from lack of sleep, from too much beer and dope, from the let-down after so much anticipation. Some of the unshed tears are relief at having time to rethink their plan to start an affair. Though she'd intended to, and she knows she'll have to live with her intention even if she doesn't ever sleep with Pete, she hadn't yet betrayed anyone.

She hopes Pete will at least tell her what happened. Cold feet, perhaps. Or maybe he and Lunch Box Man got stoned; she sees them shooting the shit at the kitchen table, and suddenly it's too late to go anywhere. Maybe Lunch Box Man refused to bring Pete to the park. She shrugs a no-matter shrug, and stops to check for traffic before turning onto the road. The sun slips above the horizon and separates the sky, a huge swath of pale grey above a thin line of molten magenta.

"Red sky in morning," she says.

Kathy pulls into the driveway and parks close to the house. She notices the aluminum door moving ever so slightly and ever so slowly back and forth. When she gets out of the car she sees the inside door is open, too, about halfway.

She walks to the front of the car and leans her hand on the warm hood. She softly calls to Pete, but he doesn't answer. She isn't expecting him to. It's early and he should be asleep, but it's more than that. The morning breeze is gentle and fresh and the door is moving in and out.

She walks to it and waits. The sun slices the shadow between the houses, draws a line through the driveway, half light, half dark. She waits and watches the door move, an inch this way, an inch that way and back again.

Kathy's already sure there's nothing she wants to see on the other side of that door. She should get back in her car and go to her mother's. Instead she opens the outside door enough to slip inside. The house is quiet, an ordinary quiet. Pete's just waking, about to get up to shower before he puts the coffee on and makes some toast.

She takes the three steps up from the landing and there he is. He's facing her, lying on his side, left leg pulled up, right leg straight and turned out. His right arm rests on his chest; the left is thrown out upon the floor, the palm cupped toward the ceiling. His eyes are open, fixed. His mouth is slack, his tongue a swollen purple thing between his lips. Kathy's hockey stick lies near his feet, the broken blade still held to the shaft with hockey tape. Pete's face is recognizable, but what Kathy can see of the rest of his head is a non-shape, a pulpy mass of skin, bone and blood.

Kathy turns from him, takes the three steps down to the landing and the seven to the basement. She counts to keep from thinking, one-two-three-four-five-six-seven. She goes into the bathroom. There on the shelf is her deodorant and Barry's almost-empty bottle of aftershave, the green bath towel she used yesterday askew on the rack, the rubber bathmat over the side of the tub. Two toothbrushes, one pink and one yellow, sit in a juice glass on the rust-pitted metal shelf above the sink. An open tube of Crest, the cap upside-down beside it, rests near the glass. A curled green elastic with blonde hair sticking from it lies by the toothpaste. It's all as she left it.

She takes the green elastic and makes a rough ponytail and leans over the toilet and vomits. After she stops being sick, after she's sure there's nothing left inside her, she flushes the toilet and walks back up the stairs. She stands on the landing and breathes the fresh air coming in the door.

She contemplates leaving and pretending she never came home. But her car is there for all to see. People are waking now, taking their dogs for a walk, picking up newspapers from their front steps, standing on their porches in their pyjamas, yawning and scratching their bellies, checking to see what the weather's like, while Kathy's standing on a landing not ten feet from a dead man, and there's no pretending otherwise.

The aluminum door is still open. She pulls it shut as gently and as quietly as she can. Then she takes one step, and another, and another until she's stepping over Pete. The phone is on the counter near the stove, the receiver dangling from its cord onto the floor. First Kathy hangs up and then she lifts the receiver to her ear. There is a dial tone, so she calls the police. She steps over Pete again and goes outside where she sits in her car and waits for the shit to hit the fan. Which is, of course, exactly what happens.

It isn't just the body on the floor. It's the plates and bowls and cups and glasses smashed around it, the silverware stacked like pick-up-sticks beside an overturned drawer. It's the broken furniture, the emptied hall closet, the tipped-over bookcases. Toys strewn from the toy box, food dumped from the refrigerator, the freezer door left open.

And though she doesn't want to talk to anyone, it's a relief when she hears the police siren, hears the sound of feet coming up the driveway, hears the voice asking her to get out of the car.

Kathy is told to go to her room and wait there. A young policeman is posted at her door. He glances at Freddy, but he doesn't say anything. In fact, until she is asked to come upstairs, after what seems like a very long time later and Pete's body is gone, no one speaks to her. Then it is all words, strings of them, with each sentence ending in a question mark.

There has to be a reason for the death and for the trashed house. Does Kathy know the reason? Is it drugs? Is it money? Is it a combination of the two? Does Pete have enemies? Who else lives here? Where are they? When are the wife and child expected home? Did he get along with his wife? Did she get along with him? Was he having any trouble at work? Is he having an affair? What can you tell us about Pete? Where does he work? Who are his friends? Are his parents alive? Can you tell us what his plans were for the evening before? Can you tell us where you were? Were you there with anyone? Can you give us their addresses and telephone numbers? Why were you out all night?

They write everything down.

Kathy tells them what she knows: She tells them about Al's party and the bonfire she and some friends had at Varnum Park afterwards. She tells them they had some beer and waited for the effects to wear off before driving, that's why she came home in the early morning. She tells them she doesn't know much about Pete's extended family, but that his wife and son are at her family's cottage. No, she tells them, Pete isn't having an affair, or not one she knows about.

She tells them, when pressed, that Pete dealt a little dope, just a bit now and then. But once, she says, that she knew of at least, there was a bigger deal. And she tells them about the airport and about the lunch box full of hashish and the lunch bag full of money. About the handsome muscleman with the acne scars, the one Rachel said she saw at the house the night before.

Kathy tells them what Pete told her at the barbeque, that he'd meet her and her friends at Varnum Park later in the evening. She tells them that Pete never showed up. That when Kathy got home, both the inside and outside doors were open. And when she came inside she found Pete dead.

She tells them how to get hold of Penny and Rhettbutler. Then she asks if she can call her mother. She doesn't want her to hear the news on the radio and worry. They tell her to go right ahead. She dials and Shelly picks up. Kathy can hear cartoons in the background. Shelly doesn't speak, but Kathy hears her breathing.

"Shelly, it's Kathy. Go get Mom."

Shelly doesn't respond, but Kathy can still hear her breathing so she knows she's there.

"Come on, Shelly. Get Mom, please," Kathy tells her.

The breathing stops, the phone clatters to the floor. Kathy can hear Elmer Fudd talking about the pesky wabbit. She can hear cartoon gunshots and Elmer Fudd's groans. That's when she hears Bugs Bunny say, "What's up, Doc?" Then the phone clatters again, but more gently this time.

"Hello? Who is it?" Connie asks. Her voice is sleepy, but anxious.

"It's me, Mom. It's Kathy. Mom, Pete's dead. He's been murdered," Kathy says. And that's when she begins to cry.

KATHY'S SITTING AT THE BACK OF THE VIEWING ROOM. Rhettbutler's sitting beside her, driving his orange Dinky Toy dump truck up and down the pleats of a fake French provincial sofa that's a shade Connie, when she came with Al earlier in the afternoon, described as baby-shit yellow. When Kathy asked her how she could remember after all these years, Connie said some things a mother never forgets.

At Kathy and Rhettbutler's feet, on the yellow and brown shag carpet, is an open metal Mickey Mouse lunch box with more Dinky Toys—three white and blue police cars with red plastic lights, a yellow road grader, a white ambulance, a red farm wagon without a tractor, two Mustangs, one a red convertible, the other a hardtop in black. There's an unopened package of waxed paper-wrapped cookies, maple creams, Rhettbutler's favourite, some carrot sticks in a plastic bag, half a drying-out peanut butter sandwich missing a bite and a small bottle of a juice so violently, artificially pink it hurts the eyes to look at it.

The sofa is flanked by fake French provincial end tables, dark and shiny, sprouting tall tri-light lamps (set on medium-low) with mushroom-cap shades the same off-white as the walls. Beneath the lamps, fanned out for easy picking, are prayer cards with Pete's demographics, 1946–1970, a short prayer beginning, *Let not your hearts be troubled*, and an invocation garnering the invoker time off their stay in purgatory. On the front, a long-haired and decidedly hippie-looking Jesus exposes his Sacred Heart. Beside the prayer cards sit boxes of tissues of a pinky-beige colour reserved for plastic doll's skin, and the same shade as the foundation on Pete's face, except where two rosy ovals have been dabbed on his cheeks.

Penny and Pete's mother—his father died of a heart attack when Pete was seventeen, Pete's mother told Kathy this afternoon—his brother, Ray, Penny's parents and her two sisters are up at the front of the room with the casket, which is open and surrounded by flowers. They cry and welcome visitors, who cry with them, dabbing at tears with available tissues, asking how Pete could have been murdered. Who could have done this to such a sweet and gentle man? They exclaim how lucky it is that Penny and Rhettbutler were away for they, too, might have been killed. They ask, who is the girl who found him? That's her there, Kathy Rausch, they're told, and they turn to look at Kathy sitting on the sofa at the back of the room with Rhettbutler. Kathy came home from a night out to find Pete's body lying on the kitchen floor.

After they say a few more words to Penny and give her a hug or shake her hand, they move to the casket and look in at Pete. Some of them reach in to touch his arm, or rub the cold rubbery flesh on his hands, which are crossed on his chest. No one touches his face, which actually looks pretty good considering the state of the back of his head when Kathy found him.

Tonight, while Penny's at the funeral home, Kathy's moving into the Deutsche Hotel. This morning, after she made toast and cocoa for Rhettbutler while Penny lay in bed crying, Kathy walked downtown and arranged to rent a room by the month. She's got the key in her pocket. The room overlooks Main Street and contains a double bed, a green chair, a sink, an electric kettle and a two-burner hot plate. The bathroom is down the hall and parking is free, as is the cigarette smoke, courtesy of the bar downstairs. She can get steamed rice or noodles at Tops Chinese around the corner, and newspapers and cigarettes across the street at the Eby Hotel. It will do.

Kathy will tell Connie after the funeral. Connie is beyond worry; she's pissed off. After Kathy stopped crying, the morning she told her mother Pete had been murdered, Connie told her she *had* to move home. When Kathy didn't respond, Connie shouted, "I'm losing patience."

"I have to go, Mom," Kathy told her. "The police need to talk to me."

Connie cried then, loudly and without restraint.

"I'm sorry," Kathy said, and very gently and very quietly placed the receiver in its cradle.

It would be smart to move in with Connie and Shelly, but smart's not the way Kathy feels these days. Being near her mother, even if she never said a word, would remind her how un-smart she's been. Connie wants to help Kathy, wants to give her love, which will come wrapped in kindly advice. Kathy doesn't want anything from her or from anyone, kindness least of all. Pete's dead. She didn't have sex with him, but she was going to. Because Pete was murdered doesn't change the fact they'd made a plan the morning of Al's barbeque.

When Kathy had come up to make breakfast that morning, Pete was at the table, the newspaper spread out in front of him. He looked up from the paper and as she poured her coffee, he held out his cup. He set his cup on the table and while she poured, ran his hand along the back of her thigh. Her arm weakened; the coffee pot dipped. Pete took the pot from her and set it on the table. He took her arm, and very gently pulled her to him, then down to sit on his lap. And he kissed her, pushing her hair away from her face.

When he finished he said, "Tonight."

Not a question. Not a command. He said what she'd been hoping. And she nodded, and got up, put bread in the toaster, waited for it to pop, buttered it, put one piece on a plate for her, one on a plate for Pete. She sat down to eat and read the newspaper. Pete ate his toast, and when he left to run errands, Kathy's toast was still on her plate and she had not read one word in the paper.

He hadn't kissed her again; he'd walked past her, down three steps to the landing, opened the door and walked out. When the aluminum door closed, he was gone.

While he was gone Kathy changed the sheets on her bed; she had a shower and washed her hair. She put on new underwear she'd bought but never worn, silk, a blue like snow in shade. All day she she'd been aware of her underwear, as though it was all she had on.

All day she'd thought about sleeping with Pete. And when she wasn't thinking about sleeping with him, she was trying not to think about sleeping with him.

It's funny, but her desire that day, mixed as it was with fear and anticipation, feels exactly like her sorrow and shame today, as if everything in her body is contracting and will never relax again. She isn't a suspect in the murder, but the police want her to be available to them, to answer questions as they arise, and to identify the man who gave Pete the lunch box. She hopes he has disappeared forever, because if he killed Pete, he could kill her.

There are police in plainclothes circulating at the funeral home. Kathy knows who they are because they want her to tell them if she recognizes anyone from other drug transactions. Kathy figures if the narcotics agents know as much as they say they know, they'll recognize everyone she knows without her help. She's not inclined to turn informant, except for Lunch Box Man, and she's sure the police will know him from her description if he showed up for the funeral.

But he doesn't show up for the funeral. Penny's there, standing beside the pew reserved for family. She's unable to settle, sits and rubs the tops of her legs, then gets up to move around. She's wearing a black peasant dress with a red crocheted shawl, black stockings even though it's hot, and red leather platform shoes. Kathy used to covet those shoes. Rhettbutler is attached to Penny's dress, a tail to her kite. When she sits, he's under her, squirming to the side.

Pete and Penny's families arrive to sit with Penny and Rhettbutler. Scattered through the church are school friends, neighbours—Mr. Vanderbergen and Helen and Willie Szasz among them. Teach, wifeless as usual, sits with Pete's many colleagues and clients from the university. Connie and Al and Margaret and Darlyn and Donny and Barry and Rachel—they're all there.

There are bikers who have arrived in their colours. Pete used to ride with them before he and Penny had Rhettbutler. There are cops in uniform, some in suits and others dressed like hippies, but they all look like cops. Patrolmen sit in cars across the road from the church and take pictures. There are people no one seems to know. And there are the reporters who have been asked respectfully by Pete's brother to remain outside during the service. They stand on the steps smoking cigarettes. Their smoke drifts into the church.

There are the people across the street, the gawkers and the curious, wearing shorts and old T-shirts, setting up lawn chairs on the boulevard. People drive by slowly, trying to figure out what's going on. A car stops and a man asks, "Whose funeral is this?" A gawker says, "The guy who got murdered."

Kathy stands at the open door, neither in the church nor out, and as far away from Pete as she can be. His casket is closed now, a cascade of roses over the top, bouquets arranged on plinths around him, more on the steps to the altar. Incense smoulders, votives in red and white glass flicker, servers light the altar candles.

That morning at the final farewell for family and close friends, before the casket lid was closed and screwed down for good, Penny came to Kathy and said, "Pete didn't love you."

"I know," Kathy told her. "He was only a friend."

At that moment, Kathy wanted to believe there had never been anything between them. There had only been that one kiss. She wanted to believe it with all her heart, so that Penny would feel better. Because someone had to feel better; it was crap feeling this terrible.

Penny really looked at Kathy then, hard and long, with the eyes Pete loved.

"He was my friend," Kathy said, pleading, fighting back the whine in her voice, "that's all."

"I'm glad you moved out before I had to ask," Penny said.

She walked away, her glossy black hair swaying across her back. The hair Pete loved, the waist, the breasts. Penny took Rhettbutler's hand and they went up to see Pete one last time. Kathy watched as they stood on the kneeler in front of the casket, Rhettbutler teetering, holding onto her dress. Penny leaned in and kissed Pete. Then she lifted Rhettbutler and as he rose, Penny's dress rose too, her thick legs exposed. Like fat black sausages, Kathy thought.

Kathy was on her way to the washroom when Teach, who had been hovering through her conversation with Penny, caught up.

"Pete did love you, Kathy," he said to her. "And I love you."

Teach was crying, inching closer and closer to her. "He loved your strong body and your naiveté. He told me, Kathy. He told me everything."

He reached out and took hold of her sleeve.

"Fuck off," Kathy said, and she shook him loose. "Fuck right off."

She walked away, along the corridor, past other reception rooms filled with mourners gathered around bodies in caskets whose lids would be screwed down so nothing could get in, and, God forbid, anything could get out. She walked to the door, she opened it. Breathe, she told herself. Breathe.

Fall, 1970

No matter. Try again. Fail again. Fail better.
                                        — *Samuel Beckett*

KATHY SITS CROSS-LEGGED ON HER BED WEARING DEAD-MAN'S clothes, the blue silk I'm-going-to-sleep-with-Pete-tonight underwear that now bags at the bum and an oversized men's undershirt worn so thin it takes on the pink of her skin. It was her father's, rescued from a brown paper bag of his clothes she found in the basement after he died. Clothes too old and worn, or too personal to give to the Salvation Army, that Connie meant to throw in the garbage. Kathy used to keep the undershirt in her dresser drawer, taking it out when she chanced on it, sniffing it, searching for her father's scent. Now she wears it all the time and it smells like her.

Kathy wonders whether, if Charlie had lived—Pete, too, for that matter—she would have noticed similarities between them. If there had been something of her father in Pete that attracted her to him. Perhaps she'd noticed how comfortable Pete seemed inside his body, so like her father's laid-back physicality and the way he did things with complete self-assurance. Doug had a bit of it too, she could see that now, at least when he was skating. And Bobby. Bobby Orr *is* Mr. Self-Assured.

Or maybe she had some distant memory of how her father and mother had been together, feisty and passionate, a little edgy, that was echoed in Pete and Penny's marriage, and that she wanted, too. It's all speculation now, a bit of a spin she tries not to indulge, though the thoughts sneak up on her now and then. That's when she tries to find a rink open to skate them away.

She's going skating in an hour, but right now she's reading her horoscope: *Whatever in your life that you dream of changing—and there must be something—now is the time to stop dreaming and start doing.*

She laughs out loud. Connie must have paid the paper to place it, a public service announcement directed at her daughter. It sounds so much like her that Kathy cuts it out and tapes it to the wall above her bed, next to articles about Jimi Hendrix and Janis Joplin. "Jimi Hendrix Dies of Drug Overdose" one says, and "Stars Pay Tribute: Hendrix Was Rock Innovator" says another, in which Janis Joplin tells the reporter that Jimi's a good friend of hers, and she'll miss him. Then Janis cries, the article says. Should have been crying for herself, Kathy thinks, because the article next to it announces Janis's death, *heroin and drug overdose*, it says.

So Kathy's is a wall of infamy and woe, for, accompanying the items about dead rock stars, she posts the weekly drug bust list, published every Friday in *The Recorder*, a Who's Who of Varnum youth. The lucky ones have charges withdrawn, the unlucky wait to be sentenced. Some get fines, on average about $300 for possessing a bit of marijuana or hashish or a tab or two of LSD for personal use, and some are put on probation, usually a year. But all of the convicted will have criminal records.

She doesn't save the articles about Pete. Lunch Box Man has disappeared, and there are no new leads and no other suspects, so there isn't much coverage anymore. There's a reward for information that appears in the classifieds every Monday, $1000 posted by Pete's family and co-workers at the university, some of whom should be worried their own names will show up in the investigation. Kathy still cries though, for Pete and Penny and Rhettbutler. For herself. She cries for Jimi, who played guitar like fury, and for Janis, whose big voice, so full of cigarettes and bourbon and grief, is silent.

Every day she cries for some reason: when the guy at the Smoke Shop gives her a free newspaper, when Darlyn brings her groceries and *Sports Illustrated* with an article about Bobby Orr, and when Shelly gives her a drawing, all in purple crayon, her favourite colour these days. She cried last week when she heard on the radio that some crazy FLQ guys had taken another hostage, first the Liberation Cell had kidnapped James Cross, and now the Chénier Cell has kidnapped Pierre Laporte.

Kathy pulls on her jeans, raggedy bellbottoms filthy from dragging on the ground. She's skinny these days and her jeans hang off her. There on the floor is the tie-dyed T-shirt she wears over her undershirt. She finds her skating socks in her hockey bag, and pulls her Kodiaks over them. She leaves the boots untied; she'll be taking them off at the rink soon. She hauls on a navy-blue wool sweater, tucks her hair under a Greek fisherman's cap and wraps a scarf around her neck. She grabs her puck bag and the stick leaning against the wall, and she's off.

"You look like shit," Connie says. She gets up from her reading chair and the newspaper slips from her lap. "You're skin and bones."

She hugs Kathy and when she pulls away says, "And you smell like shit, too."

"Good clean sweat," Kathy says. "I'll take a shower after skating. When I get home."

"That room you live in is not a home, and don't you dare call it that. This is a home," she says, throwing her arm out.

"Mom," Kathy warns.

"I certainly hope you take a shower," Connie says, giving in.

"Where's Shelly?" Kathy asks. "I thought I'd take her skating."

"Al took her to the library. They have an evening puppet program for kids on Tuesdays. Al found out about it and decided to give it a whirl. Turns out she likes puppets. Al says she sits all by herself at the edge of the group and doesn't move a muscle during the entire show. Hardly even blinks. The best part is she doesn't mind going with Al, so it gives me a break."

"Far out," Kathy says. "I'll head out then."

"Do you want a coffee? Water's hot."

"I'll miss the skate if I do," Kathy says. "Sorry."

When she kisses her mother goodbye, Connie says, "Shower."

As she backs out of Connie's driveway, Kathy turns up the heat and clicks on the radio. The heater cranks out dust on a blast of cold air, and the radio an interview with Pierre Trudeau.

"Sir, what is it with all these men and guns around us?" the reporter asks.

Kathy puts the car in gear and listens while she drives. The reporter presses Trudeau about his reasons for calling in the troops. Why can't the police deal with the situation, he wants to know.

"I still go back to the choice that you have to make in the kind of society that you live in," the reporter says.

"Yes, well, there's a lot of bleeding hearts around who don't like to see people with helmets and guns. All I can say is, go ahead and bleed, but it's more important to keep law and order in this society than to be worried about weak-kneed people who don't like the looks of..."

The reporter is insistent, "At any cost? How far would you go with that? How far would you extend that?"

"Well, just watch me," Trudeau says.

Of course Kathy cries, but the kidnappings and Trudeau's threat seem to her no more and no less senseless than rock stars living so hard and fast they kill themselves, or getting fired for wanting to be in a union, or a friend's murder. Or Shelly being born the way she is, for that matter, and their father dying. The only thing Kathy understands right now is skating. When she skates, uncertainty and sadness evaporate. There are no tears on the ice, only movement, only this foot and this foot and this.

So every chance she gets, she skates. For as long as she's allowed, one hour, two hours, occasionally a whole glorious morning or afternoon or evening. She skates with school kids, with mothers and toddlers, with retirees. If she's lucky, she's almost alone on the ice, though it hardly matters. People are nothing more than markers placed on the ice to test her skill. She doesn't hear the music over the loudspeakers, only the booming of her heart, the blood pulsing to her muscles.

Today she's skating at Sand Hills Arena, but it never matters where. She laces up and strides onto the ice with her stick, holding it comfortably, loosely, knees bent, weight well forward. She circles with the recreational skaters, then she skates to the middle of the ice and sets down her stick. She does stops and starts, back and forth in the confined space. She maps small circles, making fast tight turns, round and round clockwise. Reverse. Round and round counterclockwise. Reverse.

When she's sweating, she slows, grabs her stick and widens the turns until she joins the other skaters again. She skates backwards to their forwards, looking over her shoulder, weaving in and out and around them, always aware but hardly noting their presence. She waggles her hips, fluid and sweet, keeps her seat over the ice, keeps her legs flexible. Just like Bobby.

The Recorder says he's a natural, says he works hard, and follows his instincts and that's why he's a winner, a record breaker and a trophy holder. On skates he's exceptional in every way, reporters say, and he owns every inch of the ice. When he speaks to the press, he doesn't say *me* or *I*, he says *we*, and we means the Boston Bruins. You don't win the Stanley Cup alone, he said.

Kathy bought a ticket to a pre-season game at the Aud, Boston and New York. The place was packed, boys mostly, and some girls who came to watch the boys. The kids blocked the entrances when the players arrived. They shouted and jostled and held out sticks and hats and hockey shirts and programs, anything for their favourite players to sign. Kathy watched and waited for Bobby.

But he didn't show. An injured wrist, the announcer said. Phil Esposito wasn't there either, and Johnny Bucyk was recovering from a boating accident. Don Awrey was a no-show, and Derek Sanderson and Ed Westfall were both unsigned for the 1970-71 season, so they couldn't play. If it hadn't been for Johnny McKenzie of the Rangers bowling over a few Bruins to let Ken Hodge score the tying goal making it 2-2, the game would have been a colossal bore.

Kathy doesn't hold it against Bobby and hopes his wrist heals in time for the season opener. But just once she wishes she could see all of the Boston Bruins play. And while she's wishing, she wishes she could see them play on home ice so she could watch Bobby Orr perform his magic in the Garden to a home-town crowd.

Meanwhile, she skates. When she's not skating, she looks for work—checkout girl, meat wrapper, nurse's aide, janitor's assistant at her old high school, anything that shows up in the Help Wanted (Female) ads. She fills out applications and occasionally gets an interview. She waits for the call, and while she waits, she skates some more.

"LARRY WANTS TO TALK TO YOU."

The speaker is a woman, youngish and round, in too-tight ski pants and an orange sweater that reaches her knees. She minces on dyed-orange figure skates that look too small for her size and plunks herself down on the bench beside Kathy, who is unlacing her skates.

"I'm Bev and I'm gonna die if I don't get outta these." She stretches her legs out and lifts her orange skates in the air. They bob near Kathy's head.

"The doctor told me to lose weight," she tells Kathy. "I used to compete, trained for figures here. I've still got the moves, but it just about kills me.

"Don't ever have a baby," she groans. "I was your size and now look at me."

"It is good exercise," Kathy says. She sits up and looks at Bev, whose dimples are the size of dimes. Kathy wipes the blades of her skates with the end of her scarf. She bends to tie her boots.

"Who wants to talk to me?" She turns her face up to Bev to ask.

"Larry, my old compulsory figures instructor," Bev says. Her dimples wink as she speaks. "I'd better warn you, he swears." She laughs and adds, "A lot. But he's harmless.

"He says you're a pretty good skater. That's a compliment, because he doesn't say much about skaters, just tells them what to do."

"What's he want?"

Bev shrugs. "Just told me to say he'll be waiting outside the door."

Kathy ties her skates together and grabs her puck bag and stick. As she walks to the door the woman calls, "You *are* good. We all watch you out there."

Larry's all hard angles and bones. He buttons his jean jacket up to his neck so that it squeezes his Adam's apple, and his jean legs look empty. He sucks on a cigarette, coughs, spits to the side, takes one more drag, drops the cigarette and mashes it with his foot.

"Larry Wilkins," he says on the exhale.

"Yes?" Kathy says.

"You are?" he asks.

"Kathy Rausch."

"Want a job, Kathy Rausch?"

"Wouldn't say no, but you better tell me what you have in mind," Kathy says, and as the words come out of her mouth, she can't believe she's saying them, when all she should be saying is, yes. Perhaps it's because she's trying so hard not to cry.

"Let's get a coffee and go to my office," Larry says. He's shivering, his entire body shuddering in spasms. "Fucking freezing out here."

The sign on the door says CUSTODIAN. Either Larry's the janitor or he shares the space with him. Inside are scrub buckets and mops, cleaning fluids and folded rags. There's an industrial sink, and a drain in the middle of the floor.

"Earn more if I did that," Larry says, pointing his thumb at the pails and brooms. "This is my side. Have a seat."

Larry's side is spartan: an ancient table-cum-desk and two rusty metal chairs. An orderly pile of tattered hockey programs sits on one corner of the table, a dirty mug and a clean ashtray on the other.

"This here antique was made in Canada," Larry says, tapping the table. "Top made of Arborite developed in Cornwall, Ontario. Now don't go thinking I'm smart; I only know that because my son is smart. He's an engineer and he's helping set up a new Arborite plant in Vaughan. Told me this table is worth something these days. I found it at the dump. I like to salvage things; don't really care what, so long as it's useful."

A pair of skates, laces tied together, hangs on an otherwise empty hall tree beside the door. The room is at least 100 degrees. Kathy strips off her hat, scarf and sweater and takes off her boots. She fans herself with an old Junior B game program, one from the pile sitting on the table.

"Be careful with that," Larry says. "It's antique too, from Wally Tkaczuk's first game."

Larry visibly relaxes in the heat, like Freddy when he's content.

"I spend most of my time in cold arenas and on the ice," he tells Kathy when she remarks on the heat. "I'm such a skinny fucker I'm always chilled to the bone, so I come in here to get warm. Really warm. When I retire I'm moving to Florida with all those fat Quebecers. That'll be me, baking on the fucking beach, saying *excusez moi*, don't block my sun."

They talk then. Larry says he's offering Kathy a job assisting with his compulsory figures classes—Larry was once a competitive figure skater. Says he'd rather have played hockey, but he was on the small side back then. Unlike now, he says, and laughs. He figured what would be the point of getting killed, so he switched to figure skating. Damn near gave his father a heart attack when he told him. Called him a faggot. But he got over it.

Now he teaches and does some coaching, has a summer camp like Howie Meeker. Only he wishes he was half as smart as Howie. He asks Kathy if she knew Howie retired from playing hockey just last year, but didn't wait for Kathy to answer, told her Howie was forty-fucking-five. They were born the same year.

Kathy will also help teach girls how to skate like boys, that's how Larry puts it, while he teaches boys how to skate like girls.

"The girls come in here wanting to be Barbara fucking Ann Scott. I want them to be better than that. I want them to know all about skating, not just fucking figure skating. I want them to know how to stop without picks, not to rely on them. Boys who learn figures, and there are too fucking few, let me tell you, know how to skate on hockey skates because that's how they learned to skate. Girls never get the same fucking chance."

Kathy has never heard so many fucks said at one time. They flow like a river and seem just as natural. She isn't too appalled, really, but it's hard not to laugh, partly from embarrassment, but mostly in delight at the dazzle of Larry's linguistic repertoire. Not to mention that this man is offering her a job.

"But you'd better fucking believe," he continues, "that compulsory figures are going the way of the fucking dodo. I can see that dance is taking over and soon guys like me won't have fucking jobs. It will be about choreography, so fucking dancers will teach skaters, instead of skaters like us teaching them. But for now I teach fucking figures, and I need help, and I'd like you to fucking well help me.

"Excuse my fucking French," he says. "I get emotional."

Kathy can start in the new year, he tells her. He's got to set up the classes, get the newspaper ads ready and let the city recreation department know so they can budget for the classes and set up their schedules and announcements. Their paycheques come from the city, and they're union employees. He hopes she doesn't mind a union, some people do, he says.

They'll also teach lessons contracted by local skating clubs. For that he rents ice time and charges clubs accordingly. He does some private lessons, but he'll continue those on his own for now. If Kathy's still around when he wants to retire, he'll turn them over to her. Or she can go out and get her own students. Why not? No skin off his fucking nose.

If everything goes as planned, and the courses and lessons are well received, and Kathy does a good job—Larry says sometimes the ones who can really skate can't teach—then Kathy will have a permanent job. Or as permanent as jobs are these days. He tells her he's been watching her warm up and do her routines for weeks now. He says she's pretty fucking good.

He says he'll get the boys he coaches at his summer camp to accept a girl, leastways a girl as good as Kathy. It's the parents who might object. But he'll fix that. He'll just fucking well tell them. It's the kids who count anyway.

There are two kinds of kids who give up their summer to hockey, he tells her. The ones whose parents—the father usually—want their kid to play. Make a man of him or become a big star. Shit like that. And there are the kids who are keeners, the kind who beg their parents to let them come to camp. The ones like Kathy, who love to skate and love the game. The naturals. They're the ones he enjoys coaching most. They listen and they work hard, and he can see them improve dramatically over the summer.

They talk a little hockey, the Leafs not being up to the Bruins, the Bruins' win this year, the trades, what expansion is doing to the game. What might happen next season. He asks Kathy who her favourite player is and she tells him Bobby Orr. She tells him she liked him before Boston won the cup, before he became famous. He says good choice; he can see now where her technique comes from.

He wonders if Bobby'll last. Those knees, he says. He's gotta take care of those knees. He says he likes Boston, likes some of the quieter players, less flash and dance, the solid ones like Don Awrey, who he'd want on defence if he was playing for the team. Solid body checker, Larry says. Excellent puck blocker.

By the time Larry's finished, Kathy's damp socks are piled with her sweater and scarf on top of her boots, and she's rolled up the legs of her jeans. Larry still has his jacket done up to the neck. While she puts on her sweaty clothes, she gives him her phone number at the hotel. (He tells her he's had a few beers in the bar there, and in fact they've probably crossed paths once or twice, but that was then and this is now and they'll fucking well recognize each other next time.) And when he opens the door and the cool arena air rushes in, he shivers, and says fuck.

Once in her car, Kathy closes her eyes and leans her head back on the seat. The sweat's drying and she's chilly, but she doesn't mind. She knows she should tell Connie about the job, but she's not ready. Soon, but not right now. She wants to savour the happiness first. Doesn't want to hear out loud what's in the back of her mind: That it might not work out. That she might not be a good teacher. As Larry said, being a good skater doesn't always mean you can teach.

In the end, Kathy drives to Connie's, who's pretty happy. Not as happy as Kathy, but happy enough to cry. Blubber really, and say, oh, Al, oh, Kathy, oh, Al, oh, Kathy, until Shelly runs around flapping her arms, yelling oh-oh-oh-oh.

"Stop that," Connie shouts at her.

Shelly doesn't, so Kathy tells Al to pour Connie a big rye and take it and her mother to the rec room to watch a little TV. Then she catches Shelly as she runs by and pulls her arms down to her sides and holds her against her body.

"Oh-oh-oh," Shelly yells into Kathy's shoulder.

Kathy lifts her as gently as she can and carries her to her bedroom. She sits on the bed, Shelly rigid in her arms and her feet on the floor, and sh-shushes until Shelly relaxes and her oh-ing becomes a hum. Kathy pulls Shelly up onto the bed and reads to her.

"The night Max wore his wolf suit and made mischief of one kind or another," Kathy reads, *"his mother called him wild thing."*

Shelly listens. Kathy reads the story once, twice and is part way through the third time when she whispers, "Shelly, I got a job. Skating."

Shelly doesn't look at Kathy, doesn't blink even. She waits, so Kathy resumes the story and by the time she's finished, Shelly's asleep. Kathy slips out of Shelly's room and goes into the kitchen and calls Sally and Roy.

"Oh my dear, my dear," Sally says, "that's the finest kind." She shouts to Roy, "Roy, love. Kathy got a job out at Sand Hills Arena. She's going to be a hockey skating instructor."

Kathy talks to Roy, who tells her he always had faith in her. And she knows that's true, knows he always did. She thanks him for all of his help and kindness and asks if he would like to come and watch her first class, to give her some pointers. He says he'd be delighted, but he'll wait until she's over the first-day jitters. When she hangs up, Kathy sits a minute, listens to the muffled sound of the TV coming up the stairs from the basement, listens to the sigh of wind outside the kitchen window. Then she heads down to Connie and Al.

"Thanks for putting Shelly to bed, honey," Connie says when Kathy joins them in the rec room.

"Congratulations, Kathy," Al says, and he comes over and gives a little bow and shakes her hand. His formality makes her laugh.

"Yes, congratulations, Kathy," Connie says and she gets up and does the same thing. They bow and shake hands and laugh until they're tired of the joke and Connie turns up the TV. News of course, sports, Toronto beat Detroit 3-2.

"Guess I better figure this game out," Connie says, "if I'm going to offer a critique of your work."

Kathy looks at her mother.

"Just kidding," Connie says. "Really. I'm very happy you got a job with the city. I'm surprised it's teaching skating, that's all.

"But proud," she adds quickly. "In fact, I'm so happy I think we should have a party. No barbequing this time," she says looking over at Al and winking. "A nice party with a few friends."

They set a date—the day of the Santa Claus Parade, because it's the last time Darlyn's going to twirl. She's hanging up her baton. Too old, she's decided. They'll have a double celebration, a new job and a retirement.

When Kathy leaves, Connie hugs her and says, "You may have a job, but you still need a shower."

And that's exactly what she's going to do, go home, have a shower and crawl into bed. Al will tell Darlyn and Donny the news, and she'll call Barry tomorrow. He and Rachel had moved into an apartment together, and without telling her parents, got married at City Hall. The wedding's still on, though. Too far along to stop, and too much money spent already, her parents say. At least married, Rachel isn't living in sin.

Kathy misses Barry, misses talking to him. The last time she called, he said he'd visited Penny and Rhettbutler. Penny was still in pretty bad shape. Angry at Pete, and more angry at his so-called friends and drug buddies. Except Teach. Teach hangs around and helps the grieving widow. He was there when Barry visited. Mr. Altruistic. Barry thinks Teach has the hots for Penny, thinks the elusive Mrs. Markham with an 'h' had better watch out. Barry said he figured he was on the outs with Penny when she asked him to leave five minutes after he got there.

Teach walked him to the door. He said he knew Barry had been sleeping with Kathy. Pete told him. Pete wasn't angry about it or anything. He loved Kathy. Hell, they all loved Kathy, Teach said. But Barry had been the lucky one.

He asked Barry how Kathy was doing. Did she have a new boyfriend? Would it be a good idea for Teach to call her? He said Pete would have wanted him to look after Kathy, just the way he was looking after Penny. Barry told him, no, don't call. That's when Teach told Barry that Penny had asked him to kill Freddy, so he'd crated him—no easy task—and taken him to the university and euthanized him. He said Penny was grateful; she said she always hated that fucking snake.

KATHY CAN HEAR A MARCHING BAND. SHE TOSSES THE NEWSPAPER to the floor. She's been reading about British Trade Commissioner James Cross's captivity. He was finally released by the FLQ on Thursday after being held for sixty days. A long time, she thinks, but better than being executed like Pierre Laporte was back in October. His body was found stuffed into the trunk of a car that had been abandoned in the bush near the Saint-Hubert airport a few miles from Montreal.

Her window overlooks Main Street, one of the few things she'll miss when she moves from the hotel the first week in January. She's renting a bed-sit on Church Street, in a big old Victorian house that's been converted to apartments. Kathy checks to see where the parade is. It's been inching along Main Street since 10:00 a.m. when it left Sand Hills Square. The paper said it would be three miles long, culminating in a float with Santa, who would then proceed to greet children at City Hall. Right now the music drifting up the street is martial—bagpipes and drums. Earlier she could make out a giddy "Must Be Santa" played at a quick-march tempo.

Bobby Gimby'll be leading school kids singing endless repetitions of Ca-na-da (one little, two little, three Canadians), we love you. It might have been cute during Expo '67, but it's tiresome now. There'll be bears in cages, a plethora of politicians in fur coats sitting on the back ledges of convertibles with scantily clad girls, Miss This and Miss That. Darlyn's twirling, of course, one of many twirling, but she's leading the whole shebang. Darlyn Smola, #1 in North America. Her swan song, she told Kathy, so she's going out on a high note.

She and Donny are renting a tiny house with a tiny turret on the Sand Hills part of Main Street, not far from the Rue. Kathy meets them for a beer sometimes. Sometimes they go to The Black Swan to hear Perth County Conspiracy and sometimes to the Ground Inn where Paul Woolner plays with his little band, Kit Carson, or sometimes Joe Hall wails sad-funny songs. Sometimes Kathy stays over with them, but usually she goes home. She's getting used to her own company.

It's cloudy, 40°, a decent enough day for a parade. Afterwards, Kathy's meeting Darlyn and Donny. They'll pick up Shelly and they're all going to Pioneer Village, which is hosting a parade day celebration of carolling with demonstrations of old-time holiday activities. And after that, they're heading over to Connie's for her famous warm potato salad and sausages cooked in sauerkraut. The fart supper, Connie calls it, the big blow-out.

Roy and Sally are coming. Al will be there, of course. Margaret's been invited and may or may not come. There's a weekend-long feminist conference with a lesbian folk singer coming up from the States. Margaret doesn't think she'll have the energy to make polite conversation and dinner-time small talk, or to be nice to men, meaning Al and Donny. Men still come in for it from Margaret, particularly after she's been to a conference or a consciousness-raising session, though she remains kind enough to Al.

The music's louder and it's familiar. Darlyn did say she was working on a new routine and the music was presenting a challenge. She'd found a band, she said. They were going to play from a small float just behind her. It won't be Christmasy, she'd warned, and she'd fought with the parade coordinators to get her way. The only reason they're letting her perform her new routine is because it's her last.

Kathy can see her now, and she can hear the band. They sing, fast time, words like bullets propelled by drum beats, horns and guitars.

When Darlyn reaches the hotel, she stops. Music bounces off the buildings, angry and alive. She marches in place. Her baton flies into the air and she spins twice and catches it, her red tights blur, the double row of fringe on her white bolero jacket shakes and shimmies.

She struts and the red tassels on her marching boots bounce. Her tiny green skirt flares and her ponytails flies.

Kathy opens her window.

"Darlyn," she calls, "you're the best!" She whistles and whoops.

"Kathy," she hears below her. When she looks down, Donny shouts, "I'm coming up."

Darlyn twirls, front to back and front again; twirls hand to hand, tosses the baton and spins, catches it one-handed behind her back. She brings it under one leg, then the other, back and forth, faster and faster, until it's in front again and she throws the baton high into the air, kneels, and while she's kneeling, arms wide, waiting for her baton, she looks up at Kathy and grins.

The music hammers. She catches the baton, jumps up and spins in a circle, twirling the baton in front of her as she turns. When she's facing forward again, she rests the baton in the crook of her arm, marches in place, arms pumping, back straight, knees high, up-down-up. The band plays behind her; she turns to them and bows. She marches backwards, then spins around, leads them, and the parade is moving again.

Kathy claps. The crowd claps. They all cheer. As Darlyn marches out of sight, Donny comes in the door.

"Kathy," he says. "Grab your coat. We're meeting Darlyn at the City Hall parking lot. We'll take off from there."

Pioneer Village is one of Shelly's favourite places; when they drive up, she's rocking from foot to foot holding the door handle, back and forth like a wind-up toy. She's wearing her favourite winter parka, shiny red nylon, the hood tied so tight her face looks like a cabbage, crinkled eyes, lumpy cheeks, doubled chin.

"Is your hood too tight, sweetie?" Kathy asks. She pulls the door open.

"Ha-ha-ha," Shelly laughs and runs past Kathy to the car. She opens the back door, gets in and pulls the door shut. She sits back against the seat and puts her hands behind her head. Darlyn, who is in the back seat, turns to speak to her, but Shelly looks straight ahead and doesn't answer.

"She's been dressed to go and waiting at the door for twenty minutes," Connie says as she joins Kathy. They look out at the car. They begin to speak together.

"I'm not late, am…"

"Supper at 5:30…"

"No, you're not late," Connie says, "and supper's at 5:30. There's no holding Shelly back when she wants something. She did up the hood herself. She learned to tie a bow the other day. She might forget how tomorrow, but for now everything with two dangling ends gets turned into a bow."

"I'll see if I can loosen it," Kathy says. "We'll be back by 5:30 at the latest."

Al walks from his house across the driveway and opens Shelly's door. He leans in to talk to Darlyn. Shelly doesn't move, doesn't even acknowledge him.

"You'd better get going," Connie says.

"Hey, Mr. Smola," Kathy says as she nears the car.

"Al. Call me Al," he says.

"I don't think I can," Kathy tells him.

When Kathy starts the car, Shelly leans forward, puts her hands on the seat in front of her and laughs, ha-ha-ha, just a sound, over and over. Once they're out of the driveway, she quiets, leans back, hands behind her head again, and doesn't move until the car stops at the Village.

It's very overcast now, still not too cold. Kathy tries to convince Shelly to take her hood off but she runs to the admission booth and waits there. A woman in period dress hands them a list of events and demonstration times. The place is busy, families moving in packs. Kathy wishes she had some way of hanging on to Shelly, who can't abide holding hands.

Shelly doesn't seem to notice the crowds. She heads straight for the harness shop, always her first stop. People make way for her as if they know she's special. Kathy can't keep up and is glad Shelly's in red so she can see her at least.

"You guys do what you want and I'll meet you at the gift shop at four," she tells Darlyn and Donny, and she's off, following the red hood.

In front of the harness shop, a pair of enormous Clydesdales, manes braided with bells on red and green ribbons, stand yoked together. Their tails and the blond feathers over their hooves are brushed so that every hair is distinct and downy. Their keeper, Clarence, explains that each one of their shoes is the size of a dinner plate. That each horse weighs nearly two thousand pounds—almost a ton—and that Clydesdales were originally bred by the Flemish for use as war horses.

During World War II, he tells those gathered, they replaced tractors in many places due to restrictions on fuel. And though they are mostly used for show now, they are still strong and able work horses, and can be seen in fields and forests where they are used in logging operations. These are mares, he tells them. Genevieve on the left, the bigger of the two, is the mother of Deborah on the right. They're a good work team and they enjoy each other's company.

As he speaks, Genevieve and Deborah nod and snort and sway. Their bells tinkle softly. Sometimes they shudder, a ripple of muscled flesh. Deborah lifts her tail and turds the size of bread loaves fall from her bottom. There are giggles and groans, but Deborah just swishes her tail and lifts one foot for a moment, then the other, and is quiet again. A rich sweet scent of fresh dung, like earth and warm fermenting grain, fills the air.

Shelly is standing as close to Clarence and his horses as he'll let her. She doesn't flinch when Deborah shits, doesn't take her eyes from Clarence while he speaks. When he stops, her eyes shift to the horses, and as they sway, so does she. When one lifts a foot, Shelly does too. Kathy pushes through the crowd and leans down to her.

"How about we go into the shop, Shelly?" she says.

Shelly, without acknowledging Kathy, turns from Clarence and the horses and moves to the entrance of the harness shop.

"Clydesdale," she whispers. "Clydes. Dale. Almost-a-ton. Almost-a-ton. Almost-a-ton."

Kathy stands back while Shelly looks at pitchforks and hay bales and bits and saddles. It's peaceful watching her, she's so entirely engrossed. What's in Shelly's eyes when she looks at a pitchfork or a hay bale is the same as what's in them when she looks at Connie or Kathy or Al. There might be curiosity, though it would be hard to tell; Shelly has never asked a question. She seems to run on trust, so what she sees is only exactly what's there. A horse. A sister. A saddle.

Kathy wonders what really goes on in her head. And in her heart. What does she think? What does she feel? How is it she can tolerate being in crowds who brush against her and jostle, but can't bear to hold hands, to be touched in any way—without permission—even by those who love her the most?

Darlyn and Donny poke their heads into the harness shop and smile. Kathy nods in Shelly's direction, and they wave and head out again. Kathy would love to go with them. They're busy these days, Darlyn substitute teaching, and Donny on a contract in Fergus, drywalling an entire new subdivision. He works late and spends too much time driving, but the money is good, he says.

Kathy's dying for a cigarette, but smoking isn't allowed in the buildings. Shelly isn't going anywhere fast, hasn't moved in ten minutes. Kathy slips around the corner of the door and lights up. She has three puffs then grinds the butt into the ground and heads back into the harness shop to see if Shelly is ready to go to the Seibert House, the next stop on her favourite places itinerary.

As Kathy enters, a round-faced woman with red lipstick and teased-up hair leans toward Shelly and says, "Little girl, doesn't your hood hurt your face?"

When she reaches down to loosen it, Shelly screams as only Shelly can: loud, toneless and excruciating. The woman lets go of the hood.

"I didn't do anything," she says to the air. "I didn't hurt her."

Kathy's there in an instant. Shelly is screaming even louder.

"Yes, you did," she says, shoving her face into the woman's, staring at her. The woman stares back. There's terror in her eyes and her red lips are quivering. Kathy's furious, she wants to hit her, even though she knows it isn't her fault.

"She doesn't like to be touched," Kathy says. "It's just the way she is."

By the time she says this she realizes Shelly isn't screaming any more. She turns away from the woman to lean down to Shelly, but Shelly isn't there.

"She ran out," a man says.

Kathy runs out too, sees a red hood dart around the corner of the building, but by the time Kathy gets to where the hood disappeared, there is nothing to see. She runs around the building and still can't see Shelly. She stops. Looks around the crowd, turns and turns and turns. No red hood. No Shelly.

Kathy goes to Clarence and asks if he's seen the little girl in the red parka. No, he says. Kathy shouts, "Has anyone seen a little girl in a red parka?" She shouts it as loud as she can. No one answers, but Darlyn is there and so is Donny.

"Shelly ran away," Kathy tells them. "Did you see her?"

"No," Darlyn says.

Donny runs toward the gift shop. "I'm going to get help."

In no time that is an eternity, groups of people are setting off to look for Shelly. Kathy wants to tell them not to touch her when they find her. Wants to tell them Shelly will hide. She won't talk to them or come when called. But everything is happening too fast. People seem to know that this is an emergency, no ordinary lost child. But they don't know how extraordinary Shelly is.

When an hour has passed, when it's close to five, and the Village is supposed to close, Kathy knows she has to call her mother. Not only to let her know that Shelly is lost, but to have her here in case Shelly's found. Connie is the only one Shelly might respond to, the only voice she will ever answer to now. Kathy knows she should have called her right away, but she wanted to make everything right. Find Shelly, go home, tell the story as if it was nothing. Shelly got lost for a few minutes and we found her again.

When Kathy calls, it takes forever for Connie to answer.

"Mom," Kathy says.

"I was checking the sauerkraut," Connie says.

"Mom," Kathy says again.

"Oh, Kathy,'" Connie says, "What's the matter?"

"Shelly's lost," Kathy tells her.

"Kathy," her mother says and her voice trails off. "Oh, Kathy," she says again. "How could you?"

"Mom..." Kathy says. "Please."

Connie doesn't answer, so there's nothing for Kathy to say. No excuses: I didn't mean it. It wasn't my fault. It only took a minute. No apologies, nothing.

"I'll get Al," Connie finally says. "We'll be there as soon as we can. If you find her, if she's hiding, wait for me. Don't let anyone touch her. Don't you touch her. Just wait until I'm there."

Then there's a click. Kathy holds the receiver. Darlyn takes it from her hand and hangs it up.

"Tell people if they find her, not to touch her," Kathy says.

"Oh, Kathy," Darlyn says, and tries to hug Kathy, but Kathy moves away. Darlyn leaves to find Donny and spread the word.

In the end, it's Kathy who finds her, in the barn, tucked between several loose bales of bedding straw. No one could have seen her, not only because it's almost dark, but because she's jammed herself so far into the bales she's invisible.

Kathy found her when she went into the barn to have a moment alone before her mother arrived. She'd asked Darlyn to keep an eye out. To call her when she saw Al's car. She needed time to compose herself, to remind herself she was responsible so she wouldn't be tempted to make excuses.

Kathy was leaning against a horse stall, thinking, trying not to cry, when she heard, "Almost-a-ton. Almost-a-ton." Not really hearing the words, but the rhythm of them, a flash in memory of having heard them before.

"Almost-a-ton."

Kathy goes to the barn door and tells Darlyn, says to make sure to thank everyone, but to ask them to leave. And to tell Connie where they are.

Then, like that, Connie's beside her. Kathy points to the back of the barn.

"Back there," she mouths.

Connie's holding a flashlight, motes of dust drifting through the beam. She turns it off and the darkness is entire.

"Honey," Connie says making her way slowly to the back of the barn. "Shelly, honey."

Connie keeps walking and talking until her foot hits a bale. She kneels.

"Shelly," she says again.

There's a rustle, nothing more.

"Shelly."

"Help me," Connie calls to Kathy.

Together they lift away lengths of straw, as carefully as if they were glass. Their eyes adjust to the dark, so they can see, but only just. And there she is, lying quietly, face sideways, still scrunched by her parka hood. Connie sits beside her.

"I'm here," she says. She reaches out her hand, but Shelly moves away.

Then Shelly's standing. "Almost-a-ton," she says, and she turns from them and walks toward the lighted doorway.

Kathy will drive Connie and Shelly home. Al will take Darlyn and Donny. Shelly walks in front of them to the car and gets in the back, just as she did last time. She shuts the door. When Connie tries to get in back with her, she screams, so Connie gets in front with Kathy.

They don't speak during the drive home. When they arrive, Shelly gets out of the car and walks into the house. They follow her. The house is hot, filled with the smell of sauerkraut and meat.

Once inside, Connie takes command. Al is to turn the oven to low; Donny and Darlyn are to set the table. She tells Shelly she's going to give her a bath. Shelly doesn't protest but goes into the bathroom and undresses while Connie runs the water. Kathy stands in the doorway. Connie turns from the tub and asks her to go out, and please shut the door.

Kathy goes to Connie's bedroom and lies on her mother's bed. She listens as her mother bathes her sister. Listens as Connie makes soothing noises, as she pours water over Shelly, listens to her there-

thereing while Shelly hums "almost-a-ton." She listens to Donny and Darlyn and Al move around the kitchen and dining room, hears the murmur of their voices. She listens as her mother takes Shelly to her room and settles her there.

Then the bedroom door opens and Connie comes in. The mattress beside her compresses and Kathy smells her mother's sugary smell. She feels the whisper of her breath on her neck. Her mother's arm slides out from between them and rests a moment on the length of Kathy's body. Then it pulls her closer and their bodies are spooned together.

Her mother holds her, and she doesn't say a word.

When Kathy wakes, it's light. She can hear Connie talking and Al replying, not the words, but the soothing sounds the words make. She closes her eyes and sleeps again. Next time she wakes, she gets up.

"Where's Shelly?" Kathy asks when she walks into the dining room.

Al carries his coffee to the table and sits. Connie pours two cups from the percolator on the stove and sets them on the counter. Kathy leans against the doorway watching her mother. Connie's hair is wound in toilet paper rolls, her lipstick is on, her mascara is perfect. She's wearing a royal blue fake kimono Al gave her from his lingerie line. It shimmers in the sun from the window.

"She's in bed," Connie says. "I gave her an extra sedative in the night. She'll sleep until noon at least. But she's fine, Kathy. She's fine.

"Roy and Sally took a doggie bag home but Darlyn and Donny stayed for supper last night. They wanted to wait until you woke up but it got late. They took a taxi home."

"Mom," Kathy starts.

"We watched a movie on TV. Then Al went home and I slept on the couch."

"I feel so ..." Kathy is close to tears.

"Don't," Connie says.

Kathy comes into the room and sits. Connie brings their coffee to the table and sets a cup in front of Kathy.

"Honey," Connie says, but doesn't say anything more.

Kathy turns her coffee cup handle one way, then the other. She lifts the cup, blows over the surface of the coffee and takes a sip. It's strong and bitter. Connie sips her coffee. Kathy sips hers. The furnace comes on, a metallic pop, then a steady low thrum. Cool air circulates, then warm. Al gets up.

"I'll clean up the rec room," he tells them. He pulls an envelope out of his shirt pocket and sets it on the table.

"Your mother and I meant to give this to you at the party," he says.

He goes downstairs. They hear the clink of beer bottles and the vacuum starts up. Kathy moves the envelope with her finger, then slides it back to where Al left it.

"Honey," Connie says again. "For a long time after Charlie died I was afraid. I was afraid for Shelly. She was so difficult and I wasn't sure I could love her the way she needed to be loved. I wasn't sure I could take care of her. And I was afraid something would happen to me, because if something happened to me, what would become of Shelly?

"I was afraid we'd be poor. That I'd lose the house, that the car would break down and I wouldn't be able to afford another. I worried about everything. I was terrified of life.

"Then I hit middle age and I stopped being afraid. Oh, I know I talk about worry keeping airplanes up in the air, and I still think there's some truth to it. I keep that damned scrapbook (she waves her hand toward the refrigerator) of worry. But really, I don't worry about any of that any more. I don't worry about myself or what will happen to me. I don't worry about Al. I don't even worry about Shelly, not in the long run at least. Not more than I should. I'm not afraid of any of us dying. It will happen when it happens."

Connie gets up and pours more coffee into her cup, brings the pot over and tops up Kathy's. She sits down and pulls her kimono around her legs. She leans back in her chair.

"The only thing I really worry about is you. You're the most perfect thing in my life. I know I'd go on if something happened to you. I learned I could do that after your father. But when your friend Pete died... I realized if it had been you... I'd be so...so diminished. So entirely full of sorrow."

Connie stops then. She stands, picks up her mug and takes it to the sink. She faces the window and looks out; she pours her coffee down the drain. Kathy hasn't moved, not since her mother started talking. She's been looking toward her mother, but not looking at her. She tried to, but she couldn't bear it. All that love.

She sits a moment longer, then gets up and goes to the sink. She stands beside Connie, gently butts her mother's head with her own. A paper roller crumples, then pops back into shape. Connie laughs, shifts her body away from Kathy, rinses her mug and sets it in the sink.

"I have to get dressed," Connie says. "Al and I are going to church. You can stay and look after your sister."

"Mom," Kathy starts.

"Shhh," Connie stops her. She kisses Kathy on the cheek, holds her lips there a moment.

"We'll have leftovers for lunch," she says. "So you can catch up to us. Otherwise Al and I will do you in with our farts."

She says the last part over her shoulder, grinning as she walks away.

Kathy watches her walk out of the kitchen, watches her walk through the dining area. Watches her disappear around the corner, a shimmer of blue.

THE AIR IS YEASTY WHEN KATHY GOES OUTSIDE TO PACK THE Valiant. Weston's is baking and the scent seems to warm the still, cold air. It's dark, but the street lights are bright enough to see what she's doing. Not that she's taking much, a small suitcase with some clothes and three paper bags of candy. One small bag of Turkish delight, another of assorted cream-filled chocolates and one with five fat foil-wrapped marshmallow Santa Clauses left from Christmas.

Kathy stopped to say goodbye to Connie and Shelly last night. As she stood in the front doorway, Shelly wrapped her arms around Kathy's waist and pressed her face so tightly into her diaphragm she could hardly breathe.

"You're the lucky one," Connie said. "She must think you're going away forever."

Connie handed Kathy the paper bags.

"Snacks, for the road," Connie said.

Then she leaned over Shelly's body and hugged both girls together. Shelly squirmed, but didn't complain. Connie kissed Kathy on the lips and pulled away.

"You be good," she ordered.

Kathy's maps with the routes marked out are on the front seat, highways through Ontario to cross into the States at Buffalo, then through New York State straight into Massachusetts. There's a Boston city map so she won't get lost driving from the YWCA, where she's going to stay, to the Garden, where she'll be watching a home game of the defending champions of the Stanley Cup.

In the envelope Al set on the table the day after Shelly got lost was a ticket for the Bruins game. And there was a card with fifty dollars in it, for gas and a room, the card said, love Mom and Shelly and Al. So Kathy had checked with Larry, and he'd said no problem, take a few days. Chance of a fucking lifetime, he'd added.

Kathy throws her skates into the trunk. She intends to skate on the Garden ice one way or another, because when she gets back, she wants to tell Larry—and her students—she skated on the same ice as the Boston Bruins and Canada's own Bobby Orr. She slams the trunk shut. In the car, the upholstery is cold. Connie's chocolates sugar the air. Behind the rumble of traffic, in the pulse inside her ears, Kathy hears her own heart pounding, a little loud, a little nervous, so much good fortune.

She pulls cold air deep into her lungs and lets it out slowly, her breath condensing along the edges of the windows. When she leans forward to put the key in the ignition, the seat creaks, metal clicks on metal. A few hard pellets of snow ping off the windshield. She turns the key but the engine hesitates, it misses. She gives the gas pedal a fast tap, hoping the engine doesn't flood. It catches with a roar and then there's nothing left to do but to start.

The End

Acknowledgements

Andy Watt never gave up on me, though I believe I stretched his patience to its limit. As my first reader, he was both kind and truthful, the best help possible.

Susan Brown, without whose reading of—and subsequent enthusiasm for—the first draft of the manuscript, I might have given up, and whose comments were invaluable during the re-drafting the novel: thank you.

Librarians and archivists are the hidden help in the writing process. Between the archivists at both the Yukon Archives & the National Library, I was kept supplied with newspaper microfiche for a year. Jennifer Stephens at the Yukon Public Library, Whitehorse Branch, and Susan Hoffman at the Kitchener Public Library helped with particular questions.

Anne Knittle, Bernadette Bryans, Nancy Zettell-Pope, and Jerry and Loretta Zettell liberally shared their stories, and their home-town knowledge. Patrick, Jim, Jackie and Jerry, and Daniel and John, and the Watts remained fans even when there was nothing to get excited about. Marion Thompson, Sarah Beck, Wendy Smith and Penny Steele have walked with me through all drafts of the novel, and have kept me steady through life's ordinary and extraordinary events. Laura McLauchlan, Bonnie Thompson, Danny Robinson, Jerome Stueart, Jane Isakson, Russell Colman, Ruth Schneider, Brigitta Buehlmann, Duncan and Chrissie MacEachern, and Kathy Zinger: constant. John Roberts and Fenella Nicholson kept me attached to my garden even when I couldn't be in it. During several long Cape Breton winters, Bill Nicholson skated with me in Baddeck most Friday mornings. For helping me to keep *my* heart on the ice: thank you, Bill. The St. Ann's Bay Book Group, intelligent readers all, sustained me. Tunnel Inn and music consultant: David Papazian. One snowy February afternoon, Carol Kennedy and Deanie Cox shared deeply personal and honest memories of young womanhood. Alistair Watt shared his musing on his 1966 Valiant. Gil Levine and Brian Williamson shared their knowledge of unions. Playwright Bev Brett talked to me about dialogue.

Karen Haughian's advice throughout has been sage and kind. There would be no book without you. Thank you.

Unless otherwise noted, all newspaper reports are from the *Kitchener-Waterloo Record*: January 1970—December 1970. *Bobby Orr: My Game* (Little, Brown and Company, 1974) by Bobby Orr with Mark Mulvoy was an invaluable resource. I read *Searching for Bobby Orr* (Knopf Canada, 2006) by Stephen Brunt after I had finished a draft of my novel, which was then called, *The Bobby Orr Guide to Becoming a Woman*. It proved a wonderful read, and helped me fill out my portrait of Bobby Orr, and to more clearly understand just how complicated a man Bobby remains, and how good a skater and hockey player he was. *Proud Past, Bright Future* (Stoddart Publishing Co. Limited, 1994) by Brian McFarlane showed that despite this book's stance, women have played hockey for as long as hockey has been played. I came late to hockey through MAMMAH (Middle-aged Menopausal Mothers Attempt Hockey). All of my teammates inspired me, but special thanks to Heather, Jan, Barbara, and Robin. Although I never did learn how to twirl, *Baton Twirling: The Fundamentals of an Art and a Skill* (Charles E. Tuttle Company, 1964) by Constance Atwater provided useful information. Sections of Tim Ralfe's *Just Watch Me* interview with Pierre Trudeau were taken from *Quebec 70: A Documentary Narrative*, John Saywell, Toronto University Press, 1971.

I am privileged to live in the community of St. Ann's Bay in Cape Breton, Nova Scotia. Through the writing and rewriting of *The Checkout Girl*, I was encouraged at every step by friends, neighbours and acquaintances. I thank each and every one who said a kind word. I needed them all.

Susan Zettell is the author of two short story collections, *Night Watch* and *Holy Days of Obligation*. Her stories have also been anthologized in *Quintet, Spider Women, The Day the Men Went to Town* and *The Company We Keep*. She edited, along with Frances Itani, the posthumous story collection *One of the Chosen* by Danuta Gleed. *The Checkout Girl* is her first novel.

Born and raised in Kitchener, Ontario, Zettell has lived in Cambridge, Vancouver, Halifax, Ottawa and Whitehorse. She now lives in Cape Breton with her husband, Andy Watt.